CONSPIRACY IGNITES

To my parents, Jack and Teresa Bertucci

CONSPIRACY IGNITES

Book Three in the Conspiracy Series

JOHN BERTUCCI

First Printing: May 2024

Paperback ISBN: 978-1-955541-43-5
eBook ISBN: 978-1-955541-44-2
Hardcover ISBN: 978-1-955541-45-9
Library of Congress Number: Pending

Cover and Interior Design: Ann Aubitz

Published by FuzionPress
1250 East 115th Street
Burnsville, MN 55337
612-781-2815
fuzionpress.com

"War is peace, freedom is slavery, and ignorance is strength."
~George Orwell, *1984*

"It's the action, not the fruit of the action, that's important. You have to do the right thing. It may not be in your power, may not be in your time, that there'll be any fruit. But that doesn't mean you stop doing the right thing. You may never know what results come from your action. But if you do nothing, there will be no result."
~Mahatma Gandhi

"Even the darkest night will end and the sun will rise."
~Victor Hugo, *Les Misérables*

Chapter 1

The conspiracy began in seven sites across the contiguous forty-eight states. One of the most active was in an area of the Upper Peninsula of Michigan, deep in a primeval forest so thick that for the average person, finding it was not likely. However, Joe, a school teacher and ex-Army veteran of Vietnam, was in the right place at the right time in the summer of 2019 when he heard several loud explosions. It led him to an experience he would never forget—and to investigating seditious activities in the Upper Peninsula (U.P.).

His curiosity had almost gotten him and his best friend, Ron, killed on a few occasions. Their investigation of the people who were in charge led to the discovery of the other six secret bases. That is what they were—paramilitary bases controlled by outlandishly rich people both in and out of the country who wanted to have complete control of the U.S. Government.

Without the assistance of any local or federal help, Joe and Ron made several attempts to slow down the groups' leaders who were paying huge sums of money to their troops, anyone they could convince to work for them. The group had infiltrated government agencies to the point that they were hindering any kind of response to the insurgents. Joe and Ron could trust no one and had little support. The insurgents' plan that Joe found had to do with taking down the president and governors in forty-nine of the fifty states.

It wasn't easy trying to follow these conspirators nor to understand what exactly they were planning to do. Joe had uncovered several possible dates for the coup and was now working to destroy this menace to democracy.

Chapter 2

Washington, D.C.

It's difficult to track any secret organization as it is created, but this one was especially arduous since it had countless components in numerous areas in the U.S. Many of the sites were obscure places, not well known to the general population and were often difficult for law enforcement to stretch its long arm. Knowing what they were about to create, the originators of this wily organization kept as low a profile as possible until it became too problematic. Keeping track of thousands of "associates" became an almost overwhelming duty for those at the top.

The head man, known as the old boss, had been taken out of commission by Joe and Ron, but he was now back. He had taken power again by convincing his challenger, the new boss, that he should step aside briefly. The old boss was notorious for his planning and organization. He was also very cunning, and so he was able to sidestep several of the founders—men with money and power. Being the person he was, he controlled everyone on the committee. They feared him, but they knew he was the man to accomplish this enormous feat.

The old boss strategized for a coordinated takeover. His people were everywhere they needed to be to make him successful and to fulfill a dream he had had since he was a young man. He wanted to control the most important economy in the world. He would become a billionaire many times over, and he would be the richest man in the world, times two.

It was 3:30 a.m., and the boss had a vision, and he could see clearly as the Capitol Building was surrounded. He was with his security people waiting for a chance to move into the White House. His people were quickly making progress as they moved stealthily toward their goal.

Chapter 3

Colewin, Michigan, a hideout in the U.P., June 10, 2021
Joe was being cautious because he and his partners had attacked a paramilitary bunker in the primal forests of the U.P. The local sheriff was in collusion with the group, and Joe and his followers understood that they could not trust anyone, so were taking matters into their own hands. Joe had discovered the bunker that was used by a group of insurgents who wanted to take over the government. Joe, his best friend Ron, and a group of patriots had banded together to try to take down the people who were involved in the insurrection.

They had attacked the base and had taken the insurgents' tech person, Bates, and had him captive. They had also been able to take his computer equipment and had searched the hard drive for information.

Both Joe's and Ron's sons had also searched the dark web and discovered most of the plans for the group that was organizing a coup. Joe and his partners were now at a secluded cabin for protection since they knew the insurgents at the bunker would retaliate in some way. There were twenty-four people in the attack who were still here, and they had posted sentries outside just in case. Joe and Ron were in a discussion as to what to do. They waited to see if there would be any reaction.

The bunker in the U.P.—and 1,500 miles away

One of the military trainers at the bunker had no idea how to react to the attack. He had contacted his friend in California who put him in touch with the new boss. This was bad. The new boss had been concerned about the U.P. for months, and he could not convince the old boss to do something significant to stop the harassment of his troops and base. He was furious when he heard that their key communications manager had been captured by these simpletons. He should have contacted the old boss and told him what had happened, but instead, he decided to handle this himself.

He spoke to his first in command. "I want you to send three hundred troops to the Upper Peninsula of Michigan base, and I want you to personally go there and help with a plan I have."

"What's going on there?"

"There has been an uprising of sorts, and some group, we're not sure who, attacked our base and took our communications expert, Bates, the one who organizes and coordinates all our bases. He is a key man in the plan to take down the government, and he is now missing."

"Did you contact the old boss?"

"No need. We just need to get our communications people to take up the slack, and they will have to do what Bates has been doing, so they need to get up to speed quickly. That we can tell the old boss, but as far as sending troops to Colewin—which is what I am going to do—we keep that to ourselves. He is never in for this type of action before the event.

Months later, Spring, 2022

It was a long winter, and it took time to repair what had happened to the bunker area, and to get back to normal at the insurgents' base in the U.P. The trainers who had taken over since the attack had one hundred men armed and loaded in trucks, and they were headed to Colewin, a small town not far from the bunker. It was time to retaliate.

Bill, a lifelong inhabitant of Colewin, had joined with the people at the bunker. He gave the trainers names of people that he suspected were part of the attack. He knew Matt and Charlie and a few others from Colewin who probably assisted. They were out to get them.

The trucks rolled into Colewin. The head trainer was livid. Earlier when he had contacted California, the new boss had blown his top and said, "Shoot anyone and everyone you suspect or even if you don't suspect, if they are in your way. This base has been a headache all along. We don't have these problems in other places. Maybe the event has to start earlier."

The trainer agreed, "We won't leave anyone to tell any tales."

Trucks full of armed troops headed for Colewin, searching for anyone who might have had anything to do with the attack at the bunker. Since the leader had orders to shoot anyone on sight that might have been involved with the attack, he was excited and finally satisfied. In fact, he was overjoyed. The trainer was overzealous and took the plan to a level that even the new boss would never have approved.

Earlier, Lansing, Michigan, 2022

Loretta, an FBI agent out of Lansing, Michigan, had been searching for her best friend, Ann, also an agent, who had gone missing. Ann had been working with Joe and Ron for some time, and she had discovered a militia in Lansing like the one in the U.P.

Ann had learned that her boss had flipped and joined the insurgents, and he had been keeping Ann hostage. He had a young agent, Aaron, watching her. Loretta thought that Ann may have been eliminated, but she found out that she had been taken to another spot in Lansing and was being held there.

The boss selected Aaron to watch Ann again. He had watched her prior to learning about the boss joining with the militia groups. Loretta had worked with Aaron, and she knew he was not part of the boss's plan, and so she convinced him about the boss—and that he should work with her.

Aaron was now assisting Loretta, unbeknownst to the boss. He and Loretta devised a plan to free Ann. Unfortunately, the next day when Aaron went to tell Ann how they would rescue her, she was on her way out with several militia escorting her. Fortunately, she was savvy enough to leave Aaron a note.

Aaron was stunned, but as he scanned the note, he noticed that Ann had given him all the information they would need to find her.

His boss wanted to get rid of Ann, but he felt he could not do it in Lansing, so he was having her transferred and taken off his hands. That made the boss feel better. Now, it would be just as if she disappeared, but he also knew he had to slow down Loretta and her partners.

Loretta had Aaron, and Jerry, another agent, working with her to try to find Ann, and Loretta had sent them to the place where they had learned Ann was being held.

Colewin

They entered Colewin, a small town in the U.P., and drove down the main drag. It was early morning, 6:15 a.m. The sun had come up at 5:52, so it was getting light enough to see. The head man, a key trainer for the insurgents, was in charge and he was angry. They had lost their computer expert and most of his computer equipment, and now they were really on their own as far as what to do. He had spoken to the boss and had been given the green light, but what that meant to his boss and to him—well, who knew?

Since Bill was from Colewin and had been a part of the bunker troops for a while now, he knew where everyone lived, but they did not want his input. They didn't like the fact that he was from Colewin, and he might lead them astray.

Bill was dismayed that they did not have him involved. He had been loyal to this point, but he was from Colewin, and he had known most of these people his whole life, so he was not too keen on giving away where they might be. He was getting a bit leery of the tactics the group was using, and he did not think that this was the goal of the entire operation.

As the troops drove down the main street, they noticed little activity, so the trainer decided to park all the vehicles on a side street and have his men dispersed around the town. The shooting began around 7:00 a.m. The town's gas station owner was opening for business when ten armed troops accosted him.

He was not happy and started yelling. "What the hell are you doing? You can't be military! Get off my property and let me be."

One of the troops did not like his attitude and lifted his rifle, aimed, and shot a bullet over his right shoulder, very close to his ear, and then slammed him with the stock of his weapon. The man fell instantly.

The shot startled the owner of the grocery store across the street as he looked out and saw the armed men. He quickly locked the door he had just opened. He called the state police in New-berry—and they were on their way. He also called anyone that might be in town and told them to stay inside. Word spread fast after that, and one person who had partnered with Joe, received a call. He immediately hustled to the cabin to tell Joe and Ron.

In the meantime, the troops in town were banging on doors and dragging people out of their homes. They soon had one hundred troops on the main street in Colewin. Most people had gotten the message, so the troops could not rouse many others besides the few they had. They had people in the streets and were threatening to shoot them if they didn't tell who was behind the attack on their bunker. However, very few people knew anything, and so they had few answers.

Just before 8:00 a.m., Don, the mayor, arrived and addressed the leader. "We don't know what you're talking about. None of us have ties with the group. Charlie and Matt are friends of ours, and we know that they have a group that is paramilitary, but that is all we know."

The leader of the troops stepped up to Don and spit in his face as he yelled. "Where are these people right now? If you don't tell me, it'll be you next!" And he pointed to the man lying on the ground at the gas station.

Don was nervous and he could taste the bitterness in his mouth from the adrenalin in his stomach. He was on the verge of a panic attack. "We're not sure where they are now, but Matt lives in Poplar and Charlie has a place out north of here."

"Where exactly?"

Don looked at him and said, "Get out of my face! You have no right to come here and harass our citizens."

The leader just laughed. "We don't care."

A screaming police car came rapidly to a stop not far from Don. Out jumped Sheriff Daryl. "What's going on here?"

Don turned to him. Sheriff Daryl had been his friend for many years, but he had not been much of a friend during the past year and was now firmly entrenched in the conspiracy.

The leader, who had worked with Daryl on several occasions, spoke, "Daryl, last summer we had someone attack our base. They killed several of our troops and took our computers from the bunker."

"What!" is all Daryl said before he turned to Don and asked, "What's going on with you guys? I told you not to mess with the bunker."

"It wasn't me or anyone I know," Don snapped.

"Well then who could have done this? Was it that Joe again? I hear he's back."

As Daryl said this, two state police cars came flying into Colewin, sirens blaring.

Chapter 4

Lansing, Michigan, May 2022

Loretta had just gotten off the phone with Joe. She and Joe had been in contact over the paramilitary groups that had been infiltrating Michigan, and Loretta had learned of a plot to abduct the governor of Michigan. Loretta's work searching for Ann, and her work assisting the governor, had gotten her in trouble with her boss who had joined with the local militia. Loretta's investigations led to getting her boss incarcerated. Her boss knew that Loretta was getting too close to uncovering what was going on, so before he was apprehended, he had her on his list to be taken, and now she was being hunted.

Since Ann had disappeared, Loretta and her partners had been working to find her, but now Loretta had lost contact with the two agents. Loretta was concerned.

She was in touch with the governor of Michigan for support, since she was now being hunted by the militia. She had been given a temporary safe place to stay until the governor could ensure her protection.

As she ended the call with Joe, she saw several armed troops leave a military type truck and head to her hiding place. Loretta had to move quickly if she was going to reach the governor's arranged place. She turned around and moved to the back door only to see several other armed troops heading there. *Where could she turn?* She pulled out her phone and called the number the governor had given her.

A deep voice croaked, "Sargeant Miller," and then the connection was lost. Loretta tried again, but there was no service. "What the hell? How did that happen?" she yelled into her phone. She knew she had to do something quickly. The safe house she was in had an attic and a basement, but she knew they did not offer a solution. She thought, *I need to set a trap and get the hell out of here. Maybe set the place on fire, cause a diversion, and exit through an upstairs window?*

The safe house had loads of equipment for Loretta's protection. She had military style weapons, Kevlar vests, knives, rope, and she had prepared the house for an intrusion. She thought, *This is not unlike a movie,* but this was no movie.

Her car was parked in front of the house next to the military vehicle that had brought the troops. She would not be able to get to it. She would need to exit and run.

Her plan had been to stay inside if there weren't many assailants, but there were more than two or three, so her plan was to cut the gas line, go upstairs, open the window on the side of the house, light the curtains on fire, and jump for the tree in the yard several feet away. That is if all the troops entered the building.

She checked to see how many troops might be there. She saw several moving to the front door, and she heard loud crashes as the front and back doors were rammed. She went to the kitchen, cut the gas line, grabbed a utility lighter from a drawer, ran upstairs, and opened a window on the side of the house.

She did not see anyone outside, so she slipped the sling of her assault rifle over her head, opened the window, tore off the curtains, lit them, threw them down the stairs, and then jumped for the tree. She caught a branch, split her lip, and banged her head on another large branch. Then she slid down a bit and fell to the ground. The only thing that saved her was a branch as it broke her fall.

She twisted an ankle, landed on her side, and swore. She did not see anyone and began to hobble as quickly as she could to the neighbor's yard. She shuffled to the back of the house and rested behind a shed. Then she heard a loud explosion.

Chapter 5

Joe's hideout—and downtown Colewin

Word had gotten around that the troops at the bunker were on the prowl, so a few individuals were at the hideout with Joe, and they were now on high alert. Charlie and Matt, who had both been a part of the attack, went there to find out what they should do next. Most of the original group that had attacked the bunker was scattered around Colewin. After a few weeks, they had assumed that there would be no retaliation for what they had done to the bunker, so they went about their normal lives. Now after a quiet winter, they were on high alert again. Joe and Ron had decided to keep lookouts in place, but they did not have as many as they had prior to the attack.

The first response was to arm every person at the hideout to assist the lookouts. The lookouts there were positioned around the perimeter to guard against an attack. Ron decided that he and some others should quickly jump on vehicles and begin some type of surveillance to see just what the opposition was. How many troops did they send into Colewin, and where were they right now? They decided to use four-wheelers and take a back road into Colewin, one that the troops probably did not know.

Ron took three others, all of whom had been involved in the attack on the bunker. They were all armed and dressed in camo, and they left as soon as they drew up a plan with Joe.

Matt was not surprised at what was happening. "This is about what I expected from these people. They kept getting closer and closer to running our community, and now they're not only going to run it, they're going to destroy it."

"That's what it looks like," Joe said.

Charlie was nervous, but at the same time concerned for his friends and community. "We need to do somethin' to help the people in town."

"Ron is there now with several others, and they're going to report in as soon as they know anything."

"Do we just sit tight until then?" Matt asked.

"Yes. Until we know what's happening, we need to stay put and get everyone ready in case they head here. If we get the word to move to town, that's what we'll do."

Charlie was pacing around and mumbling to himself, but he agreed that they could not go to town without knowing what was happening, especially if the troops found the hideout.

Joe told Matt and Charlie to go out and make sure all their personnel were situated to cover every direction, and to put up road blocks heading into the hideout. They left immediately.

Joe waited another fifteen minutes when his phone rang. "Hello."

"Joe, this is Ron. We're on the outskirts of town watching what's going on. It looks like the troops have hurt someone at the gas station, not sure if he's dead. Daryl is here, but you know he won't do much. It looks like they must have about one hundred troops going door to door, harassing the citizens."

"Do you think we should head to town to help out?"

"Not right now. Two state police cars just pulled up and they're talking to Daryl. They're pointing to the man on the ground, and it looks like Daryl is going to take over, but the state troopers are walking around and talking to the troops."

"Can you get closer to listen?"

"I'm doing that right now. I have Tommy with me and we're sneaking up behind the gas station. We were able to slip inside the back door, and we're heading to the front of the station." Ron and Tommy were crawling to get near the front door. They opened it a crack and were able to hear Sheriff Daryl talking with what looked like the leader of the troops.

Daryl walked close to the leader and said, "You need to get these guys back to the bunker and stay there until I hear from the new boss."

"We have permission from him to do what we want and to take out anyone who is in the way. You need to give us an alibi for the gas station attendant. It was just an accident."

"Is he dead? We need to get him some help. He was cracked in the head, and it split open. How do I explain that?"

"Don't know. Just do it."

"These state troopers are not satisfied. They're going to do some investigating themselves, so you need to leave and give us the person who injured the gas station attendant."

"Can't do that. We'll move out for now, but we're not going back to the base. We're going to hunt those guys who took out some of our troops and destroyed our computer equipment. And where is Bates? Do they have him?"

"I sure as hell don't know!"

"Well, if you had been around this winter, you could have helped. He's a missing person from our base. We need to find him pronto."

"I'll get the state troopers on that."

"No. Keep them out of it. Just send them back to Newberry."

Daryl knew he was in a predicament. Usually, he could just come up with a story when it came to these situations with the people from the bunker, but with the state troopers, it might be a bit more difficult. He walked over to the Lieutenant from the state police. "Say, Lieutenant, I think I can take care of this. I can work with the leader of this group and take the person who hurt the attendant to the lockup in St. Ignace."

"What about the rest of these guys? They're not the military, and they can't be running around like they have some kind of permission to do this stuff."

"I get it. I'll send them all back to their area."

"No. We'll get them to disband. Where did they come from anyway? Who gave them permission to harass citizens for no reason?"

"I think they're working with the government."

"Really? Which part of it?"

Daryl realized he was in a spot and had to come up with something quickly. He walked back to the leader and had a quiet conversation with him. The leader was not going to back down. Daryl did not know what to do. As he considered his options, an ambulance pulled up to the gas station to attend to the guy on the ground. Daryl hoped he would live, but the gash in his head looked bad.

As Daryl turned to speak to the leader again, before anyone could say or do anything, the two state troopers were on the ground, tied and gagged. Even Sheriff Daryl was shocked.

Chapter 6

Colewin

Ron and Tommy heard everything and saw what just went down. They were surprised, but at the same time they knew this might happen. Before they could even turn to leave, the two state troopers' vehicles were on their way somewhere, as were the two officers.

Ron called Joe and explained the situation. He knew now that if the leader was willing to take state troopers, he would go to any lengths to get whoever caused the attack on the base.

Tommy spoke as he and Ron left the station. "We need to protect the people of Colewin. These guys will do anything, and the lives of the people around here are in jeopardy. We need to contact as many as we can and have them lock their doors and hide. They probably need to arm themselves, too."

Ron said that Joe had told him to return to the hideout and to make plans for what they should do next. Tommy agreed, but he also thought they should contact people right away. "We also need to contact the state police to see what they can do."

"Right. Joe is on that already. Let's try to notify more people on this street. Can you call Wendy and some other locals and get them contacting people too? We can't go door to door with these guys here. Our best bet is to call people we know and tell them to call others."

"Why don't we get the rest of our people out here and pick off these guys one by one as they move down the street?"

Ron was doubtful. "They have about one hundred troops here. We might have about two dozen if everyone can get here. How would that work? Even if we could stay hidden, they would quickly plan an attack against us. I think we have to be smarter."

"I'll call as many people as I can then. Hopefully they can stay safe if we give them a heads up."

"Let's get back to the other two guys and our machines. We should be ready to move if anything happens." When they arrived at their four-wheelers, they had the two other men make calls too. Soon they had notified several people in town."

Joe was having everyone do the same thing. Unfortunately, a lot of people just laughed at them. Some just did not believe that this could be happening. Joe called the barber, Jack, and asked if his son had any information. Jack's son, Peter, had infiltrated the bunker and was inside during the attack. He had not reported for a while.

"Jack, have you heard anything from Peter yet?"

"Nothing yet. I hesitate to text him right now because I don't know where he is or who might be near him."

"If you get any information, let us know right away. We need to find out what these troops are planning to do in town, and how long they'll be here. We know they're looking for us after what we did, but I'm not sure how we can go after them, but we need to do it soon."

"I agree. I'll keep you informed if I hear anything."

Chapter 7

Lansing, Michigan

Loretta was working on her ankle, trying to loosen it up to see if she could walk. As she sat behind the shed, she saw three of the troops move for their truck at the front of the damaged house she had just left. They were talking and yelling at each other as they moved toward the vehicle.

She heard one of the men yell, "Have you seen anyone else who might have made it out?"

His partner said, "No one else could have survived. We were lucky we were where we ended up, or it would have been us too. She could not have made it out, so let's get out of here."

They jumped into the vehicle and roared off. Loretta took a deep breath and stumbled around the shed and out from behind the house. Her car was still in its original spot, so she hobbled to it, but when she got there, she could not find her keys and the car was locked. She did not want to spend a lot of time in that area since she heard sirens, so she started shuffling down the street, found a spot to stop and rest and made a call.

Her first call was to the number the governor had given her, but she had no luck. No signal. She had to get out of the area, but she couldn't be seen lugging a rifle down the street. She decided to head back to the car, smash the window, and try to start it. She limped back hoping to beat any police or fire trucks.

Loretta had been taught to start cars in the past, but not the newer ones. She had a 2020 model and thought she might be able to start it. She played around with it for a few minutes and had some success. She drove off in the direction of the Capitol Building, passing police cars and fire trucks speeding to the house.

As Loretta was driving, she was thinking about Ann, who had been missing now for some time. There was a lot of speculation about what might have happened, but no real results. The two agents she had been working with also had not reported. She thought she should look for them too, but where to start?

Loretta drove on, and was near the capitol when she saw the truck that had been in front of her safe house.

Chapter 8

Near Colewin

Ron was trying to think of a way to get the group to leave Colewin. He talked to Joe, and together they could not come up with anything. As Ron was talking to Joe, Tommy came up with an idea that he thought might not get these troops out of the town, but it might get something started. Ron and Tommy moved back close to the main street.

"Say, Ron, do you see Bill over there by the grocery store?" Ron was not sure who Bill was, so Tommy pointed him out. "Right next to the window with the ad for cereal."

"I see who you mean. What's your plan?"

"I'm going to try to get his attention to see if he can tell me what's going on. He can't like what they're doing to our town."

"If he's wearing that uniform, then he's with them. It might be a bad idea."

"It's worth a try. Don't you think?"

"Let's clear it with Joe first."

"Sure, go ahead."

Ron called Joe and they spoke for a short time. Joe thought it would be worth a try if he could get him away from the rest of the troops. "And, Ron, do not let Tommy get himself in a jam. Back him up the best you can."

"Will do." Ron ended the call and turned to Tommy. "Go ahead, but we're going to back you up."

"Let us work our way past this street and cross up ahead near the school. That way we can get behind Bill."

"I'll get the other guys here. Wait until I get back."

It took a few minutes before Ron had everyone, and they walked briskly to the spot that Tommy had selected. They were able to get behind Bill without any trouble. Tommy had the others stay hidden close by, and he moved ahead to Bill.

"Hey, Bill, can I talk to you?"

Bill turned and did not see anyone, but he thought he recognized the voice, so he moved in that direction. When he was at the corner of the building, out of sight of the others, Tommy stepped into the open and waved Bill over. Bill saw Tommy and immediately knew who it was. He turned around to make sure no one was watching him, and then he walked briskly toward Tommy.

Tommy spoke first. "Bill, what the hell is going on? Are you guys going to destroy the town and hurt a lot of people?"

"What are you doing here, Tommy? You could get hurt. You know these guys mean business."

"I do, but I've had enough of them, you included. What the hell is happening?"

"I know. This upsets me. This has been my home my entire life. I know all the people on these streets, but shit, look what they did to our bunker."

"Your bunker? That was Charlie's before it was taken by these hooligans. You know that. They took over and turned it into something that it shouldn't be."

"Well, we've got to change this country."

"Like this? These are innocent people you're harassing! What did they do to deserve this?"

Bill was troubled. "It wasn't them. It was Charlie and Matt and whoever else is with them. Are you with them?

"If I am, what are you going to do?"

"Right now, nothing. I told them that I knew this town, and I could get them the people they were looking for, but they don't want my help. This makes me sick. I want out now, but if I try, I'll be the next one to die."

"Bill, you could help us end this."

"So, you're with them?"

"Doesn't matter. What matters is that we stop what's going on right now."

"I agree."

"Listen. You're a Yooper and have always been from Colewin. Stick with us to get rid of these guys. They're trying to take the country down. We have proof that they want to destroy everything and set up a dictatorship. Is that what you want?"

Chapter 9

California

The new boss was at the California base, one of the seven they had around the country. He had gone there to check on the training and readiness of the troops. He was anxious to get the event started and was not happy with how things had been going. He was at the same time directing the troops in the U.P. where some group had attacked the base. He had a man on it now, but he was very disappointed with what had happened.

The old boss, who was trying to take complete control again, was also in on the discussions of what to do and had been informed about what was happening in Colewin. He thought that the troops should head back to the bunker and do it quickly. He was on the phone with the new boss and told him so. "This will just give us a bad name. We need to end it right now and send the troops back to the base. We can't be taking local law enforcement every time they show up and don't help us."

The new boss said, "I knew you would say that, but we need to show these people who have been fighting our base there in Michigan that we are in control."

"We've had trouble with that base since those two teachers tried to infiltrate our base years ago. They were nothing but trouble. Your men were supposed to take care of them and anyone who was in our way."

"We took care of them. That place is just trouble, so we need to find the people who are causing this trouble and end it."

"What you are doing will not work. We cannot just wipe out a town and call attention to our cause. We have been able to keep our bases quiet for several years, and all we need to do is keep our cause hidden and our bases secure for a short time more."

"I understand. What do you propose?"

"Just what I said. Send the men back to the base. I will have my contacts take care of the detained state police officers as we have in the past."

"Okay. I'll give the order to return to the base, but this is not over."

"It has to be over until we begin our biggest event. Can you hang in there for a few more months?"

"I'll give the order to return to the base, but I am getting impatient."

"As we all are, but just follow my directives, and we will be all right."

"For now."

"That is all I ask."

The new boss made the call.

Colewin

Before they left Colewin, Ron and Tommy saw the leader call his troops back. They loaded into the trucks and left the injured man for Daryl and the EMTs to figure out a story. Daryl was confused on how he would handle this situation, but he knew he had to. He was a bit concerned about how the state troopers' situation would end, but he knew they had help in high places, and that it would be taken care of.

It didn't take long before all the troops were gone.

Chapter 10

Colewin

When Ron and Tommy returned to the hideout, they told Joe the entire story. Both men were dismayed that the bunker people would head into town and be so belligerent in front of the local people. They had always visited Colewin, but they had never openly harassed the local citizens. Might this be the time they could get some of the locals on their side? For so long they had been indifferent about the troops in town. They thought it was good for the economy, and they ignored any situations about the troops when anything went wrong.

Tommy repeated his conversation with Bill, and he thought they could get Bill to help. He was really upset about what they were doing. "We'll have to be careful, but maybe Bill could assist in some way, but first we need to find out what happened to the state troopers."

Joe decided that they should call the state police post.

"Lieutenant Carney."

"Hello? Is this the Newberry State Police Post?"

"Yes, it is."

"Say, Lieutenant, we had a problem down here in Colewin. A couple of your cars came down to look into these paramilitary guys around town, and we saw that they were apprehended and their cars driven away. Did you know about them?"

"Our boss from downstate just called, and he said everything was taken care of, and he had the two officers on their way to another situation. I'm not sure what it is, but that's all I know right now."

"Are you sure they're okay?"

"Yes, my boss has it under control, but I'm going to keep an eye on the situation if I can."

"Could you let us know if they are all right then?"

"I cannot be making calls to people about police business, but if you call back in a day or two, I'm sure I'll have information for you."

"All right. Thanks."

"You're very welcome."

Joe hung up and explained what he had found out. Tommy was very doubtful. "That's the kind of stuff that happened to me and Wayne back in 2019 when we were trying to help you. There were two state troopers who just disappeared when we asked for help. What the hell? Is that happening again?"

"Something is going on, but we have a bigger problem right now, and that is the troops at the bunker. They're headed back right now, but who knows if they'll be after us again. We need to get reinforcements and get the ear of the governor. We can trust her. I'm going to call Loretta to see if she has any information about Ann, and if she can get our information to the governor."

When Joe was finished, Ron said, "I'll contact our partners and let them know what's up. I think we should all stay together for another day or two, and then we should all go back to our normal routine. They don't know all the people involved, so everyone should get back to regular activities as soon as possible."

Tommy agreed. "I also think they should each try to recruit a few people and inform them what these guys are trying to do."

"Good plan," Joe said. "Ron, let's get ahold of Loretta and see what we can find out."

Ron had a new burner cell phone, and Joe thought they should use that to contact Loretta right away. "Could I use your burner?"

"Sure."

Joe called Loretta. It rang several times. "Hello, Loretta?"

"Joe? Is this Joe?"

"Yes."

"I was afraid to pick up because I didn't recognize the number."

"I understand. I used Ron's burner."

"Say, I was wondering if you had any news about Ann?"

"Nothing yet, but let me tell you what has happened to me since we last spoke."

Loretta explained her situation and told Joe where she was. "I'm afraid to leave my vehicle right now. I'm near the Capitol Building waiting for the truck to leave. I see several of those paramilitary guys moving around outside there. Do you think the event is on?"

"I highly doubt it because of the information we found, but there are two bosses fighting to be in charge, so who knows for sure?"

"Right."

"Loretta, if you can get to the governor, I've got some information she might be able to use."

"I was just going to call her. I was unable to use my phone for part of the day, so I haven't talked to her today, but I hope to get her soon."

Joe told her all he had just learned about the U.P. paramilitary group. He had talked to Loretta several times before, and she was knowledgeable about the event.

Little did Loretta know she was not going to get ahold of the governor.

Chapter 11

Lansing, Michigan

The governor had been at the residence in Lansing. She was preparing for her day. Her entourage included several Michigan troopers assigned to protect her from future kidnappings or other violence against her. This had been ongoing since an attempted abduction earlier.

Two men had been watching her for days, looking to find some weak spots in her protection, but there were none. They had been assigned to take the governor, but they were not to make a huge scene. The new boss wanted this to go down quietly. He had his reasons.

They followed her to work, shopping, home, and her children's activities. Anywhere she would go, they would be right there. They were not worried about when they would take the governor. They wanted it to be swift and quiet, when there was no protection nearby.

So they waited, day after day, but she always had someone nearby. They wondered if they could distract some of the guards, but that would cause a problem. So, they just hung on.

Then an opportunity presented itself. It was a weekend. There were few people around, and her guards were parked near the front of the residence. That is when they saw the governor alone in the back yard. They were down the street a bit, but they had a clear view of her. She was by herself. Yet, there was no way to get at her without causing a problem.

They waited some more. It was a week later when she was shopping for a birthday gift for her daughter. When they entered the store, she was by herself. Her guards were in a car outside. They approached when she was looking at some clothes. One distracted her as the other approached from behind and grabbed her. As she turned, a hand grabbed her mouth and her waist. She was thrown to the ground and pinned there as someone rolled her over and zip-tied her hands and taped her mouth. It did not take much to get her out of the back door where a van was waiting, and no one saw a thing.

As she was carried from the store and dragged to a vehicle, she thought, *How could this be happening? How had these people bypassed her security?* But as she was thrown roughly in the vehicle, she knew her security people were waiting patiently in their cars as she had asked. Then the doors were slammed shut, and the vehicle roared off.

The man in charge laughed as he turned to his partner who was driving. "This was too easy. I guess the planning this time was perfect. Those guys who tried this in the past were just amateurs."

His driver asked, "Why did we move this up so much? I thought we were going to wait until later next year."

"Humph, this ass was going to try to take us down. Word has it that some FBI agent tipped her off to what is going on, so we needed to stop that in its tracks."

"What kind of tip?"

"Not sure, but this was the head boss's plan. You don't know him. I guess I don't either, but after what happened in the U.P. at that key base, he ordered things to start. We've got a man we want to get elected once we get rid of her. That'll change everything.

We're all sick and tired of her crazy laws. Thinks she can do what she wants."

"You think this will ruin the big plan that's coming down the pike?"

"Not sure. I don't really care as long as we got the governor. I'm happy."

"Where we taking her?"

"Not sure. The warehouse in Cheboygan has been compromised, so we will need to wait for word, but right now to the planned hideout in Ohio."

"That's a long way. You think they'll have someone after us?"

"Not for a while. We have the right people on our side. No one will hear about this for a while, and we'll be long gone. The new boss is hoping that this really riles up the troops on both sides of the aisle. That's what he wants. He thinks if it gets bad enough, they'll be blaming each other—and we'll walk right in. He'll be the president, and we'll have things our way."

They drove on in silence for the next hour. They had a little over two hours ahead of them, and they did not want to stir up any suspicion, so they drove the speed limit. They knew they had a lot of time on their side, and it was only a little over an hour to the border where they would change vehicles. There were a lot of places to hide in Ohio.

It took some time for her security to realize that the governor was taking much longer than they felt safe. They entered and searched the place, but they did not find her anywhere, nor did they find any evidence that would indicate foul play. They were mystified. Where was the governor?

Chapter 12

A Hidden Location

The new boss was happy. His team in Michigan had done its work. He decided to call the old boss who was back at his headquarters. "We had to speed up our activity in Michigan."

"What do you mean our activity? Do you mean what you had them do in Colewin?"

"No. That's taken care of. We have people in the right places there. The troops are back at the base getting ready to ship out."

"Then what work are you talking about?"

"Well, that FBI agent in Lansing had the governor on speed dial, I guess. She found out about the group that was meeting with the head man in the Lansing FBI. She ratted him out, and she was going to meet with the agent today, so we had to act quickly, but the FBI agent was not apprehended. Somehow, she escaped, so we had to stop what she was planning to do. The only way to do that was to silence the Michigan governor."

"Are you kidding me? What did you do?"

"We got the governor. She is in a secure place."

"What? That is not a good move. We are scheduled to do those types of actions much later. Sometime in late 2023 or 2024, before the election. Remember, we are going to make the move for every governor around the same time. The idea is to move at once, so no one has any idea what is about to happen. Now, we might have let them in on part of our plan. All the governors will be prepared and have security."

"I do not think so. We will just play this up like it was the original militia that took the governor the first time. They will get all the blame, and we should be all right. We need to stop her from sending more people after the groups we have in Michigan, or it will blow up the entire Midwest."

"Listen, we have a lot of work to take care of. We need to work on getting me on the ballot for November 2024. We have many people gathering signatures where they are required. I will be running as an independent candidate, so we must petition each state. You probably would not be eligible since you have only been in this country for five years. I am the best bet."

"I have seen the requirements, and I agree that you must be the one, but you must give me a key position in your government."

"Of course."

Chapter 13

Colewin

A while back, Tommy, his girlfriend Wendy, and his best friend, David, had delivered Bates, the communication expert at the bunker, to Loretta in Lansing. She and the governor had decided to have him locked up. They had not been able to get much out of him, and they knew he probably did not know much more than what Joe and Ron had already told them about the event, so Bates became a non-issue. He would probably rot in jail for a long time unless he could come up with something new for them.

Joe and Ron were concerned about Ann, and after what happened in Colewin, they decided to take a trip to Lansing to see if they could assist Loretta. Their wives were not happy with their decision and said that they would go along. They insisted on having backup again, since Joe and Ron seemed to continually get into trouble. The situation in Colewin had cooled, and their contact at the bunker, Peter, told them the current plan was to lay low for a while.

Joe thought this was the best time to move to help Loretta. He and Ron took the advice of their wives and planned for Tommy, Wendy, and David to go along. They would work together to find Ann.

Before they left, Loretta called and said she had to go after her two partners. She had sent them to an address in Ohio where Ann was supposedly held. She had help from the governor's office and was already on her way to check out the place where they might be. She thought it best if Joe and Ron stayed put for a while until she knew more. There was not much they could do unless Ann was not found. She would let them know.

1,500 miles away

The committee was overseeing the old boss's effort to get on the presidential ballot in 2024. They had pumped tons of money into the effort. Secretly, they had millions come from overseas from their members and countries that wanted someone who would lean favorably toward them. That is, they hoped for favorable status with the U.S., and this was the only way forward for them.

They had been able to skirt many of the laws. They had set up PACs, trusts, and partnerships, and they had the new boss himself make huge donations from his "own" funds that they had created over the years. They had helped him build a billion-dollar reserve. Many of their funds came from overseas, but they were well hidden through years of planning and pumping money into the established partnerships all over the country and the world. Money was not going to be a problem.

They had also moved thousands of people into positions of power in states, something they continued to do each day. Getting their people connected to the election process was important if they needed them to do something in a state to turn an election their way. It would not be difficult. They had backed many elections and, at first, they lost quite a few, but then as they learned the ropes, they began to see their people win. They had also spent tons of money to put their candidates faces all over the map.

As a prosperous CEO of a huge and successful company— showing profits year after year through their manipulation of funds—they had created this persona for the new boss that was quite honorable.

Now they needed to make sure his face showed up on as many electronic sources as they could. They had him traveling the country giving speeches about how to be an effective leader, and he often gave his assessment of the current administration, pointing out its weaknesses and problems.

The committee had hoped, as they got nearer to the election, to plan some false information incriminating the president and people on his staff. What they had to do was up in the air, but they had their people working on it.

It was all good.

Chapter 14

Earlier

Aaron and his partner, Jerry, had a lead—a note from Ann that she would be taken to a home south of Lansing in Ohio, so they were going to investigate. They had phoned Loretta and told her of their plan. She was supposed to go, but she was separated from the two, and now she knew they had to move quickly. She said to be careful and not to take any chances.

"We'll be careful. You know where we are so if you don't hear from us in several hours, you know we're in trouble."

That was the last Loretta had heard from her FBI partners. She had waited for quite some time, but then she ran into trouble of her own, and had all she could do to escape. Now, she knew she had to get in touch with the governor's team, and they would have to search for her two partners. She knew where they had gone.

Ohio

Aaron and Jerry were close to the residence that they had learned was where Ann was being kept hostage. They had driven straight from Lansing, and they arrived near the house around noon. They decided to attack the home as if it were being guarded by armed individuals.

In the house three men were playing cards at a table, and two others were keeping watch around the house. They had been instructed to take care of some hostages, and they were awaiting several barrels of acid in which to dispose of some bodies. Then they were to take the barrels to a spot near a railroad crossing, and they would get directions on how to load the barrel on a car.

Aaron knew enough not to pull up to the house, so he parked on a side street.

Jerry was nervous. "It's way too quiet here. No one is out or around. It looks deserted." He looked around the neighborhood and saw no people anywhere. Lawns looked like they were over-grown a bit, but not so bad that they had been abandoned. It was daylight, so they did not have a lot of cover, but everything looked so peaceful around the neighborhood and the house that they let their guard down a bit. "What is this place?" Jerry asked. "No one's around."

"That's for sure. We should treat this like any crime. I'll take the front door, and you go around to the backyard and look."

"All right. Let's keep in touch. Have your phone handy."

They both exited the car, and Aaron walked stealthily to the front door while Jerry snuck into the backyard. Aaron tried to see if there was any movement in the building, but he could not see anything. Jerry was doing the same thing in the back, but he could not make out anything inside. All the blinds were pulled, and it was very quiet.

Aaron called Jerry.

Jerry picked up when his phone buzzed.

"You see anything?"

Jerry answered, "Nothing. It's so quiet. Do we have the right place? Maybe we have the wrong address."

"No, I'm sure this is it. Maybe everyone has gone. I hope it's not too late. Why don't we head back to the car and wait for some-thing, anything."

"Waiting might just make us late to save Ann. Don't you think?"

"Well, we can't just ring the doorbell if the people are here and they're armed. We need backup. Something just doesn't seem right. It's too easy. Like we're being set up."

"Right. Let's wait for a bit and make a better plan. Maybe we can get ahold of Loretta and some help."

Aaron walked slowly back to the car keeping an eye on the house and the surrounding area. He reached the car, opened the door, and sat in the driver's seat.

Jerry decided to walk around the other side of the house to see if anything was there, when a hand grabbed him from behind and someone threw something over his head. It was lights out.

Aaron waited a very long five minutes and then called Jerry. The phone rang, but Jerry did not pick up. Aaron panicked. He immediately jumped out of the car and ran around to the back yard. When he arrived, there was nothing there. No sign of a struggle or anything to identify Jerry. Aaron decided to walk around the house, and as he passed the back door, he was hit on the head and he was out.

Inside, Ann sat in a room all by herself. She had been thrown into a van and taken here by some very military-looking men, but it wasn't U.S. Military. She wondered why her boss had kept her locked up for so long, but she realized he didn't have the nerve to get rid of her. He was leaving it to someone else.

When she was moved to a new place in Lansing, she was relieved when she was able to get a message to one of the agents, Aaron, who was watching her. He had watched her in the first building she was in, and then she was moved. When Aaron showed up to watch her again, she knew she had to get a message to him—and she did. When Loretta had once snuck in to see Ann, she and

Loretta had planned that if anything went wrong, Ann should make sure she left information in some way.

Before she was transported to Ohio, she overheard her captives talking about the new place in Ohio. She even heard the address. She knew she had to get this to someone, and the only person she could think of was Aaron since he had been sympathetic with her situation and had agreed with Loretta that something was wrong.

Ann knew that she was not the only one being held captive in the house because the night before, she had heard another woman screaming. She must have been put in a room next to her because she continued to scream at the person who put her there, and she was kicking and pounding on the wall. It didn't last long though because suddenly it got quiet. She thought, *They must have drugged her or worse…!*

Ann tried to contact her using morse code, but there was no response. The only response she received was yelling from the men in the kitchen to stop the pounding.

Then, she heard what sounded like more bodies being brought into the house. She heard a man's voice, "Put them in the bedroom on the end. Tie them together."

Another said, "You sure that's a good idea?"

"Take the zip ties, bind their feet and hands, cover their heads, and tie them together with that nylon rope. Do a good job. Make sure their mouths are taped before you cover their heads."

"Will do. I'll make sure they can't move."

Ann froze. She muttered, "Were these people coming to help me? I know that Aaron and Jerry work together. I hope this isn't them, and they didn't get in trouble with these bastards."

Chapter 15

Colewin

Joe and Ron were wondering what they could do next to really help end the event. That morning, they had heard from Peter, and he had told them that all the troops were still at the base, but he did not know what the next move would be, if there would be one. He had learned that the trainer in charge had been told to stop what he was doing and just keep training the troops at the base.

Joe asked, "Ron, do you think we should begin some type of investigation with the governor?"

"We need to do something. This event is really going to be bad if everything goes as we have understood it might."

"It looks like they are already spreading false information about the left and right, trying to get them to hate one another and blame each other for all the bad things that are happening."

Lansing

Loretta had waited long enough. She finally got ahold of someone in the governor's office, and she was able to get the twenty soldiers assigned to her by the governor to help her track down Ann. It would be a very risky endeavor, however. Loretta was worried that crossing into Ohio might be a bit tricky without Ohio's governor knowing what they were doing, but she and the Michigan governor's office agreed that they needed to keep the situation quiet since they did not know yet whom they could trust.

The governor's office in Michigan was working on contacting the president's people to see if everything would be legal.

Loretta knew they had to hurry. They wanted to keep as quiet as possible, so they had the team load into commercial vans, and they drove to the site. It took them two hours. In that time, a lot had changed.

1,500 miles away

The old boss was livid. He had been agreeable up to this point, but when he heard that the new boss had agreed to eliminate three FBI agents and the governor of Michigan at this early date, he could not go along with the new boss anymore.

The new boss was in Montana now, and the old boss called him, "We need to meet! I am on my way to Montana to meet with you, so stay put."

After a plane ride and then a lengthy trip in a black Suburban, he met with the new boss. "So, you want to eliminate these four people without any thought about how it might look a year before we want to take over?"

"Yes. Why?"

"We cannot do this now. It would look bad for us. You need to let these people go."

"And then what? If we let them go, they might catch on to us, and then it would set us back—big time."

"Not if you do what I am planning."

"And what is that?"

"We let the four of them go, and we blame it all on the militia in the Upper Peninsula. There are several up there, but I think we can connect the one in Colewin with the others, and then we can make it look like they did this to put our people in a bad light."

"That could work?"

"Yes. I have already contacted Sheriff Daryl in the Eastern Upper Peninsula. He works for us up there, and he said he would be happy to start arresting people and putting the blame on them."

"Really? How will he do that? You can't blame both the militia and the governor!"

"We will post all kinds of information on the web and on social media platforms about how the militia pulled it off, and we will contact newspapers and television. We can say that the governor was in on it because she was upset about what had happened to her earlier. We will also contact news outlets and post everywhere how she tried to set up the militia. Who cares what people really think? They can draw their own conclusions, but we will have both sides in trouble."

"Now, I am interested."

"We know that there is a group headed to your place in Ohio, and they are going to try to free the four of them. We need to have your men leave, and they need to clean the place completely of any of their stuff, including fingerprints, food, garbage, anything that might be able to identify them. Then they need to leave immediately, but they should leave the four tied up, but make it so they can free themselves after our guys leave. They should make sure there are no vehicles around, so the four of them will be stuck there until the cops arrive."

"That's doable."

"Then we contact the authorities in Ohio that this group is planning to set up our organization. We will connect with some of our people in the Ohio government and let them know what our plan is, and they can help to facilitate all of this. Hopefully, the public, especially the Michigan Governor's opponents, will believe that she tried to have them set up, and that no one was holding them hostage."

"Could they arrest the ones who are headed there?"

"That will not be necessary. What is necessary is that the blame falls soundly on the people in the U.P. We can say that the governor gave the FBI false information."

"Who is going to believe this?"

"It does not matter. If it is out there, there will always be uncertainties, and that is what we want. We need to get false information to instill doubts, create conspiracy theories, and get people talking, especially after Sheriff Daryl arrests some of the militia. It is going to work."

"It sounds good, but I am not sold on the idea that you can keep these people in jail if they are arrested."

"It does not matter. We just need to keep this going until the event or the election, and then all will be well. If the event works, we will not have to worry about the election."

"Good point. I think you are right though that people will believe it if we can convince them that the governor is doing this out of retribution for what happened to her earlier. Can we leave anything at the hiding place that could implicate these people?"

"We do not have a lot of time, but if we can come up with something, then sure. Why not do that?"

"We need to think and get this done."

"The best part of this is that we will have the people who attacked our bunker in the U.P., and we will be free of those scoundrels. They keep messing up what we have there. First it was those teachers, then whoever spearheaded the attack on the bunker. We need to get back to controlling that place. It is a key base."

"We will need to have the tech person back, too. Whatever happened to that guy, Bates?"

"They have him in Michigan. We will see if we can also get him out of their custody. He was an asset."

Chapter 16

Somewhere in Ohio

Ann was going crazy wondering who had been brought to the house earlier. She had heard a lot of commotion, and then it was all very quiet. The day passed with very little noise. It was strangely quiet. She had always been able to hear her captors talking and moving around, but now she could hear very little.

Aaron and Jerry had been tied back-to-back and could not move. They could not speak or see anything. It also seemed too quiet to them.

The governor was in the same boat. They had drugged her the night before, and she was just coming around. Her head was still fuzzy, but she was beginning to feel somewhat awake. She was gagged and blindfolded too, but she could hear.

Ann wanted to start morse code again, but she was afraid that the captors might get violent if they heard it again. Then, as she sat there thinking, she heard doors open and close and a commotion begin that lasted quite a while. She heard a lot of yelling, cursing, and running around. By her guess, this lasted for several hours. Then a funny thing happened. Someone came in and ripped the tape off her mouth and cut the zip ties on her legs and cut part way through the ties on her arms. She was not free, but she could see that she would be able to break the ties if she had time.

She asked, "Are you helping me or are you hoping I try to escape and then you kill me?" The person looked at Ann, laughed, and left the room. *What the hell was happening?*

Once the person left, she heard some commotion, doors slam, and all was quiet. She was able to stand for the first time in several days, and it felt good. The zip ties on Ann's arms took her about five minutes, but she was able to break and remove them.

At this point she knew something was up. She moved slowly to the door. She stood in front of it and listened. Nothing! She slowly opened the door. She could not see anyone. She looked around and then crept out of the room, keeping low so as not to be seen. When she reached the living room, she saw that all was quiet. It was clean and empty. She checked the kitchen, nothing. She glanced outside. All was quiet. After a thorough inspection of the front of the house, she decided to look in the back bedrooms. She felt dirty and disheveled after being held for such a long time. She had not showered for days, maybe weeks. She had not been able to use any facilities, and as she looked back in her room, she could smell the stench. How had she survived in there?

On the road

Loretta was getting anxious. They had been on the road for over two hours, and they were getting close, but she was afraid that the time it had taken them to get here might have cost Ann and the others their lives. She knew this was the only way to get there without alerting any other people, and she had to hope that what they were doing would work.

Loretta tried to call Aaron and Jerry again, but it went right to voice mail. "Where could they be?" she said out loud.

The driver looked at her and said, "Did you say something?"

"No, I was just thinking out loud."

The journey continued. They were close now so Loretta began to go over the plan. They would not just drive right up to the house, but they would park a few streets away and proceed on foot.

She contacted the leaders in each of the three vans. She was riding in the only car. "Is everyone ready?"

The responses came back that all were ready. They just needed the word.

It was not long before they pulled up to a spot that had been preplanned, and Loretta had the driver pull up in a wooded area that would conceal the vehicles. When the vehicles stopped, Loretta told everyone to stay put until she checked the area.

Loretta wandered down the street. As she approached the house, she saw lights flashing on several police cars.

Earlier in the house

Ann walked to the bedroom next to where she was staying, and she found someone tied up and blindfolded. She looked around the room to make sure no one else was there, and then she went directly to the person and pulled off her blindfold and took the tape from her mouth.

The governor's first response was a very nervous, "Who are you? What are you going to do with me?"

"My name is Ann, and I have been held in the room next to you. I know who you are. How did you get here?"

"I'm not sure how everything happened. It was all so quick. I was thrown into a van, and they drove for hours. Where are we?"

"I'm not sure, somewhere in Ohio, I know that. There are some other people in the next room. Maybe they know."

"How did you get free? Where are the people who have been holding us?"

"I don't know. I checked the entire house, and there are no other people here. I guess we better check the next room."

Ann found some scissors in the kitchen, and proceeded to help the governor out of her zip ties. The governor was relieved, but she was still panicked. "What now?"

"We check the next room. The only weapons we have are these scissors. I did find a small knife too. Here. You might need it."

They walked out of the room and moved to the third bedroom. Ann opened the door and stepped back, just in case. Nothing happened. She peered into the room. She saw two men tied back-to-back, sitting on the floor, feet and hands tied, faces covered with cloth bags.

Ann decided to say something as she glanced around the room, but she stayed in the hall checking to make sure no one else was there. "Who are you? Are you all right?"

One of the men tried to answer, but he could only mumble. Ann was cautious, and she kept watch at the door as she motioned to the governor to take off the blindfolds. The governor moved slowly and removed the coverings. The governor also removed the tape from one of the men's mouths and then the other, then she quickly stepped back.

As soon as the tape was off the first man, he said, "Who are you? What are you going to do with us?"

"I'm Ann, an FBI agent. I've been held captive for months in different places."

As they turned to look at her, both men yelled her name at once. "Ann…."

"Ann, you're alive?" Aaron said, "What's happening? This is us, Aaron and Jerry."

"What?" Ann took a good look and recognized them. "Thank God you guys are okay. We're not sure what's going on either."

"What do you mean we? Who else is here?"

"It's the governor of Michigan."

Jerry spoke, "No kidding. Are you okay?"

"I am."

"Let's get you guys out of these zip ties."

The street

Loretta thought at first that something bad had happened. Were they too late? Are they all dead? She knew she had to be careful and not give herself away. She contacted the vans and told them not to act. There was a problem. Loretta got as close as she could without anyone noticing her. She listened, but nothing was happening. Several police cars were sitting in front of the house, and the officers were in their cars.

Then, one man exited, and he walked to the door and knocked. It was the sheriff. He also wondered why he had to take so many of his deputies to this place. It was probably just a few squatters again. He was tired of having to run out here every so often to deal with these homeless people.

Loretta thought, *If this is the house and something bad has happened, why is he knocking? Something is up.* She entered the yard next to the house and walked to the side of the house the police were investigating. She saw the door open—and there was Ann. *What is going on?*

Chapter 17

Prior to Loretta's arrival

Ann and the governor helped Aaron and Jerry out of their restraints. When they were free, they could not thank Ann enough. She thanked them in return for trying to find her. They talked for a while when the governor broke in and said, "Do any of you have a cell phone?"

No one did. They had all been taken. Ann said, "Let's see what we can find here. We'll need to get out of here and notify our people."

Aaron thought they should call Loretta if they could. "Do you think some of the homes around here might let us use a phone?"

Jerry said, "Well, when we were first here, we noticed that there were no people around, and no one on the streets. Our captors picked a place that was abandoned. I doubt if there are any phones around."

"Well, we need to do something." The governor was frustrated.

They searched the house, but they could not find anything. Just as they were assembling in the living room, they heard vehicles approaching and then a knock on the door.

Ann walked to the door and opened it.

On the street

Loretta watched for a while as the man spoke with Ann, but as several of the officers left their vehicles, she decided to walk over and talk with them. She knew they would not know who she was and so she could play dumb.

"Hello, say what's going on?"

An officer looked at her and said, "Who are you? This area has been like a ghost town for the past few years. You cannot be living around here, are you?"

"No. Why?"

"Then why are you here, and how did you get here?"

"I drove here, but I left my car a few blocks away. I was hoping to find a friend of mine, but I cannot find anyone."

"Yeah, this area is kind of dead. You should go back to where you were. There's no one around. It's abandoned."

"It doesn't look abandoned."

"No, a company keeps it up in hopes of selling off the homes. So far, no luck. Hey, I said you should head out."

"Okay, I will. What are you doing here if no one is around?"

"We're picking up some fugitives who decided to squat here from what I gather, I guess. I'm not sure. You'll have to ask the sheriff."

"Why so many cop cars?"

"I don't know any more than you do right now. Say, why all the questions?"

"Oh, nothing, I'll head out. Good luck."

Loretta walked back the way she had come, but she did not leave the area. She kept hidden nearby in some lilac bushes and watched. As she watched, the officers who had left their vehicles, began to head toward the house, and they all entered.

Inside

The sheriff was being quite gruff. He asked how many people were inside. Ann told him, "Just the four you can see."

"What are you people doing here?"

"You don't know? We thought you were here to rescue us. I'm an FBI agent as are these two guys. That woman over there is the governor of Michigan."

"Sure she is, and I'm the president."

"No seriously. We were being held here against our will until the people who were holding us left. I was able to get out of the zip ties they had put on me, and I was able to release the others."

"I don't see any bindings."

"Just look in the bedrooms."

The sheriff went to the room in which Ann had been held, and nothing was there except for the stench that remained. "What am I looking for? I don't see anything here. Wow, this place reeks."

"Well, look in the other rooms."

He did. The same was true for all the rooms. Ann realized that his men had been all over the house while they talked. "Did some of your men remove the zip ties and blindfolds?"

"Nope. They were just looking for other people, but I'll check with them."

"Something's fishy here!"

Aaron spoke up and said the same thing. "Hey, we were being held. My buddy, Jerry, and I were trying to free these two, and then we were taken."

"Okay, okay. Let's just pretend that it's true. Then what in hell is the governor of Michigan doing here?"

"I was taken by some militia types. It has happened before."

"Well, the word I have is that you guys have been pulling a fast one. You're setting someone up."

"What!" screamed the governor.

"Bullshit!" said Aaron.

Chapter 18

Montana

"So how is this going to work now? We have people in Ohio ready to arrest the people who are there, and I can see that we can make this look like they planned this, but if they do, then is Charlie's militia off the hook?"

"Yes and no. For some people, they will believe that the governor and her friends are guilty, but others will believe that the militia is guilty of abducting her. We will fan the flames of both in the news, and we will have our people proceed with both arrests. That will confuse people, but they will believe what they will believe. We have documents drawn up by our people in Michigan to show that the militia had a plan to snatch the governor, and we have detailed plans that will be planted in the house in Ohio showing that the governor wanted to entrap the militia."

"And this will convince everyone?"

"It will, because again, they will believe what they want to believe. There are no facts except those that we manufacture."

"I guess that is why we need you. You know how to work the system. I am not adept at that, so I am glad we are working together."

The new boss was not entirely certain that he wanted to be the number two man, but he knew that he needed the old boss right now because he had great ideas.

Ohio

Loretta saw that several of the officers entered the house. While the sheriff was knocking, one of his deputies went in the back door for some reason. He left just as quickly as he entered, walked to his patrol car, threw something in, walked to the front door, and went in.

Loretta was surprised by this, and she knew it was not a good sign. She waited a while longer and then she saw Ann being led out of the house in HANDCUFFS!! Then Aaron and Jerry. Same thing. Handcuffs! *Where was the governor?*

The sheriff had checked and none of the people inside had any type of identification. He was doubtful that they were squatters, and he looked at their wrists, especially Ann's, and he thought they might have been held captive. He was also sure that if this was the governor of Michigan, he was not going to handcuff her.

He had sent the others out with his deputies, and he checked if anyone had found anything, but they said they had only found a few items in the kitchen. Now, it was only him and one other deputy and the governor. "Say, I don't know what's going on, but if you're the governor, I'm not going to be the one to cuff you. In fact, let's call someone to verify."

Upon hearing his boss, the deputy disagreed vehemently. "No, sir, we should just cuff her and take her away. These four are criminals."

"Are you telling me how to do my job? You think this is my first rodeo? I've been doing this for years, and I have a gut feeling. You can go out with the others."

"But sheriff…"

"Now. I said now."

"But…"

"Now."

The governor did not know what to think. She just stood there and hoped she could make the call. "Are we going to call anyone to verify who I am?"

"Here, I have a phone. I'm going to call your office. You stay right there and don't move." The sheriff looked up a number that he thought would get him to the governor's office. He called. It rang a few times and someone picked up.

"Hello. You have reached the Michigan State Capitol Commission."

"Say, this is Sheriff Sutton from Fulton County, Ohio. May I speak to someone in the governor's office?"

"Just a moment." As the secretary put the sheriff on hold, she contacted the governor's security since everyone was on high alert since she was taken. "Hello, security, I am one of the secretaries at the Capitol Commission. I have a sheriff from Ohio asking to speak to someone in the governor's office."

"Put him through immediately."

"Yes, sir, just a moment." The secretary patched the security through.

"Hello, this is Trooper Carlson."

"Hello, this is Sheriff Sutton from Fulton County, Ohio. I have a woman here who claims she is the governor."

"Is she all right?"

"Yes, but I need you to verify her. I'm not sure who she is."

"Could we see a picture or video?"

"Sure. Well, let me see if she can work that magic." The sheriff handed the phone to the governor who told Trooper Carlson what they needed to do, and in a minute, they were face to face.

The trooper instantly recognized the governor. "That's her." They spoke for a few minutes, and he said he would contact a group that was on the way to Ohio, and that she would be escorted back to Michigan. "I just want to thank you sheriff for what you have done for the governor and Michigan. A group is on the way there right now to pick her up. I'm not sure where they are, but I'll check, and I'll get back to you."

"You're welcome. We have other people who were with her, and the word is that they were in cahoots with a group to take your governor."

"Really. You have them?"

"We do, and we'll lock 'em up."

"But, sheriff, they were not the ones," the governor exclaimed.

"Well, then were you conspiring with these people? Were you doing this to throw the blame someplace else?"

The governor could see where this was going, and she realized she would be better off to just go along with the sheriff until her help arrived.

The Michigan trooper called his man in Ohio. When he answered, he told the trooper that they were right where he had just indicated, but that the FBI agent was checking out the place. As he was speaking, Loretta showed up and explained what had happened. The driver relayed what he had just been told, and they drove with their entourage to the house where the governor was.

Montana

The old boss was smiling as he watched the news. He had delivered what he thought would end his troubles in the U.P., and it would get the country focused on these people rather than his group. Now was the time to throw the other story out there. He thought, *I must make sure that the governor and those FBI agents stay in the custody of the police, so now is the time to send information about how the Michigan governor and the FBI have worked together to make sure the Michigan militia, and for that matter, the Midwest militias were blamed for her abduction. If the*

Ohio

Back at the house, the sheriff had given the word that the governor would go free, and he thought the others might too. He called his deputies, "Send those others in here for a bit."

"What? They're already on their way to jail. Cliff took 'em."

"Well, I guess that's why we came here. I'll let the governor know, and she can deal with them."

As the sheriff ended his call, an officer came in and said, "An FBI agent and an official representative from Michigan are here to pick up the governor."

"Wow, that was quick. All right, you're free to go, but you are on our radar because someone said that you were in on the plot, so you might still be in some trouble. We'll let you know."

The governor was not happy. "A plot? You know we've been set up. Why would we do something like that?"

Loretta had walked in and overheard the conversation. She got the governor's attention and said, "Let's just get out of here and head to Michigan. We can talk later."

The governor agreed and they left.

Chapter 19

Colewin, Michigan, a few days later

Sheriff Daryl had gotten a message that he was to head to Colewin to pick up the people who were responsible for planning and carrying out the hostage situation with the governor. He had a smile on his face as big as any he had ever had. He was tired of Charlie and his crew creating situations for him to placate all the time. He felt overjoyed.

The old boss gave orders for him to do it soon and to get the culprits behind bars. What they had done was bizarre, and he would make sure they were locked up for a long time.

Joe and Ron had been watching the news with their wives when a bulletin came across. It said that a group of the U.P. militia was responsible for taking the governor hostage. They listened as the newsperson named three people: Charlie, Matt, and Tommy. The anchor spoke about the plot and how Colewin had been the hotspot for the plan. Joe looked at his wife and then at Ron and Shanice. "What in the world is this about? Where did this come from?"

Ron responded, "This is pure fabrication. I'd like to know the source."

Joette could only look and wonder. She knew this could not be true, and she said, "How had the national news even gotten the names of these guys in Colewin?"

Shanice agreed. "How would anyone know about them unless they were a part of this community? We've gotten to know them, and Charlie and Matt have never been anywhere except Colewin. They've worked their entire lives right here."

Joe was watching the news, switching from channel to channel to catch as much information as he could on the various networks. He was also checking any outlet with news, including the internet. On one news outlet, he had heard that Sheriff Daryl from the St. Ignace police station would head to town looking for some locals who had been a part of the abduction of the governor.

Joe and Ron and their group were keeping an eye on Sheriff Daryl's moves, and so far, he was not able to find Charlie or Matt, the two people he wanted to arrest first.

Sheriff Daryl knew he had to go after Tommy, but he also knew that getting Tommy would be difficult. He had too many friends, and they would protect him. It would cause an uproar in Colewin if he took him first.

Joe understood the sheriff's predicament, that apprehending anyone in Colewin would be a problem, but he could not understand how Colewin had played into the report about the governor. He knew there were other militias that had been responsible for the governor's problems a while back, but Charlie's group was not part of that, so why go after Charlie?

Ron had the same thoughts, but it was Shanice who came up with the reason. "This is retaliation for our group attacking the bunker. I'm sure of it."

Joe had to agree. "You're right, Shanice. That's it."

Joette was sitting quietly on the sofa drinking a cup of coffee. She took a sip and then said, "Do you think they will come after us next? Are we still safe here?"

Joe said, "If the people who are spreading this information are the bunker leaders, then we are safe. They think we're dead, so we might have an advantage here if we can keep it that way."

There was a knock on the door. Ron said, "Come in."

It was Matt.

They all turned and stared. Joe said, "What are you doing here? We heard that you were being sought by the sheriff. Shouldn't you be hiding?"

"I just had to come and find out what you guys think. Do you believe this stuff? We didn't have anything to do with the governor."

"We know. These are fabricated stories."

"Have you heard the latest one about the governor?"

"No. What have you heard?"

"I was watching one of the networks, and I heard that the governor was in on the plan. She wanted to take down the militias, so she faked her abduction."

Shanice said, "No way!"

"Well, that's what's out there. Maybe that's it, and she thought it was us in the U.P. Maybe she just wanted to get even with all the militias, and we were easy picking."

"No way," Ron said. "How would she know who to point out to the authorities?"

"I don't know, but if it's true…"

Joe looked at Matt and said, "Do you really believe that?"

"I'm not sure what to believe any more."

"We know you're innocent, and you have to protect yourself. I don't like having to go against the law, but you know that Daryl has been in on this for some time. Even Charlie says that he was deep into the organization to take down the government."

"I'm not worried. I know where to hide, and they'll never find me. I can survive for a long time until this is all cleared up. You probably won't see me until I get word that this is over, so thanks for your help. I'll be in touch through my family."

"Matt, you take care, and let us know what we can do to help."

"Just figure this out and clear us if you can. Maybe check with the people you know downstate who would know if the governor is in on this."

"We'll try," Joe responded.

When Matt left, they could hear his four-wheeler pull away as they all looked at each other in dismay.

North of Colewin

Charlie had heard from the news that he was being hunted. He could not believe it. He was spinning out of control, and he did not know what to do. He had contacted Matt, and Matt said he was going into hiding, and they would never find him. He was not going to allow these bastards to get him. He was furious, but he always thought something like this could happen, just not to him.

Charlie, on the other hand, was being himself. He did not really believe that they would come to get him, but he was preparing if he had to defend himself. He had called his friends and relatives to see if any of them would help. Most of them were sympathetic, but they did not know what they could do.

Charlie had stockpiled weapons and ammunition, just in case. He had also buried money and survival equipment in his root cellar for just this type of situation. He felt prepared if he had to defend himself.

Charlie contacted Joe to see if he knew any more than what he had heard on the news, and he wondered if he could help him. "Joe, this is Charlie."

"Hey, Charlie, what's up?"

"Well, I'm wonderin' if you got any ideas about these here news bulletins that we got about us. What the hell are we gonna do? It sounds like they're comin' after us?"

"We need to make sure the three of you are cleared of everything. Ron and I are working on getting the FBI involved, and we will check if the governor can help. We have friends in Lansing who might be able to assist us too. I just spoke with Matt and he's going into hiding. I'm not sure that's the answer, but I get it. Tommy is out of the area. He's also hiding. I doubt they'll find him."

"Well, I'm not movin'. I got all the preparation I need: good protection here, food, water, ammo. I'm stayin' put."

"Be careful Charlie. We'll get back to you if we find out anything."

"Thanks…and, Joe, sorry about how we got started. Same with Ron. You guys have had my back now for a while, and I appreciate it."

"Thanks, Charlie, we'll do our best to help you."

Ohio

The governor walked out with Loretta, but she was not in a good mood. "I have had it with these people. They just keep trying to destroy the government. Me included. We need to get a handle on this, and we need to do it right now. Whoever is masterminding these insurgent activities must be neutralized." She reached the vehicle, and the driver opened the door for her. She slid into the back seat and breathed a huge sigh of relief.

Loretta agreed. "I know. Let me tell you what happened to me since we last spoke." Loretta went into detail about the safe house and the group of men who came after her. "And that is how I lost track of Aaron and Jerry. You do have my boss though, and he must know something that can help us weaken or destroy this plot against you and the government."

"Yes, we need to work on that guy. We also have that young fellow, Bates, from the bunker who was involved, but he might not be a big help."

"We'll also have to check on my partners, the three who were taken."

"Definitely."

The driver had been on the phone outside of the car. He opened the front driver's side door and said, "Governor, we have contacted your security, and they are sending a helicopter for you. They will be here in five or ten minutes. There will only be room for you since they have security with them."

"Thank you." She turned to Loretta, "I will need you to be at my side for the next few days, so we can figure out some of what to do with my security force. Report to the Capitol Building when you arrive."

Lansing

Loretta rode back in the car. She was very tired and took a short nap on the way. When she arrived, she went straight to the place that the governor had indicated earlier. As she walked in, her phone buzzed. "Hello."

"Loretta?"

"Yes."

"Joe here."

Chapter 20

St. Ignace

The new boss kept in touch with Sheriff Daryl. Daryl thought he should take at least ten deputies with him to Colewin. The new boss thought he was crazy. "You need eleven men to get these guys?"

"You haven't been to Colewin, have you?"

"No."

"These guys are crazy over there. I need at least ten, especially for this guy, Charlie. He probably has an arsenal of automatic weapons, and who knows what else. Then there is that kid Tommy. He's lived in Colewin his whole life too, and he knows the area. He guides people on bear hunts, so he knows the woods, and he's got firearms. I'm not sure about that Matt guy. I don't really know him."

"Just get it done."

"I will with ten deputies."

Lansing

The governor was at home to clean up and get ready to go back to work when her security people knocked on the door. She was thinking about all that she had to do after being away for a while, and a few of her key people were at her home updating her prior to heading to the Capitol.

They were going over recent information when one of the assistants stopped everyone to check on a news article. She said, "Everyone look at the news on this network. It's saying that several members in the Michigan House are asking for the governor's resignation. They say she is actively working to show that the militia abducted her, but they say she planned the whole thing and had help from the FBI."

"What? Who said that and where did they get that false information?"

"This person, whom they have not identified, said that he spoke to some FBI boss who is incarcerated in Lansing. He says some of his agents worked with the governor to take down the militias as retribution for what some of them did to her."

"Do you mean that FBI boss that Loretta gave us?"

"I believe that's who it is."

"That guy is bad news. He was working with a local militia to bring down the government. We have investigators working on that right now. How did they get access to him, and how do they even know this?"

"It doesn't give many details. It just says they want you gone."

"It has to be the guy in the House whose friend ran against me, and who has been crying about my victory since day one."

"He also indicated that your entire administration is in on this. He gives names and dates and places when you worked to conspire against the FBI boss. Wow, he even says that you freed the three agents who helped you, and that they were in on this plan."

"I just exonerated them. I sent word to the Ohio authorities that those people were heroes, not crooks. The two guys found me and that agent, Ann, and they were even held captive. We were lucky to escape!"

"How did you escape?"

"Well, Ann was able to free herself. The men who were holding us had left. We don't know why. They just cleared out and left us there."

"Are you sure they were not setting you up?"

"Who?"

"The people who allegedly freed you. Maybe they were in on it. This looks bad. What should we say in response?"

"Just say it is all lies and sour grapes because I won the election."

One of her assistants who had not spoken said, "Governor, this is very distressing. Are you sure that those people who freed you were not part of some plot to get your administration in trouble? I mean, it sounds bad."

"Now you have me wondering. What really happened? I know I was taken, and I know that others were held in that house, but that's really all I know."

"And that agent Loretta. What about her? Do you know if she is telling the truth, or is she in on this?"

"I don't know. We had better do some checking."

Montana

"Our man in the Michigan House is going to throw out some conspiracy theories. We are going to try to take down the governor and her whole administration. We should be able to do it, too. Once we can get our man to convince his party and get them on board, we will be home free in Michigan."

Although he didn't agree at first, the old boss thought he might be able to get some traction out of the new boss's development in Michigan. He was extremely happy about the way everything was going. He knew if he put juicy information out there that people would bite. He realized that the country was so divided that anything anyone said *became the truth*. He was just adding to the turmoil and the division. The old boss had been in government for many years himself, and he knew just how to inject this information.

"Boss, the governor of Michigan just said that the U.P. militia did not have anything to do with her capture—and that it was another group closer to Lansing."

"That is all right. Let it just play out as it will. No one will believe her if we can show that she was planning her abduction. It will be her word against everyone else's. I love it. She cannot win this."

"I hear that the sheriff in the Eastern U.P. is right now trying to arrest the guys we identified out there as the perpetrators. If he is successful that will help."

"I do not know if it matters if people believe that they might be involved. It will be good either way."

St. Ignace

The word came in that the three people who had been accused of abducting the governor were innocent. The governor cleared them, and she said they should not be arrested or harassed in any way, and that the people responsible were not from there.

Sheriff Daryl heard the news. He was immediately on the phone to the new boss. "Did you see what the governor just said?"

"I did."

"What do you think?"

"I think you should arrest them."

"That's what I thought. These guys are nothing but trouble anyway. We need to silence them."

"Don't say anything, just arrest all three and start with that Charlie guy. Your old friend."

Daryl had his orders, and he was hoping for the same thing, but he wasn't sure where to start. He decided to ask around to see if anyone knew where Charlie might be. He had been friends with him, but he had never been to his house.

Daryl's first stop was Colewin to find Mayor Don. He would put some pressure on him and hope to get some information about Charlie. He and his ten deputies pulled up to the town hall where Don usually spent a lot of time, but he wasn't there. He turned to one of his deputies and said, "I should have guessed. I bet he's at the Sportsman's Bar and Pizzeria. Come on with me, just in case. The rest of you guys stay here and be ready for anything. Who knows in this town?"

Daryl and his deputy crossed the street and entered the bar. It was noisy inside, music playing, people talking, and some yelling, and Daryl saw Don sitting by the window with several other guys. They were in a very heated discussion. Hands were flying and faces were red. It looked like they were ready to take somebody out. One guy was half standing and leaning over the table.

Daryl approached. Everyone quieted instantly.

Lansing and Colewin

Loretta had just gotten the news that the governor had given the word to free Ann, Aaron, and Jerry. She had heard the news about the U.P. militia and knew that she had to call Joe. The word was that they were not responsible for abducting the governor, but she knew what she had seen on the news, and she was concerned. She called Joe.

Joe was sitting watching the news with Ron, Joette, and Shanice, and when he picked up his phone, he decided to put it on speaker.

"Joe, this is Loretta. I'm calling to see how everyone is doing there. Have you heard what happened with the governor? We believe that someone is working against her and trying to get her thrown out of office."

"We've been following the information on the news. Depending on the channel, the story differs. What's your take?"

"I sense that the people who took the governor are trying to create more divisiveness in the country. There's already enough. Politicians can't get along and won't compromise on most anything. I'm afraid that whoever is behind this is fanning the flames and hoping to get the governor impeached."

"That's what it sounds like here, too."

"What about the people there who have been identified as the ones abducting the governor? She cleared them, but are they all right?"

"We'll have to see. The information we are getting is that some people in the government believe the governor is lying. We have a couple who are hiding somewhere and one who is standing his ground. I'm afraid if this goes much further that there's going to be some bloodshed. We know Charlie has built a barricade around his home, and he has enough weapons, food, and water to hold out a long time. It's Charlie and his wife. They won't take this. They'll go down swinging."

"Can you get the local law enforcement to help?"

"That's the problem. They believe he's guilty from everything we've heard. I have word from some of our people that the sheriff is in town right now asking questions."

"Let me get ahold of the governor, and I'll inform her about what's happening. I know she will not want this to end like that."

"That would help. There isn't much we can do here. We have people ready to help, but the sheriff brought about ten deputies according to what I heard, and that would mean our people would have to fight the law. Ron and I are hoping to contact Charlie and talk him down, but so far, we haven't had any luck."

Loretta did not say much, so Joe continued.

"It's complicated. These guys have been preparing for something like this for a long time. Charlie informed us that his old militia members all had arms and munitions buried on their property along with money and supplies. Some have even built what they refer to as "bomb shelters," but not the ones you might picture. They are more like fortresses to defend themselves in case the government goes after them."

"You're kidding, right?"

"I wish. I have never seen one, but Charlie once went into some detail about them. They say that's why they need the second amendment, so they can have arms and weapons to defend themselves and, for some, to begin the next civil war."

"What?"

Sitting next to Joe, Ron was nodding his head. He said, "What Joe is telling you is the truth. These guys are ready, but Charlie has lost control of his group. Most of them have turned to these other guys because they pay, and they feel that they'll get the government where they want it. Under their thumb."

"How do we stop these guys? Obviously, Charlie is not a part of them. The people who are driving this—the ones who abducted the governor—I'm sure they are one and the same."

Joette spoke up, "You're right. It's been years of these guys making plans and getting ready for this event that they always talk about."

Joe sat thinking and everyone was quiet for a short time. Then Shanice said, "Really, what are we going to do? We must do something!"

Loretta repeated what Shanice said, "Yes, we must do something!"

Joe looked at Ron. They were the only two who had gotten close to the old boss, and they knew the type of person he was. They had heard it from his own mouth back in 2019 when they tried to take him out. He had talked about control, and how he would divide the country further until people were at each other's throats. He felt he just needed to keep at it, and he would eventually win.

Ron said, "You know he wants to destroy the Constitution and take full control of the country. The only way he could do that is if he eliminated our current government, and he became the head man. I say head man because he would not be a president as we know it today. He would be a dictator."

Joe agreed. "That's it. That's what he wants. They have billions of dollars behind them, and they can control people's minds that way, plus he feeds into the people who already are dissatisfied and others who just want minimal or no government. Some want their states to secede from the union and become their own country. Who knows what else?"

Loretta said, "Our job then is even more difficult than I thought. I wonder if Ann, Aaron, and Jerry will ever be released if these people have a say. I'm going to work on helping them with the governor's assistance. I'll check in with you guys if I learn anything else."

"We will do the same if we hear anything. Be careful, and give our best to Ann."

"Will do."

Chapter 21

Colewin

Joe sat pondering the situation. He knew that they had to do something to help, but he wasn't sure what would be best. Should they jump in their vehicle and head to Charlie's to assist him? Would that even make sense? When Joe turned to Ron, they looked eye to eye. They knew what had to be done, but they also understood that it would be riskier than anything they had ever done.

Ron spoke first. "You thinking what I'm thinking? The governor's hands are tied. So are Loretta's because they'll work within the law, but that won't stop these guys."

Joe shook his head as he stood and stretched, "That's what I'm thinking. We tried once to stop them, but we didn't get the jugular. We went for the knees. This time we have to figure out how to cut the throat of this organization."

North of Colewin

At home, Charlie and his wife had just finished supper. They looked around the place. It was a bastion. He had a view in every direction. He lived on thirty-eight acres and had piles of wood that he used to heat his place in the winter. There was a garage, well more of a barn, where he kept his vehicles and other military trucks, jeeps, clothing, and other military equipment. As he looked around, he saw two machine guns mounted on tripods. One facing the front or south of the house, with the other facing the north. Both could easily be swiveled to face a new direction.

Charlie would man the M240. His wife would handle the lighter M240L. Both had enough rounds to last a long time. Charlie had taken the two guns when they had attacked the bunker. They had been mounted in the two towers, and Charlie had two of his people take them along with as much ammunition as they could find. He had added to the ammunition supply since, and he figured he would have to be blasted out of his house because no one was getting in.

Inside the Sportsman's

Sheriff Daryl was speaking with some of the men in the Sportsman's, and he was having little luck learning where Charlie might be. He moved from individual to individual, but no one would give him the time of day. He was in Colewin, and the people knew he was not a local. He had never been. The sheriff checked with everyone in the bar, and he was about to leave when someone said, "You and your boys had better move out of Colewin before you have yourself in a heap of trouble."

The sheriff turned to see who had spoken, but everyone was sitting mute, and not one set of eyes were up to meet his. "Who said that? Come on. Don't be a coward! Tell that to my face!"

Don was uneasy in his chair; he squirmed and bent down even further, but then he spoke. "Daryl, why are you here? You've caused enough trouble around here. You know none of us are to blame, and throwing the blame on the three people you did, or someone did, won't get you any favors here in Colewin or Poplar. Just hate." Don fidgeted again and dropped his head.

"That you speakin' Don, or is that your friends? We've known each other a long time, and you've never had that tone in your voice."

"Sorry, but you're messin' with my people."

"Do you know what they did? They abducted the governor!"

"They couldn't have. They've been here all along. I hear the governor ended up in Ohio. How the hell can Charlie, Matt, and Tommy be here and there at the same time? They haven't left town, and we'll all agree to that!"

Sheriff Daryl looked around. Now all the faces were on him, and not one looked friendly. He thought he had better leave well enough alone and find the three without local help. "You'll be hearing from me and so will those three—soon enough." Daryl walked to the door, turned around to say something, but, instead, he just grunted, "Ugghhh," opened the door and slammed it shut.

Ohio

Cliff was one of those guys. He had always been angry with just about everything. Most of his life he had hung with the "wrong crowd," according to his parents and teachers. Even before he joined the group to get paid to take down the government, he was ready to do that. Everyone was so happy when he decided to join the police force after his four years in the Marines. His parents felt that he had finally found his way.

Unfortunately, that was not the case. He was still angry, but his anger had turned toward his government and most people. He complained about taxes, guns, immigrants, politicians, even the cops. What? Why join then?

Cliff thought if he joined the police, he could legally carry a firearm anywhere or anytime he wanted, and he could be on the front lines of change. The kind he wanted was a complete change in the system, so he wanted everyone to think he was on the government's side, but he had other plans.

He had stockpiled weapons and ammunition for a time when it would be necessary to use them. He had purchased a plot of land that was just over forty acres. His plan was to change the farmhouse and barn into a fortress. He didn't care what anyone else thought about his plan—but he found people who thought just like he did, and they became a force in his life.

Cliff had sped away with the three captives taken in Ohio—Ann, Aaron, and Jerry—and, after transferring them to a van, drove to his hideout. His buddies were there. Interestingly enough, they were the same people who had kept the four captives at the house.

Cliff pulled up to the farmhouse, jumped out of the car, and went straight to the door. "Hey, you doofuses get out here and help me."

He turned to make sure his captives were still all right in the van. He walked over, opened the front door, and looked in. They were sitting there trying to get free.

Someone from inside said, "What do you need now?"

Cliff answered, "I need some help."

One of his friends came to the door and looked. "What? What do you want?"

"Help me with these three."

"What three?"

"You'll see." And he pulled the van side door open, and there on the floor were his captives.

"You gotta be kiddin' me. We just got rid of those people."

"I know, but we didn't finish the job."

"Cliff, there was no job to finish. We got the word to let them go. To get the hell out of that place and get our butts as far away as we could."

"But they're trouble, and they're the establishment—FBI and all. We need to start getting rid of these people one by one."

"For being a cop, you are one stupid man."

The other guys inside heard the yelling and came walking out of the house. One by one they all echoed the first guy. "What the hell, Cliff?"

"You're gonna get us in a heap of trouble. The sheriff is going to be after you, and that means that he'll be after us. You idiot."

Cliff did not care. He grabbed his pistol and walked to the barn. He yelled, "Bring those three here, now!"

The barn

Ann, Aaron, and Jerry were separated. Each was in a cell alone, if one could call them cells. Deputy Cliff had sped off with the three and had them locked up at a location where the five men who had been at the house had gone. None of the three prisoners knew that the governor had pardoned them. They were getting angrier and angrier as time went by. They knew something was up because they were not taken to the local lockup.

The place was just a dirty old barn, formerly a horse barn, and it smelled like it. The stalls had been reinforced, metal had been added over the doors, and the floors were poured concrete. Inside and outside steel mesh had been added to the whole structure. The entire building still looked shabby and dilapidated, but the cells would do the job. Ann yelled to Aaron and Jerry. "Anyone else in here?"

Aaron heard. He yelled back, "Is that you, Ann?"

"Yes! Have you guys seen anyone else here?"

"No one is around. I can't see much, but I think the guy who took us is with those other guys we saw when we arrived here. They were the same ones who were at the house."

"We have got to get out of here."

"How?"

Jerry heard them talk and said he had an idea. "Where I am, I can see a way to get out of this place. This barn is old and has some weak spots in the walls."

"Yeah, but our hands are zipped tied, and there is steel mesh on all the walls. How can we do anything?"

"I'm going to get on the ground and kick the hell out of this wall. If you have any walls that look rotten, give it a try."

Aaron knew that Jerry was not going to be able to get out, but he felt it was good that Jerry kept his hopes up.

Ann was just sitting on the floor shaking her head.

Colewin

Joe and Ron wondered if they should take a chance and go out to Charlie's place and try to talk some sense into him. They knew if he took a stand that he and his wife would not make it. As they were discussing what they should do, the news switched to a politician talking about possibly running for the White House. Ron was the first to notice.

He jumped out of his chair and yelled, "Joe, look! Look who's on the news."

Joe turned and looked at the television. His eyes almost popped out of his head. "That's him. That's our guy. We tried to take him out in 2019. You mean he's still around and kicking?"

Joette and Shanice were both watching, and they reacted too. Joette said, "You mean that's the person you met in Tampa? Sounds like he's in the Florida legislature."

"Yes!" Joe jumped out of his seat and turned the volume up on the television.

They listened. One reporter was asking the man, the old boss, questions about how he would fix the country. "What would be your priorities?"

The old boss looked right at the camera, and with a stern face and wide eyes, he said, "I will change this country. It is going downhill. My priority will be to reinforce the Second Amendment for starters. I will make every attempt to give the people the final say. Enough of the Supreme Court telling all of us how we must live and how we should act. That should be all of us who decide that."

The reporter asked, "Isn't that democracy? The voice of the people."

"Yes, but you can see what the politicians do. They are all the same. We do not need the Legislative and Judicial branches. We only need the Executive and the cabinet. That is enough. What we have now is a farce."

"Yes, but the government is spelled out in the Constitution."
"And?"

"Well, that gives everyone equal representation."

"We do not need that, and a lot of people agree with that."

Joe turned down the volume. "This is outrageous. We must get people involved to take him down. He will destroy our country. How did he ever get elected to such a position?"

"We know he has connections, and he has access to a lot of money. Someone could be bankrolling him. We know that he was in charge back in 2019, and he has control over these bases all over the country, but how can he pay for all of it?"

"Let's get our sons on this again. Maybe they can investigate where his source of financing originates. Is he that rich?"

"Joe, I'll give them a call and see what our boys can do."

"We need to get involved with this guy again. This time we need to do a thorough job. Last time we thought we could slow them down, and they would not be a problem. We saw what that did—not much. They are stronger than ever."

Chapter 22

Ohio

Sheriff Sutton had just received word that the three individuals that Deputy Cliff had taken away should be released. He had his best men working on determining where Cliff might have gone. It didn't take long before they had a lead. It was an old farmhouse, not far from where they had been earlier when they had found the governor.

"So, you believe they are west of here in that old farmhouse? What makes you so sure?"

"We found the abandoned squad car, and we decided to search the area. We put out a bulletin for all our people and other agencies to be on the lookout for any suspicious activity. We had a call from a group camping nearby who gave us a tip. We followed it and found the abandoned farm."

"Let's get as many officers as we can—and let's go."

Sheriff Sutton was on site at the farm in no time. His team surrounded the farm house where they found several vehicles parked, one was the vehicle the two men, Jerry and Aaron, had driven. When everyone was in place, Sheriff Sutton announced their presence and asked for everyone to come out with hands up.

The only response he received was a volley of shots that tore into the sheriff's vehicle. He was lucky and was not hurt. "Come out with your hands up," he said again. His answer was another volley.

The sheriff knew he was in for some kind of stand-off. He figured that there must be around a half dozen inside, so he sent a message to several agencies in the area, including the FBI, and in no time, he had a sizeable force. They waited a bit and once again the sheriff said, "Come out with your hands up!" He thought he would get a different response. He did not.

Ohio, the woods

Jerry had continued to pound on the wall with his legs and had broken a few boards. Now he had to pull off the wire. If he could do that, he would be able to crawl out. The three captives had discussed if anyone came for them that they would probably be sent to jail or eliminated, so the plan was to escape if they could.

After what seemed like an eternity, Jerry pulled up the steel mesh and snuck out of the barn. He slid around the back to the front, and crawled in the door. He stood and looked for his partners' prison cells…well stables. He saw Aaron.

Aaron was looking through the small opening covered with wire mesh because he had heard the pounding.

Jerry slipped to his left and Aaron jumped back terrified. "What the hell! You scared the shit out of me! How in hell did you get out?"

"I told you there was a weak spot in the wall. It took me quite a while to kick a hole in the boards and pull up the wire, but I got the wire high enough to crawl out. Not the best construction."

"Can you get us out of here?"

"I think so. I saw a shovel while crawling here. If nothing else I can use that to cut these zip ties and then pry the door open. It might work." Jerry moved his hands back and forth over the sharp edge of the shovel. It took some time, but he was able to cut through the ties. Then he looked around for any other tool or something to help him pry the door. Whoever had built the prison had used some good construction materials on the front with only small holes to look out.

As Jerry searched the barn for something to help him get Aaron and Ann out, he heard sirens and vehicles. Now he panicked.

The three captives heard the sheriff talking and then the shots. Ann was the first to yell, "Hey, help us, we're in here!"

Of course, no one could hear with all the gunfire. Ann yelled and yelled as did Aaron and Jerry, but they feared the bullets, and finally all just hunkered down and lay low on the ground in hopes they would not get hurt.

Jerry got up, grabbed the shovel, and went to Aaron's cell and started pounding on the wire mesh. It started to give, but he realized Aaron was too big to crawl out of the hole. He kept looking and found a hammer, rake, some metal, and an old galvanized pipe about three feet long. He knew he could not pound too long with the hammer if the shooting stopped, because it would bring the authorities there, or worse, his captors.

As Jerry continued to look, the shooting stopped, and he could hear yelling coming from the farmhouse. Then all hell broke loose and the shooting started again, so he was able to make as much noise as he needed.

The stable doors had been covered with studs and plywood and would not budge as much as he tried. The door on Aaron's cell had two heavy locks. He grabbed the shovel and pried the door open a little, enough to get the metal pipe inside. He put it inside the door about a foot and cranked as hard as he could. No luck. Then he put his two hundred pounds into the bar and one of the locks on the stable door popped. It took several tries, but he was able to pop the second, and the door swung open and Aaron was able to get out. Jerry helped Aaron get his zip ties off.

Next, they went to Ann's cell. She had been talking to them through the wire mesh, encouraging them. The two of them had her out in no time and cut her bindings. Ann's first thought was to find out whose sirens had arrived. She felt she could talk to the sheriff if he was there, but when the shooting started, she felt their best move would be to escape and somehow call Loretta. That is what they decided to do.

During the standoff, Cliff had crawled between the barn and the shrubbery. He could see what was going on, and he knew he had to get out of this place and head to the woods. He slipped away as the gunfire increased and everyone was focused on the house. He had a great place to hide, and he wanted to take out the three agents in the barn, but he could not risk getting caught. Maybe he could burn the barn with them in it. Great idea, but he had no time. He was in the woods, and he headed for a spot he knew would be good, not far from the barn.

Cliff had prepared this hideout with guns, ammunition, and food—just in case. Regrettably, he had only a few cans of food there. The guns amounted to one old pistol with some ammunition. He had his own service revolver and some ammo. That would have to do.

As Cliff crawled into his hiding place past the barn, there was some activity.

Ann, Jerry, and Aaron kept hearing the shooting get louder and louder. There was a lot of yelling that they could not make out, so they agreed to crawl around to the back of the barn, and then they sprinted to the woods. "Keep low," Ann said as they made their way to the tree line.

Cliff saw the three as they ran through the woods trying to get away. "Perfect," he said.

The farmhouse

It turned out to be a gunfight. It lasted quite a while until a unit arrived with tear gas and a ramming vehicle. They sent in tear gas followed by flash-bang grenades. They knew the individuals inside might have some protection from the tear gas, but they knew the combination would do the job.

A couple of the men came out shooting. They were quickly taken down. Two others had been hit and were down. The sheriff thought that if he was right, there should be just two others. Cliff had snuck out earlier and was hiding near the barn. He would not give up, but he realized that he was stupid for taking the three hostages.

The shooting had ceased almost entirely, and one man was taken by the police. The sheriff gave the order to enter the premises. It did not take long and all five individuals were either dead or cuffed—but Cliff was not among them. The sheriff knew he had to be here. "We need to find Cliff! Spread out and look everywhere."

The FBI agents searched the barn and did not find Cliff or the three captives as they thought they might. The sheriff immediately turned to his deputies, and with wide eyes said, "We're too late. They must have gotten rid of the three agents. Man, this is going to be trouble. I can already feel the pressure from our director."

1,500 miles away

The old boss was finally back in the legislature and was working to boost his standing among all the delegates. His idea was to improve his image and attract as many bodies as he could before he registered for a place on the presidential ticket. He knew he had little chance of being on either major parties' ticket, so he knew he would have to run as an independent. He wanted it that way. He did not want to be affiliated with the status quo in any way, but he would need allies.

The old boss was a smooth talker and a very likable guy when he wanted to be. He did not ooze any of his hidden animosity for the government or for its people. He was always gregarious and kind, so everyone thought he was a wonderful politician and friend.

The old boss was strategizing. He asked, "How can I get these people to back me?" His entourage, usually made up of several of his closest admirers, was there, and he asked again, "What do you think? How can we get these people on our side? What will work best?"

One of his closest associates chimed in, "Can we pay them off? I mean a lot of these guys will do just about anything for a buck."

"That's a possibility, but I hope we can win them over in other ways."

"You mean like supporting them in whatever they want, especially back them when voting on issues?"

"Exactly. We need to start small though. Currently, there are several bills. Could we start with one of those?"

"I'm sure that would work for some, but we'll need other issues."

"Right. That is what I am talking about. What are the issues we can back to get these people on our side?"

"Once you have established yourself with some of these people, we can take on the more prominent issues like immigration, the second amendment, the national debt, to name a few. There are so many issues, but we need to move slowly and take them one by one."

"Absolutely. I do not want to ostracize anyone right now. We could take either side of the issues, maybe both, depending on how this works out. I want to make sure I enlist as many elected officials as I can, so I will sometimes talk *left* and sometimes *right*. Keep them guessing."

"That's a great strategy. It will work. No one should think that you are not on their side."

"Let us see how it goes in Florida. We will make sure that I am the only voice of reason. The one to listen to. We will say one thing in private settings and another in public. Keep them guessing."

"It might backfire though."

"No, because we are just trying to keep the divisiveness going. Keep both sides fighting, so we can sneak in under their radar."

"Hmmm, interesting."

Lansing

Loretta had not heard from the sheriff in Ohio, the governor, or Ann. She was really beginning to worry. She decided to check with the governor. Her call took a while to get through because there were so many layers of security now, but eventually she got to a person who could help. "Hello. Governor?"

"No, this is Lieutenant Carlson. To whom am I speaking?"

"This is Loretta. Remember me? I was the agent that helped to rescue the governor. I spoke with you when I met the governor at the Capitol."

"I remember."

"I was just wondering if you had any news about the three agents who were with her in Ohio."

"Nothing yet. Why?"

"I thought she had cleared them, and they would be on their way here."

"We haven't had any correspondence with Ohio, so I am not sure what to tell you."

"I guess I need to somehow get ahold of them. How can I find out where they are?"

"Not sure, but let me know if you find out anything. We could help if you need us to get involved."

"I'll let you know what I find out."

Loretta hung up and immediately called for information for Sheriff Sutton, but she was sent to voicemail. She left a message and then decided to visit Ann's husband to see if he knew anything.

Lansing, at the capitol

Two lawyers walked into the Capitol and sought access to the governor. They were not allowed to see her, but through an assistant, they gave her their request. It was to release Bates immediately, or they would sue for wrongful imprisonment. They had a whole list of issues, and they were not being friendly.

It took some time, but they were given what they wanted. Bates would be released by noon the next day. The lawyers were satisfied and sent a representative to the jail where he was being held, and he was to bring Bates to them immediately upon release.

Bates had been incarcerated a while back shortly after the attack on the bunker in the U.P. He thought he would rot in prison, but, as it turned out, the authorities really had nothing on him. The old boss and Bates had been friends for a long time and had worked together since the old boss had been hired to take over the first time. When the old boss was sent to the hospital in 2019, Bates worked with the new boss, but he never really got along with him like he did the old boss.

Bates was a key individual for the organization. He had routed many of the troops to their assigned places after training, and he worked closely with the old boss after he was reinstated as the leader. The old boss needed Bates back, and he had some of his best lawyers working on that for some time.

It was shortly after Loretta returned to Lansing that Bates was freed. Since they had no legal grounds to hold him, they had to let him go. Plus, there were some politicians who were backing Bates. They knew his value to the organization, and they wanted to get him back where he belonged in the U.P. It took some doing, but the day arrived and Bates was freed. He was met by two people that he did not know, but they informed him that he would be heading back to his old job.

Bates was not extremely happy to be going back after what had happened to him, but he was anxious to inform the old boss what he knew. He realized that the old boss would want some revenge on certain people, and Bates was still pissed that he had been interrogated by those two guys, Joe and Ron. He wondered, *How had they survived? Vince had killed them, or so he said. That moron probably screwed that up too. Well, obviously, he had. That idiot!*

Bates was handed over to two guys. He was ecstatic that he would be able to continue his work at changing the country for the better.

The bunker in the U.P.

Peter had infiltrated the troops at the bunker prior to the attack. He had been able to give Joe and Ron valuable information about the bunker, how the troops were training, and the number of new people arriving. Now he was just biding his time to find out what might happen next. He was surprised when the troops had left the base to head to Colewin months after it had been attacked. They had all returned, and his contact had said that they had hurt one man and frightened the citizens, but they had not hurt anyone else, and they had left Colewin suddenly.

All had been quiet at the bunker, but he knew the trainers were up to something because they were spending a lot of time in the bunker, and they had brought in more and better computers than they had previously. He knew he had to tell his father if he could get a message out soon, but the trainers had them practicing for several hours a day, and he had little time to be alone.

Chapter 23

Colewin

Joe was not clear on what they should do about the situation they knew was brewing because the government did not have a handle on what was going on. He knew this was a real problem. Like last time, he and Ron had to take matters into their own hands, but they had failed. They were lucky to get out alive. He knew that if they were to do something this time, they would need a lot more help, and they would once again have to travel. Where? He had no idea.

Ron was pacing back and forth, and Shanice finally said, "Sit down, Ron. You're driving all of us crazy with that pacing."

"Sorry, we just need to come up with something. We took out the bunker for a while and sent Bates to jail, but this whole event keeps spiraling, and we don't have any idea what to do."

Joe agreed, "We know this group is going to do everything they can to keep the division going in this country. That is the problem. How do we combat that? When we were first involved, we didn't know how enormous this group was."

Joette had been sitting quietly on the sofa next to Shanice. She too was concerned, but she felt that doing something this time might be out of their control. "You all know that the last time we tried to help, we almost didn't come home. If you plan something, you'll need a lot more help. Can we get ahold of Loretta? Could she assist us?"

"Her hands are tied. What needs to be done would not pass for legal. She needs to work within the law. This group will not, so we need someone who can take them down, but outside of the law. It's the only way. I hate to say that, but they don't play within the rules."

"Joe, are you saying you want us to operate outside of the law?"

"I guess I am. We have before. If the government doesn't learn enough from Bates to take this group down, then we'll have to do something."

"You and Ron have done that often in the past when you had the backing of the government, but you don't anymore. This isn't some clandestine operation that was put together by the CIA or FBI. It's you and Ron. You guys are no spring chickens. You need a lot of help."

Ron said, "We could see if Loretta might be up to doing something. Otherwise, we need to depend on the people we have right now. Peter is still in play as are his two buddies, Michael and Tony. No one knows they're on our side. Plus, we have our team here."

"True, Ron, but Sheriff Daryl is out to get Charlie, Matt, and Tommy. I guess we should be focusing on helping them first."

"The word is that the sheriff cannot find Charlie's place. No one will tell him. Charlie has kept his place like a fortress hidden in the woods. It's difficult to get there, but if the sheriff does any research, he'll be able to find the place in no time." Even though Ron was not a fan of Charlie, he felt they had to do something. "We probably need to help."

Joe was certain that if the authorities took Charlie, any of the others could be next. Sheriff Daryl wanted to break the resistance that they had shown for the past few years, and Joe knew the sheriff was a part of the plan to keep the bunker safe. "You know what? We do need to help Charlie. We could head there and let him know how things stand. Maybe he will be able to stand-down and hide instead of taking a stand that could end in tragedy."

Lansing

Bates was happy to see the light of day again. He had been in solitary confinement because he kept arguing and fighting with everyone. He knew they could not legally keep him in jail. What were they going to charge him with? He had not done anything illegal! Well, not that anyone knew.

As he walked out of the prison, he had one thought—and it was revenge. Revenge for those people who had taken him. He knew who they were now. It wasn't just those two guys, Joe and Ron, it was Charlie and his friends. Most of them Bates knew from his association with Charlie before they took the bunker from him. As he left the prison behind, he began to mutter, "I never liked that bastard. He'll be the first to go, and that Joe guy and his buddy. They're toast." He screamed, "I'll kill them all!"

"Whoa, take it easy man. They can hear you," said the man who stood next to the vehicle that would take Bates to the U.P.

Bates turned and looked and saw three cops standing next to the gate he had just left. Concerned, they were shaking their heads.

Bates opened the passenger door and hopped in. He was still mumbling and cursing, and then he said, "I don't give a damn! Just take me back, so I can do my job and help get rid of some pests."

Bates was quite bitter and wanted to get started right away. His first request was to talk to the old boss, but it was a long trip to the U.P., and he knew that would have to wait. But he would get revenge—somehow!

The old boss was excited to have Bates back. He knew that he could not replace him, and that he could never train anyone fast enough to get on board right away. *This is the best thing that could have happened,* he thought.

The boss's plan would be easier to pull off if Bates was back. He had to get in touch with him as soon as he was in his old place at the bunker. He knew that the U.P. bunker was a crucial place for the final stage of his plan, and he wanted someone there he could trust. He knew that there was some cleaning up that had to happen, but he had Sheriff Daryl on that. He needed to wipe the area of those people who had attacked his bunker, so everything would go smoothly when the time came.

Colewin

Joe and Ron made the decision to go to Charlie's place and talk him out of a possible disaster. They had no backup this time, but they thought if they could get there before the sheriff, they would have a chance to talk him out of what he was planning on doing.

They decided to take a truck, a crew cab they had recently bought, and head out right away. They were both hoping to get there as soon as possible because they knew Charlie would not tolerate the sheriff, his old buddy, coming to his place to take him to jail. The two had a falling out when the sheriff decided to move away from the militia that Charlie had created, and he joined with the group that eventually took over.

"Say, let's try to have Charlie move someplace north. Maybe he could head to some of the area near Lake Superior in the forests up there. It's very dense, and there are few roads in some areas. He could blaze a trail on some of the old logging roads and hide out there. We could help build a small shelter, so he wouldn't be out in the elements. It shouldn't take long to clear these three guys, and when we do, he could come back."

"I hope you're right, Joe. This bothers me that the governor cleared them, but a lot of key people want them taken down. Charlie still pisses me off, but he does not deserve this. He did not do what they're saying. They're just trying to spread lies about everything, so they can swoop in and take over."

"You're right."

They drove for a while and finally came to the road to Charlie's place. Anyone who was not from around there might never find the place. Charlie and his wife had built it in the middle of a forest. He owned about thirty-eight acres, and his wife's family owned another fifty acres butting up to his. There were no other roads besides a few small logging trails that had mostly grown over. Charlie loved the spot because no one ever bothered him, and he could do what he wanted when he wanted.

Joe drove up the road. He realized that he had better let Charlie know he was heading that way in case he thought he was the sheriff. He might just open up on them.

"Hello, Charlie."

"Yeah."

"It's me, Joe."

"What you want? You alone?"

"It's just me and Ron. We're headed to your place. We need to talk."

"There's no need to talk. I'm all set here. Can last a long time if I have to. Don't even need to do any loggin'. Planned for somethin' like this for a long time. I have supplies and ammunition for the long haul. Matt gave me a lot of stuff when he left, too. He said they would never find him. This is shit, you know."

"I agree, Charlie."

"This is why I started the militia here. The government gets too big and powerful, and then it takes what little we have."

"Charlie, we're pulling up close right now. Can we come in?"

"No!"

"Can we talk outside then?"

"Pull up close to the house. I'll go to the window. Can't trust anyone right now."

"Got it. We'll pull up by the window."

Joe and Ron looked around. There wasn't that much here. Joe noticed Charlie's logging equipment by the far right of the house. Things were just scattered around and the house looked like it had been there a long time. Part of it was log cabin, and another part was newer, but it had tar paper as siding. Nothing fancy, that's for sure. There was an attached garage with two doors and a large pole building farther on the right behind the logging equipment. The pole barn looked like it was in really good shape.

Joe just shook his head. "Man, you wonder how people keep going and live out here. I give Charlie a lot of credit. He works hard and enjoys what he has. I can understand his fears sometimes."

"Right. Hard to believe he lives way out here like this."

"But he loves it," Joe said.

"That's good right there," Charlie yelled from the window. He had an assault rifle in his hands.

"It's just us, Charlie."

"You sure there's no one else with you. The sheriff?"

"No, but Sheriff Daryl is in town asking a lot of questions. I guess he's trying to find your place."

"Hope he doesn't."

"For sure."

Ohio

Sheriff Sutton had all his men searching the woods. They went in all directions. Some went right where Cliff had hidden. Then they heard shots from deeper in the woods. They radioed Sheriff Sutton. He responded, "Get several of our deputies together and find out who's doing the shooting. It isn't any of our men, so it could be Cliff. We haven't found him yet."

The deputies pulled together and planned their hunt. A few more shots were heard in the direction they were heading. They kept going.

Ann, Aaron, and Jerry were on the run. Cliff was close behind. When the shooting stopped, Ann had the three huddle a minute. "You guys run ahead. I'm going to hide in these bushes and tackle him. I'll yell when he's down."

Aaron said, "No, I'll hide. You and Jerry run. I'm a lot heavier and can knock him easily to the ground." Another shot. "That's close. Get out of here!"

Ann and Jerry began running, but Cliff had almost caught them. He shot several times, and this time someone yelled. Jerry was hit.

Aaron was about to jump out and knock Cliff to the ground when more shots rang out. This time Cliff fell. He jumped up and started shooting in the opposite direction. Then he turned and tried to run, but he was hit and dropped, yet he kept shooting. At the same time a volley came from the deputies—and Cliff was down for good. Several deputies were on him instantly. He had been shot many times. His fury was over. He would no longer be angry.

Aaron stepped out of the bushes, and he was immediately grappled to the ground. "Hey, let me go. I'm one of the FBI agents who was taken by that guy."

"Oh yeah, where are the others?"

Aaron yelled, "Ann, are you guys all right?"

"Over here. We're both hit. Jerry's real bad."

Lansing

Loretta received a call from a hospital in Ohio. It was Ann. "Loretta, I'm calling you because there's no one else I trust. Jerry and I are in a hospital because we have been shot by a rogue deputy. I'm fine, but Jerry was hit in the hip and lost a lot of blood. I was lucky. I have a leg wound. It will be a while recovering, but they say they were able to repair the bone that was hit."

Loretta half choked as she said, "Shit! Will Jerry make it?"

"Not sure."

"Where's Aaron?"

"He's with the sheriff who's been great and has been a big help in getting us out of the custody of the law down here. He believes us and knows the governor has cleared us."

Loretta was somewhat relieved. "So, you'll be free to leave when you're discharged?"

"Yes, I have been in conversations with the sheriff here, and he is as concerned about what is happening as we are. He says he cannot trust anyone anymore, including some of his deputies. He's not sure where to turn. He's seeing a lot of these actions where some group is trying to cause confusion and division in the country, and he says they are well-armed and ready to do something violent."

"That's what we've been dealing with since you've been taken. I have been in touch with Joe in the U.P., and he has stories I just can't follow. We haven't been able to trust anyone. Aaron and Jerry were the only two I could trust who would work to find some answers. Right now, I'm not sure who to trust. I can't even trust everyone in the governor's office here, and neither can the governor. She says that since her first abduction, things have gone crazy."

"What can we do?"

"Not sure, but I know I can trust you, Aaron, and Jerry. It's a start. Joe and Ron in the U.P. have several individuals that they trust, but Joe says they are afraid to bring in just anyone because they have the same problems up there. They say they need to thoroughly vet each person, and that takes time."

"Lorretta, can we trust any of the leadership in the FBI in Lansing?"

"Not sure. I found out that our boss who's in custody, and his boss, are both in on something—not sure if it's the same thing."

"Would you be able to come down here and work with me on some investigations? I'll be out of here in a week or so, and then I'll have a cast and will be on crutches for a while, but I can plan and investigate."

"Let me give you a few days to rest and then we'll talk. Take care and keep me posted about Jerry."

"Sure, but I better call Joe and let him know what has happened. Talk to you later."

Colewin

As Charlie began to loosen up a bit, he decided to meet Joe and Ron at the front door. Charlie had really been their enemy from the first moment he had met them. However, since they were thrown together trying to save the bunker for Charlie, and through Joe and Ron's investigations of the people at the base, they had become partners—in a way. Charlie now trusted both, and they kind of trusted Charlie.

Charlie walked to the front door, his wife, close behind. They were both still nervous and both held automatic weapons. Charlie spoke first as he exited the door. "This whole thing is out of hand. How can they say we had somethin' to do with takin' the gov'nor? We haven't even left this area for one day. They must be settin' us up for somethin'."

Joe had the same feeling. "I know someone is setting you up, and I'm sure it's the people behind this bunker. You realize that, right?"

Charlie's wife peeked around Charlie and said, "We're sick of this stuff. Ever since they took the bunker, we've had nothing but trouble. Charlie hasn't even been able to work his regular hours, and we keep falling behind on everything. Lucky for us we've been able to maintain for ourselves, but we ain't givin' up this place. No way." Charlie's wife looked determined and stood rigid right next to Charlie.

Joe could tell she was a strong woman. One who would stand by Charlie to the end. No way they were going to be taken by anyone. These were two staunch Yoopers. The epitome of self-reliance.

Joe agreed and tried to calm them. "No one is asking you to give up your place. We're just concerned that Sheriff Daryl is going to take Charlie, and then who knows what could happen. We have gone through that a few years ago. Once you're taken, there's no way out unless you have some lucky event to get you out. We think that Charlie should hide until this is over. The governor has already said that you are innocent."

Charlie's wife looked right into Joe's eyes. "You can sit there and say that, but you don't really know."

"I'm sure of it. We've been watching the news and talking to people in Lansing. He should be free, so we think it's the sheriff who has some reason to take Charlie."

Charlie was listening, and he was sure there was more to it than what Joe was saying. He had been good friends with the sheriff for years before he turned on Charlie. "I don't trust that guy. We'll lose if we stay here. I know it, but what can we do?"

Chapter 24

The bunker

Bates was back. He was firmly entrenched in his old job. The only difference was that now he was super aggravated and ready to do anything he could to advance the old boss's agenda. He knew that his old nemeses, Joe and Ron, were back. He had almost gotten rid of them on several occasions, but the plans always failed. This one would not. This was the only base where the organization was having trouble. Nowhere else was this type of opposition present. He asked for reinforcements for the bunker and some firepower, just in case.

Bates did not like the fact that he had to return to this area, but it was better than the time he had spent in jail, being interrogated with little hope of escaping. His resolve was increased tenfold now to bring the event to reality.

He knew he had a significant role in the coming event, but he did not know exactly what it would be. He didn't care, as long as he was free and back making really good money.

He had not been in direct contact with the old boss, and he felt he needed to check in. He called. "I'm back in place. Is there anything you need me to do right now?"

"Nothing special. Do you have the troops on the way that you requested?"

Bates said, "I do. I ordered three hundred to come to this site for the duration. That is until we need them for the event. That should keep us safe and keep me online with this new equipment. We have much better support. No one will attack us with what we have."

"That is good."

"Any other changes since my incarceration?"

"Some, but nothing you need to concern yourself about. We are watching the activities around the country as they unfold, and they are playing right into our plans. Things are getting very easy to manipulate. In fact, we have not had to do much of anything. We have the left and the right at each other's throats. They cannot get along for anything. We do not have to even throw out any misinformation. There is so much out there already. My plan is working smoothly because of all the dissention."

"That sounds good for us, right?" Bates asked.

"The more disagreements among them, the easier it will be for us to slide in and win big. We will still have to use some of our tactics that we discussed, but they should all work."

"Great. I cannot wait."

"Seriously though, it will be a while yet. I see things going well, but it is going to take until 2024, so hang in there."

"I will. Anything you need right away?" Bates inquired.

"We are low on troops in California. You will need to send additional troops there too. Not sure how many yet, but you can figure that out. Speak to the man in charge at our base there and find out what he needs."

"Will do."

"That is it for now. I have a lot of work to do."

The old boss disconnected the call, and Bates sat back, feet on his desk, beer in hand, and a smile on his face. "This is going to be fun."

Lansing, several weeks later

It had been a while, and Ann had recovered nicely from her wounds. Jerry was not doing as well. It looked like he might be in rehab for a long time. He still could not walk alone and needed a lot of help.

Loretta had visited Ann, and together they had decided that they were in a situation that they could not control or figure out. They had gone over and over what had happened, and they were trying to decide who they could trust, but outside of Aaron and Jerry, they could not come up with a single name except for Ann's husband.

When Ann was back in Lansing, she returned to her old FBI office. When she arrived, her boss called her to his office where she was informed that she was no longer an agent. She would not get her badge and gun. She was asked to leave. She questioned her boss, but he said he had nothing to do with it, and that it had come from the top.

"What the ...? I've been part of this office for more than twenty years. What caused this? I need to speak to someone."

"No chance. They said to get your stuff and leave immediately."

"You mean I cannot even find out why?"

"Not sure. I just have my orders and you're gone. Pack up and leave in the next fifteen minutes, or I will have you escorted out."

Loretta was standing outside of the office, but she could hear what was going on since the door was ajar. She just shook her head and waited close by. She knew Ann would go to her first.

Ann looked at her current boss, shook her head, and said, "This is just sad. You're in on it, aren't you?"

"I don't know what you're talking about. In on what?"

"Sure, play the dumb role. You have not heard the end of this."

Loretta was perplexed, but, at the same time, she knew what was up. As Ann walked out of the office, she walked straight into Loretta. "Did you hear that?"

"Yes, I did. Not what I expected."

"Come to my office as I pack. I need to talk to you."

Loretta agreed and walked with Ann down the hall to her office.

Colewin

Joe tried to convince Charlie that hiding was his best option. Charlie stood there and looked around at his place. He could see his logging truck, empty right now since he had no time to work. He thought about all the time and effort he had put in to make his place habitable. He had started with nothing, raised enough money to put a downpayment on some land, working weekends and nights. He had built his little house on five acres, now much bigger since he had purchased more land as the years went by. He and his wife had struggled for years to get the place as it was. Did he really have to leave it all?

Joe brought Charlie back to reality. "Charlie, listen. It's for your own good. We can back you up as much as possible, and I will have our group help. What do you think?"

Ron fidgeted as Joe kept trying to talk Charlie into hiding. Ron was getting nervous, thinking that the sheriff could be there at any time. "You guys, we need to decide soon. The sheriff will figure out where you live, and he has several deputies with him. He will not play by the rules. You know that."

That made Charlie mad. "You know, you're right. He won't play by any rules. He never has. That SOB turned on me the minute he had a chance. Why? No, we're stayin' put. If I have to, I'll go down with the place."

"But what about your wife?" Joe pleaded.

"I'll be right by his side. If'n we win, we win, but if we don't, so be it."

Joe turned to Ron. "I can't come up with anything else. Why don't we try to head off the sheriff, or at least get him lost out here?"

"We could try."

They talked a little longer; then all four decided it was time to end the conversation. Charlie insisted they would be all right. Joe and Ron turned their vehicle around and headed out. They drove until they hit the main road where they ran into Sheriff Daryl and his posse. Too late to get him lost or delay him and his deputies. Joe and Ron could only hope that all would go well.

They kept driving, not slowing at all when they saw the sheriff. Joe knew where they were headed, and he did not want any trouble with Sheriff Daryl. He would find Charlie's place, and Joe was afraid what might happen if Charlie and Sheriff Daryl could not come to some sort of agreement.

Lansing

Ann and Loretta walked to Ann's office where they shut the door and looked at each other wondering what the hell had just happened. "Loretta, we need to do something, and we need to do it quickly. I know that I'm being let go, but not because I have done anything wrong. They know that I would have too much power in my position, and I could do damage to their organization."

"I agree, Ann. We need to begin to build some opposition that can take these guys down. We have had clues all along that there were traitors working with these guys, now we need to find and push them out."

"Sounds easy, but it'll be a very difficult task. Just look at what Joe and Ron have been going through trying to take down the group in the U.P. They have almost been killed, and Joe says that their attempt to take out a leader only led to more of their own problems."

"They have had to move several times to keep safe. Right now, Joe says that the organization thinks they're dead. I'm not sure why, but he said he and Ron are trying to keep hidden so they can work to damage this revolution. I guess that is what it is."

Loretta turned as the door on the office was quickly opened. There stood the boss who had just fired Ann. "You two need an escort out?"

Loretta looked at him and said, "What do you mean? I'm just helping Ann pack. She will be out in no time."

"She has five minutes! And you, you had better watch your step, or you will be next."

"What? What do you mean, I'll be next?"

"Just watch your step. I'm in charge now, and things will be different around here."

Ann had finished packing her things and turned to the boss. "I have my things. I'll leave, but you will be hearing from me and a lawyer."

"Bring it. There is nothing you can do. You have made too many mistakes, and they have finally caught up with you."

"Mistakes?"

Loretta eyed Ann, and shook her head. Ann picked up the box she had filled and headed to the door. Loretta followed as they brushed by the boss who stood half in and half out of the room. Loretta gave him a good elbow as she moved him aside.

"Better watch yourself, little woman," the boss said.

"Will do."

Ann chimed in, "Little prick."

The boss was red with anger, but he did not say another thing. He just motioned to two security guards nearby to escort Ann out. "You are for sure next, Loretta. Better be careful."

Colewin

Joe was concerned. "What in the world can we do to help Charlie?"

"I'm afraid it might be too late. That sheriff is not going to just let Charlie take out his men. I'm not sure he can arrest him without a fight. The sheriff will drive them out and then probably shoot them. He knows that Charlie knows too much about him."

"Let's get the group together and see if we can help Charlie."

"Joe, most of the people are still hiding from the after effects of the attack. It has been months, but the heat is still on. Our man at the bunker, Peter, said that they are getting more troops sent to the base."

"I know. How did that happen?"

"Let's see what we can find out."

"We need to get organized, and we need help. Let's see if Loretta has found out whether the governor can help us."

Joe and Ron arrived home where Joette and Shanice had been preparing lunch. Joette seemed a bit shaken. "You're never going to believe what Peter's father just told us."

Shanice chimed in. "It's pathetic!"

"What?" Joe asked.

"That guy Bates we captured and sent to Loretta and the governor. He's back!"

"No. That can't be. We had Loretta hand him over to the governor, and she said they would get something out of him, and, if not, he would remain in jail for a long time."

"Sorry, but Peter's father just left, and he said that his son had just seen him arrive, and he was back in the bunker again."

"No way," Ron said.

"You can contact the barber if you want. He was just here and gave us the information."

Joe looked angry. "No. We believe you. I'll call Loretta and see what she knows."

When Joe called Loretta, the phone rang several times before it was picked up. "Hello, this is Loretta."

"Loretta. Joe here. I hope Ann and her friends are doing better."

"Ann has recovered, but things are not going well."

"That's not good. Say, did you hear about Bates?"

"Yes. We were meaning to call, but we have been tied up with what happened to Ann and Jerry and their recoveries. Bates was let go from what we heard."

"That's what I heard, but I didn't believe it."

"It's true. They sent some lawyers here, and they were able to get him released. I thought you guys had been given the word, or I would have called sooner. Right now, we're trying to figure what to do next. Ann has been given her walking papers. They wouldn't return her badge or weapon, and they made her clean out her office."

"What? Ann has been a part of that department for over twenty years. Who could have done that to her? Didn't her boss get sent to jail?"

"Yes, but the new one is even worse. He threatened me too. He's ready to give me the same treatment he gave Ann. He's with this group that we have been fighting all along. We're trying to plan some way to organize and take them down, but they're everywhere. They were part of the plan to take the governor, and they had Ann, Jerry, and Aaron locked up in Ohio. We're sure they were eventually going to be eliminated."

"This is getting worse all the time," Joe said. "What are you planning now that Ann is not in the Bureau?"

"Like I said, we're trying to organize and build our group, but we need to vet everyone as best we can, and that is difficult. We don't know who is with us or who is with them."

"We have the same problem. Right now, the sheriff is after one of our people. He says that he was responsible for taking the governor, but he was nowhere near there."

"Well, the governor has kind of been wishy-washy on the topic of who took her. She changed her story from what she had said earlier, and so she left it open that it may have been someone from the U.P. group who took her previously."

"Is Ann there with you?"

"No, I just dropped her off at home. Her husband is furious. He wants to do something crazy. We had to talk him out of it. He would have gone right to the office and confronted the boss. His name is Blake. We don't know if he's in the group, or if he's just doing what he's told."

"You have to make sure that Ann's husband doesn't do anything stupid. You're all probably on their list of people to be terminated. Who knows what they might do? I'd be very careful. Try to stick together and help each other through this until we can figure something out. Maybe we should all meet somewhere."

"I'll talk to Ann. I need to go right now, but I'll be in touch."

"All right. Be careful."

Chapter 25

The bunker

Bates was sitting at the computer, thinking about what he could do now that he was back. He knew he had to get caught up with what had happened since he was taken, but his mind was wandering, and he had a bitter taste in his mouth that one gets when angry. It was more anxiety about the two men that he thought he had ordered killed a few times, but who seemed to survive like cats with nine lives. How was it possible that they are still around? He was worried that they would show up again, somehow to be spoilers in his effort to make good in the organization.

The bunker was repaired and resupplied, and the word was that it would become the home of a huge cache of munitions when the time came. The bunker had been increased in size prior to the attack, and it had held many vehicles and other supplies. Now, it would hold more aerial attack capabilities, and the base would become home to some helicopters and drones that the organization was having manufactured nearby.

His boss, the old boss, had given him a position of power at the bunker, and Bates was happy to use his new power to eliminate anyone or anything that would stand in the way of the organization's success.

Bates had also asked for a special group to be added to the base—a sizeable force that was trained like Army Special Forces or "Green Berets." He knew this was what he needed in this area that would be pivotal in the final days leading up to the event. He was also responsible for the other bases around the country where troops were being trained for the event. After his many sessions with the old boss, he knew he had some time before the event would take place, and he wanted to make the most of it here. *How would he get rid of the people who attacked the bunker?* He had a plan.

Colewin

Charlie and his wife had settled back after Joe and Ron left. They knew they had decisions to make. Charlie did not want his wife to have to end up a statistic. They had both worked too hard to build what little they had. He had worked for his father as a child to help build his father's logging business, only to lose him to a widow-maker on the job, a broken limb high in a tree that fell on his father.

"You know, we do have a choice of sorts," Charlie said.

"And what's that?" his wife asked.

"We could hide out until things cool off a bit. You know, like Joe said."

"That sounds like runnin' to me. We ain't run our whole lives. We worked hard to get what we have. What's that gonna do?"

"I know. I ain't likin' the thought of it at all, but I don't wanna put you through what I think is gonna go down with Sheriff Daryl."

"He's an ass! He threw ya away when he saw he had a chance to make more money and move up in that group he was always spoutin' about."

"Yah, that's true."

As the two were talking, several vehicles pulled up to the front of their home. They looked out and saw men running in every direction. It looked like they were surrounding the place. Three patrol cars were out front with men standing behind them. A few more were on the west side of the building and one on the east. Charlie could make out three men behind the house. There was no way for a vehicle to get there, so the men scurried there and were making some kind of barrier to hide behind.

Sheriff Daryl stood behind his vehicle and pulled a bullhorn from the front seat. He spoke into it, "Charlie, you in there?" There was no answer. He repeated, "Charlie, this is me, your old friend, Daryl." Still there was no answer.

Charlie and his wife stood next to the big guns they had set up in their home. Charlie looked at his wife, and she looked at him, a hardened face on each one. Then his wife spoke. "He isn't your friend. I tole ya that years ago. He just used ya and threw ya away when he didn't need ya. Bastard!"

"We were good friends at one time. I just don't know what happened. Everythin' just kind of fell apart all of a sudden."

Another blast from the bullhorn sounded and reverberated in the house. "Charlie, come on, man. We've been friends for years. I just want to talk to you a bit and ask a few questions."

Charlie peeked out of the front window. "Sure, you do. Just a few questions."

"That's it, and then I'll be on my way."

"What about those other deputies you got out there?"

"No problem. You come out, and I'll call them off."

"Ain't comin' out. You haven't been a friend for a while."

"Now, Charlie, I've just been busy. You know that. I tried to help you get the bunker back, and I'll try again if you want."

"Shoulda done that a long time ago. Ain't much left there now."

"Sure, but do you want to control it again?"

"Not sure it's important anymore, but I would like my things back. We lost all kinds of weapons, vehicles, ammunition, clothing, and more. It took years to get that stuff, and now it's gone."

"I'll get it back for you. I know how."

"You do? And what would that be?"

"Trust me, Charlie. Like you used to. We were best of friends. We still are."

Charlie stepped to the door, opened it, and took a step out.

Charlie's wife looked through the door and whispered to Charlie. "He's lying, Charlie. Don't listen to 'im. He's no friend o' yours."

Charlie looked at his wife and then looked at Daryl. "You sure you can get the bunker back, and you'll stick by me?"

"For sure. We can work together."

Charlie took a step closer to Sheriff Daryl, "How is this gonna work?"

The sheriff walked closer to Charlie.

"Just you listen to me." He walked even closer to Charlie. "Put that gun down, Charlie. I don't have mine out. You see all I have is this bullhorn."

Charlie's wife said, "Don't do it, Charlie!"

But Charlie lowered the weapon pointing it at the ground. "A'right. Let's talk."

Sheriff Daryl walked up to Charlie. As he did, two of his deputies came around the house. One from each side. Charlie was focused on Daryl, and he did not see them. He was looking directly into Sheriff Daryl's eyes. Charlie saw something he didn't like, and he turned back to the door. As Charlie was about to enter, the two deputies grabbed him and had him on the ground in cuffs in a matter of seconds.

His wife was right there and charged at one of the deputies. "Let him go, you monsters!" She tried to reach Charlie, but he was being dragged to a vehicle. She pushed and shoved the deputy again. This time he slammed her on the ground and cuffed her.

"There, now you can go with your husband."

Charlie yelled and cursed Sheriff Daryl. "Let her go! We haven't done anythin'."

Sheriff Daryl stood over Charlie and smiled, "Oh, yeah, Charlie, you're both under arrest."

Central U.P., summer

Tommy had been hiding for some time now. Since Charlie, Matt, and he had been identified as the perpetrators in the abduction of the Michigan governor, his only choice had been to hide. He knew that there were forces out there that could not be controlled, and his only chance of escaping was to hide. Wendy and her parents had joined him there.

Joe had arranged the place with his brother who had a very large cabin deep in the woods north of Ishpeming. Joe, Joette, Ron, and Shanice had stayed there during the pandemic, hiding out themselves after they tried to take down the old boss.

Tommy was not himself. He felt that in hiding, he had abandoned his friends. He wanted to return, but Wendy and her parents had told him about Sheriff Daryl snooping around Colewin. They knew that Matt had gone into hiding also, and that Charlie was turning his home into a fortress, and that Charlie would never run. He just wanted to be left alone.

"Is there a way we could get some information about what is going on in Colewin?" Tommy asked Wendy's father, Paul.

"I can get ahold of Joe if you want to talk to him."

"I would like that. Could you call him right now?"

"I could. Are you sure?"

"Yes, the sooner the better."

Paul brought up Joe's number. It rang, and Joe answered.

"Hello. Is this Paul?"

"Yes, I'm here with Tommy. He wants to speak with you."

"Put him on."

"Hello, Joe?"

"It's me, Tommy. What's up?"

"I'm bored here. Wendy and her parents are here now, but what I mean is I feel like I deserted everyone."

"No, don't think that way."

"I can't help it. I'm worried about everyone, and who knows what might happen. We all have to stick together."

"I agree."

"How are Matt and Charlie?"

"We just came from Charlie's, and he's holed up at home. He won't leave, and he doesn't trust anyone. Sheriff Daryl is here snooping around, and that's why we went to Charlie's place… to warn him."

"You don't think they'll find Charlie, do you? I mean a lot of people know where he lives, so it won't take Daryl long to figure out where to go."

"The sheriff is almost there. We saw him as we left Charlie's place. We couldn't convince Charlie to go into hiding. I'm sure this will eventually go away, but there is confusion about the governor's words. Some people say she isn't sure who took her, so they're covering all their bases."

"I can't believe what's going on."

"You know this is all because of the people we've been fighting. We took down the base, but the word is they are sending more troops here. The people who are in charge of this are powerful. Stay in hiding for a while yet, because if you're caught, you'll be in the hands of these guys. They're everywhere."

"I hear you, but I'm not sure how long I can take this."

"Be patient. I'll get back to you as soon as we know anything about Charlie."

"Sounds good."

"Talk to you later."

Joe dropped his phone on the table and turned to Ron, Joette, and Shanice. "We need to get organized better than we are. What we really need is for all of us to get together and form a group with anyone who thinks the way we do. We need to be a force ourselves, but we don't have the resources that these others have. We can be a force if we work surreptitiously. Maybe like they're doing, except we can't pay people, but we could build a network.

"Joe, we would have to include every state in the union. How would we do that? We can't just have our small group. This is a nationwide attack on our country."

Joette said, "Joe, how would we be able to trust any other people? We wouldn't even know them. Are people aware of what's going on?"

"I'm with Joe on this," Shanice added. "We can start small and maybe get help from Loretta and Ann and anyone she knows. She might have contacts around the country."

"I'm not sure how we will do this, but, Shanice, you're right. We start small and keep adding people as we're able."

Chapter 26

Marquette, Michigan

It had been a long recovery in the hospital for Wayne, and he and his wife, Cathy, had decided to remain in Marquette for his entire physical therapy rehab. They had rented a small home on Presque Isle Avenue and had lived in Marquette since Wayne was taken there after he was shot by two assassins from the bunker. Wayne had made some serious progress from his wounds. He would never have the same use of his left arm and hand, but he could function quite well, considering.

Cathy had fallen in love with Marquette. She loved Lake Superior and the walks they took around Presque Isle as part of Wayne's rehab. They had not made any decisions yet on whether to move back to Colewin, but Tommy and Wendy had contacted them and hoped they would return someday. However, now Tommy was on the run. Some sinister plot had gotten him, Matt, and Charlie in trouble for abducting the governor.

Wayne knew this was crazy. Tommy would never be a part of anything like that. He just wanted to fill the shoes of his late uncle after he was murdered by that man, Wyatt, from the bunker. He had also heard that the attack on the bunker had been successful— but now the guy they had taken, Bates, was back at work. How did he get away?

"You know, Cathy, we're safe here. Few people even know where we live, but I have to believe that we need to get involved some way to help the people in Colewin."

"Just what might that be, Wayne? We've been happy here. I've been able to return to a job teaching and, although we're not rich, we can survive on my income until you can find something."

"I can't go back to my old job, but as soon as my arm is a little better, I could do a lot of other jobs. And I want some revenge! Not just those guys who had a hand in this, but I want to take down the boss. Joe knows who he is. The last time I spoke to him, he said that the guys who shot me are dead, but the group is still strong, and they're moving ahead with their plan about the event."

"But why?" asked Cathy. "I'm happy here. Why don't we just decide to stay?"

"Because they're everywhere!"

"Wayne, wanting revenge isn't healthy."

"Maybe not, but I can't get it out of my mind. For the time being, let's think about staying here for some time. Maybe I can get a job here and still help our friends."

"That sounds better to me."

"Then, someday, I'm going to kill that SOB!"

Colewin

Joe was stewing. He had called Charlie, but there was no answer. He tried a couple of times. He turned to Ron. "We should have confronted Sheriff Daryl. We need to go back to Charlie's place. There's no answer."

"I'll get the truck ready. You pack a few of the guns. We may need them."

"You're right. We'll probably need some protection."

Shanice jumped off the couch. "You guys cannot go to Charlie's with the idea of confronting the sheriff. We heard earlier that he has several deputies in town with him."

Joette agreed. "That's right. What are you going to do? Have a shootout with them?"

"No, but we may need protection. We have faced Sheriff Daryl before, and he has no qualms about what he does. He just covers it up, so we'll need to be prepared."

"You two are crazy. That's not protection. That's asking for trouble."

As they argued, someone pounded on the door. "Joe, let me in."

Ron was on his way out and opened the door. It was the barber from town whose son was an informer at the bunker. He looked at Ron and turned to Joe. There was fear in his eyes and he kept swaying from side to side and shaking his head. "You guys need to do something. They got Charlie, and they're taking him to St. Ignace. His wife was let go with a warning, and she came to town to talk to Mayor Don. He sent me here to tell you. Charlie will not last a week if they cage him up. He'll go insane. The man's never been out of the area."

"Okay, calm down. Come on in and let's all talk. We need to do something fast and we need to get help."

Ron shut the door behind the barber, and they all sat down at the kitchen table. Joe's heart was pounding and he was angry, but he kept his head. "We need to contact Loretta or Ann—someone who can talk to the governor. She needs to say something to clear our people. We have two in hiding and one going to jail."

Ron was shaking his head, and he pounded his fist on the table. "We need to do something now. Just like we did with the bunker. I guess it's time to begin to join forces with anyone we can get to help us."

"But we're all up against such powerful people who have so many resources." Joette knew that they were facing insurmountable odds.

The barber wasn't having any of it. He was annoyed, and he knew they had little time. "We still have to do something. We need to get Charlie out of jail before he does something outrageous, and they have a reason to hurt him. You know they take people out."

Joe was furious. He stood up and said, "I'll call Loretta. Hopefully, she and Ann can help us. Maybe they can join forces too. The least they can do is try to convince the governor to clear Charlie."

Joe picked up his phone and made a call. "Loretta?"
"Yes."
"We need to talk."

1,500 miles away

The boss was talking to several members of the committee, those people who were providing most of the financial support. They wanted the event to bring their man, the old boss, to power. They knew they had a chance to get him elected if they proceeded carefully with his plan. The man was a genius.

The old boss spoke, "It's time to begin training the people we will need who will get involved in the next election. If we can get people in every state on election boards, we can do some real damage. We also need to work out a strategy for intimidation. We have time to do this, so we need to get started right away. We can still create some violence at voting places, but I would rather not have as much violence if we can avoid it. However, if the event is completely successful, we won't need an election."

"Yes, if it is, but what will you need if it is not?"

"If you can finance the training, I can arrange setting up each training site with my people. They are very much into this."

The committee head responded, "We can provide that, but you have to guarantee that you will deliver."

"We will succeed. Then the intimidation could be through these people. They can send threatening letters and confront those who will not do what they say. We will be in charge in no time."

"You think that could work?"

"Yes, but you need to make sure none of this is linked to me in any way. I need to remain squeaky clean. Remember, I'm the guy who will run for the highest office in the land. I need to look the part and be the part. If anyone vets me, I cannot be connected to your group."

"But you are already part of our group."

"I am, but I cannot be connected to any other groups that are trying to change the election. I will have all the money we need. You have guaranteed that, but we will not be free from scrutiny, and so from now on, you cannot contact me. Go through the new boss. He'll field all questions and direct all of our moves. I will stay in the background and do my thing."

"Are you sure you want him in charge? He is a very aggressive person, and he will take people out if he wants to."

"Whatever he decides. As long as it helps the cause. He is the best person we have right now. If he does stupid things that will be on him, but I will remain clean."

"Well then, that's the plan. We will move forward as you suggest. By the time the election rolls around, we'll have our people in place everywhere, and we'll intimidate in all states. You need to make sure you can move people to vote for you. We can do a lot on our end to change votes, but you will still need millions of votes."

The boss smirked. "Don't you worry about that. That is what I am good at."

Chapter 27

St. Ignace

The sheriff had Charlie, who was locked in a cell near the front office. The guards who were nearby kept telling him to shut up, but Charlie would not.

"You asshole! I don't belong here, and you know it. Get me out of here now. Daryl, you slimy puke, get me out of here!"

The yelling kept on until one of the deputies walked over to his cell and said, "If you don't shut up, we're going to shut you up."

"What you gonna do? Shoot me?"

"If we have to."

"You know ya won't, and ya can't. I want a lawyer!"

Sheriff Daryl was informed of the disturbance that Charlie was causing, so he decided to go and talk to Charlie. He had known Charlie for many years, and for a good part of those years, they had been friends. He thought he could talk some sense into Charlie, so he would quiet down. He walked through the office doors to the cell area. He was in uniform and had both his weapon and taser on him. "What's the problem, Charlie? Why you cryin' like a baby?"

"I ain't cryin'. I'm pissed. You little pussy. Get me out of here!"

"Not going to happen."

Sheriff Daryl was standing close to the cell, and Charlie sprang toward him, threw his hands through the bars, and grabbed his neck with his hands. He was choking him, moving him up and down, and pounding his forehead on the bars. Years of working in the woods made Charlie very strong. He pulled the Sheriff's face into the bars, back and forth until he was bleeding badly.

Sheriff Daryl was stunned and shocked, but he had enough sense to grab his taser and let Charlie have it. Charlie immediately fell to the floor writhing in pain. When his head hit the concrete floor, it bounced hard. Blood trickled from his head. He shook violently.

Sheriff Daryl was bleeding and angry, but he laughed at Charlie as he kept the shock on for about fifteen seconds. Then he stopped and looked at Charlie. Again, he laughed. "Get up you old fool!"

Charlie just kept shaking and moaning. Then he seemed to shut down. Sheriff Daryl called for assistance. "Get an ambulance here. I think he needs help. He called for the guard who unlocked the door. Sheriff Daryl and the guard entered and rolled Charlie on his back. He was not breathing. "Sheriff, he has no pulse. What should we do?"

"Give him CPR, you fool. You know how, right?"

"Yes, but I haven't ever done it for real."

"Do your best."

"All right, all right!"

The deputy kept compression going the best he could. Sheriff Daryl said, "Breath into his mouth. That's supposed to help."

"I'm not breathing into that old guy's mouth. Are you crazy? Does he have a pulse yet?"

"I can't tell. I don't feel anything."

Then the door flew open and the paramedics entered the cell quickly and began work on Charlie. They worked on him a bit, loaded him on a gurney, and took him to the ambulance.

Sheriff Daryl kept asking, "Is he all right?"

"We don't know. We're taking him to the hospital right now. We'll keep you informed." They pulled away with the siren shrieking.

Colewin

Loretta listened to Joe. She had the same thoughts about calling him and organizing people to fight the group that was causing all the trouble. She thought, *How in the world would we do this?*

"I know it won't be easy, Loretta, but we need to do something to fight these people, or our country is going to be in big trouble."

"Joe, do you read the news? Our country is already in big trouble, and these people are preying on that. As I see it, they are trying to use the divisiveness as a weapon. They know that the people in the middle are not active, so the far fringes of each side are running the country now."

Joe said, "I know that, Loretta. What does Ann think?"

Loretta put the phone on speaker, so Ann could be a part of the conversation. "She believes that we need to do something too. She knows that this organization is powerful. You can talk to her. She's right here, and the phone is on speaker."

In the background, Ann asked Joe, "Do you have any ideas? You were always the one with a plan."

"This is so much bigger than I ever suspected. The more we deal with these people, the more power they seem to have."

"I agree."

"We've been talking about getting our own people together and organizing better, but the problem is that we need people who believe us, and we need to make sure they aren't being paid by this group, so we should check each one thoroughly before we add them to our own organization."

"That's right. We should join forces and begin to organize."

"Ann, why don't you and Loretta meet us somewhere, so we can plan this?"

Ann was quick to agree. "We'll need to do something. What are your thoughts?"

"I really don't have any right now, but if we can put our heads together, we can come up with something. Maybe we should meet up here somewhere. Get as many people together as you are able, and we'll do the same, then we can plan a meeting."

"That's a good idea. We need to know if we have any type of force to begin combating these guys."

"Can you involve the governor?"

"We can, but we can't trust the people around her. We think a few of them are in on this whole attack on our country, so we need to meet with just the governor somewhere other than the Capitol Building—or we might be playing into their hands."

"I hear you."

"Let's work on our ends and see what we can do. I'll keep you informed. Once we have some idea of the number of people who might help us, we can do some planning. It'll be difficult because we'll need people in every state."

"For sure."

Chapter 28

The bunker

Bates was back to work full-time, and he had caught up on most everything he had missed over the past weeks. Now he was planning revenge. He called the head man's number one—the new boss. "I need you to hear about what is going on here. I know the old boss is putting you in charge until the event, so I want your take on my idea."

"What idea?"

"Well, I was taken captive as you know, and do you know what I found out? Those two guys who started this chaos around here are still alive."

"Who do you mean?"

"That Joe, and his friend, Ron."

"I thought you told me that they had been taken care of a long time ago."

"That's what I thought. Remember Vince? He called me and said he would take care of them, but he didn't. I don't know what happened, or where Vince is, but these guys are back."

"They are the two who tried to take out the old boss, right?"

"Yes, and we've had nothing but trouble from them."

"Well, we need to get rid of these two because we can't have people like that snooping around and messing things up. The next thing you know, they'll be looking to destroy our organization and stop the event."

"That's my thought too, so I'm asking you for permission to go after them."

"You have enough troops there now, and you will get more, plus you have several shipments of armaments heading your way. Make a plan, and use what you need."

"Oh, I already have a plan. I just need permission to go after them."

"You have that, but what is your plan?"

"You know that shipment of drones we received?"

"Yes, I'm the one who had them sent."

"I'm going to use several of those to end this problem. What do you think?"

"If you can get rid of those two, do it."

Later that day

Bates kept thinking that he had to find out where these guys were, and he also wondered if they were still in the area. If they were, he knew what he had to do. His first thought was to involve someone from Colewin whom they could trust. He checked with his trainers who came up with two names.

"There are two guys here from Colewin. One is Bill. We tried working with him, but we don't trust him."

"There's another troop, Peter. He's from Colewin. He was one of the last locals we allowed into the group. So far, he's been a model soldier. We can trust him."

"Can we put him on surveillance with a few other guys to find out where this Joe person is?"

"What are you thinking?"

"If we could send a few guys into town and have them find out where these people are hiding, then I have a plan to eliminate them. It'll be quick and easy."

"What should I tell them?"

"Say that they are looking for Joe and his buddy. We need to know for sure if they are still in the area. Have them find out where they might be staying. They don't need to do anything else. Just find where they are. Since Peter is from there, he will know the area, and he could pinpoint their hideout. We'll keep three or four guys with him to make sure he's with us and doesn't do anything stupid."

"The best bet would be to send one of us trainers along to make sure all of them are not out to hurt the bunker."

"Good idea. If he seems reluctant, or it he pulls anything, we can eliminate the problem right away."

"Sounds good."

"Have them get ready right now, and send them out immediately. I don't want to wait around anymore. Let's get these guys once and for all—and anyone who might be with them."

Colewin

The barber had a day off, and it was a good thing because his son texted.

PROBLEM!

The barber immediately went to see Joe. "Joe, I just received a text from my son, Peter. It said in big letters: PROBLEM, and that's all. That has been our code for when he can't talk, so something is happening at the bunker." The barber looked nervous, but he was also determined not to let this get out of hand.

Joe was concerned. "What do you think it might mean?"

The barber answered, "Not sure at all. I need to wait until he has a chance to call or text again, but that one word means he can't say anymore right now."

"All right. We'll have to wait to see what happens."

As the barber left, he grabbed the door handle and said, "Just make sure you're all on guard, and I wouldn't show your faces anywhere in town right now."

"Got you."

Chapter 29

The bunker

Peter was unsure of what exactly he had to do, but he understood he and three others, plus one trainer, were going into Colewin. They had been issued civilian clothing, and they were all to change right away and meet at the gate. They were going to get a ride near Colewin where they would get a truck to drive into town. He knew that Bates did not want anyone to know that they were from the bunker. *Fat chance of that*, he thought.

Peter changed quickly, and while he did, he was able to leave the barracks and get out of sight for a few minutes. He texted his father, the barber.

Orders to head to Colewin. Not sure what's up, but I know they want us to look for a hideout. I'm guessing they are after Joe.

Peter put his phone away and waited.

The barber was still at Joe's, and he relayed the message.

Joe said right away what it might be, "They're after us again. Bates knows we're alive. If he finds us, we're in trouble."

"He won't find this place, and if he does, we'll get a heads up from my son."

Ron said, "If that's what it is, we may need to leave the area."

Joette had been listening to the barber and she knew it meant more trouble. "We've talked about that before, Joe. Why stay here? They aren't going to give up. They'll stay after you until they do something horrible. You know that, and it'll mean us, Ron, and Shanice."

Ron had been pacing since he heard the news. "I'm with you no matter what, Joe, but Joette makes sense. They've been after us for some time now, and they've come close to hurting us. We need to change something!"

The barber mumbled something, and then he turned to Joe. "You should leave the area. It's not worth it."

They all looked at one another, and there was a collective sigh. "We can't take these people down alone. We've been trying for a few years, and it hasn't gotten any better. Let's check in with Ann and Loretta again to see what they think, and then we'll decide." He turned toward the barber. "In the meantime, keep us informed of anything your son might tell you. We'll get ready in case we have to move out quickly."

The barber shook his head. "That's the best, Joe. It won't help anyone if they take you out. You need to work out a way to stay safe. I'm guessing a few others may have to leave the area. These people are no good. I hope I can get my son out of that place soon before something senseless happens."

On the road to Colewin

Peter was in a truck headed for Colewin. They had been transported to a spot and had changed their military truck for a civilian one. They would look like anyone in Colewin. The idea was not to stand out. However, in a small town like Colewin, everyone knew everyone. They would stand out, and the locals would know they were not from there, except, of course, for Peter.

On the way, they had been given their orders. They were to ask around for any information they could get about where Joe was. That kind of questioning would give the locals a heads up, especially if Peter could get a message to people that he trusted.

They first went to the Sportsman's Bar and Pizzeria. They were happy to sit down and have a beer. The trainer was not in agreement with them, but he had little choice. He was outvoted four to one. They were having a beer no matter what he said, so he just went along.

Peter knew all the patrons, and he struck up conversations with people he hadn't seen in a while. He pretended to be asking the right questions, but he was just playing their game. They each had a beer and enjoyed the fact that they were not on the base training for the hundredth time.

After they finished their beer and had paid the tab, the trainer stood and said they had to get busy looking for the hideout. They all knew who they were after, and they put a lot of pressure on Peter to ask around and to find out what he could.

Peter wanted to get a message to his father, so he decided he would send one if he could get away from the other troops, but suddenly it hit him. When he had changed, he had left his cell phone. He had put it back in the bottom of his boot, and he had forgotten to take it with him. This would be a problem. He stood up and said, "Say, my father is the local barber. I could talk to him and find out what he knows."

The trainer looked at Peter and said, "No way you're talking to your father. I was told to keep any family members out of this, and for you to ask around to see what you can find out. Your family is not to be involved. Too risky."

"What? How is that risky?"

"Listen, you do as I say, or you become a statistic. Got it?"

"I hear you, but it will look strange if I don't try to speak to him. What happens if we meet on the street?"

"All right, all right, but I go with you. The others should start moving around to see what they can learn."

"They're not going to find out anything. Everyone will know that they're strangers in town. They won't learn a thing."

"Really, why's that?"

"Because they ARE strangers. No one will trust them!"

"Then it's going to be up to you to find out and quickly."

Chapter 30

Colewin

Mayor Don had had enough. He and Charlie had been friends for years, and he knew Charlie as well as anyone. Sheriff Daryl had also been his friend, but he had not been around as much the past year, and Don knew he was up to something. He had spoken to several locals and had learned about the attack on the bunker. He knew a lot of it was Charlie trying to get his equipment returned. Don had been aloof when it came to the organization at the bunker, but now he knew he had to get involved.

Charlie's wife was sitting in Don's office, and she was in tears. This woman whom he had known for years was not the type to cry. She had been through a lot in her life, and she and Charlie had hacked out a life in the woods. They were true Yoopers, and they had lived in Colewin their entire lives. They were locals that Don could trust.

Don was reassuring Charlie's wife. "Everything is going to be all right. I'm going to get ahold of Sheriff Daryl and find out where Charlie is being held, and then you and I are going to see him."

"Why? Why did Sheriff Daryl come after us?"

"I'm not sure, but I know Daryl has been working with that group out at the bunker for the past few years, and he's getting himself involved in something that I think is a problem."

"That teacher, Joe, was trying to get us to hide. I'm wonderin' if that might be the best for us."

"Well, he hasn't taught here or anywhere for some time, but he's involved with this whole thing. Maybe I should go and talk to him and see what he knows."

"We were happy with our place, and how we've made it our home. It's taken us a long time, but we finally feel comfortable, and we have a place to retire someday. Charlie has worked hard his whole life, and he's never asked for anythin'. He's a good man, Don."

"I know, and I'm going to help you."

Colewin and the troops

Peter told his trainer that visiting his father would give them some ideas of where to look. The trainer was dubious. "I really doubt that this will help."

"It will help. You'll see." Peter led the trainer to a small shop on a street right off the main street. They walked slowly and Peter led the way. When he arrived, he looked around and then opened the shop door. His father was finishing with a customer, and no one else was in the shop. When the customer left, Peter gave his father a hug, and his father said to him, "How have you been? I hope everyone has been treating you well."

"Yes. Everything is great. Hey, Dad, I have some questions for you. First, this is one of our trainers at the bunker. His name is Wallace."

"Hello. Good to meet you."

"Same."

"Say, Dad, we were wondering if you could help us."

The barber was hesitant. He wondered why his son was asking for help. "With what?"

Peter shuffled his feet and looked deep into his father's eyes. "You know I've been with these people for some time now. You probably have heard that we were attacked by what we all think was some local guys."

"I've heard something about that."

The trainer interjected. "We need some information, and we need it now. Can you help?"

"First, I need to know what it's about. I can't help if I don't know anything."

Peter looked at the trainer. "I told you I can handle this."

"Then go ahead and handle it."

"Dad, we have information that the teacher that used to work in the local school is alive, and that he is one of the ring leaders of the attack. We have already identified a few others. You know Charlie. We got him, and now we are after Tommy. We hope to get the teacher, too. Can you help?"

The barber was astonished. He wondered how he was going to fake helping his son. He knew he was doing this as part of his cover, but he wasn't sure how to handle it. "I'm not sure what you need. I know that the teacher was around here a while ago. Do you mean he is still in the area?"

"Yes. Can you ask around and find out where he might be?"

"I can try."

The trainer looked at the barber and said, "Don't just try. You need to do this. We know that in this town, everyone knows everyone, so if you ask around, you can find out."

The barber looked at Wallace, then at his son. "I'll get on it right away. I'll have something for you tomorrow, I'm sure."

"That's what I like to hear," Wallace said, and then he chuckled. He knew he had reached him with his last comment. He felt he had the barber right where he wanted him. "And by the way, it'll be good for your son. We wouldn't want anything to happen to him if you say you can't find anything."

The barber froze and his knees buckled, but he realized that he had to act like nothing was out of the ordinary. "I'll find something. Be back here tomorrow when I open at eight, and I'll have something for you."

Peter said, "Thank you."

Wallace grunted, and they left.

Hideout near Colewin

The barber knew he would have to get to Joe quickly and inform him, but he knew he could not just leave his shop and head there. He would probably be followed, and what if his phone was compromised? He was worried about his son, Peter, at the same time. He would work until five, and then he would not head to Joe's, but he would travel in the opposite direction and visit with some of Matt's family. That would keep them on his trail if they were following. Then, he would have his wife go to town and talk to Don, the mayor.

The barber's wife, Agnes, pulled up to Don's home. She ran to the door and pounded. Don's wife answered. "Janice, is Don home?"

"Why, yes, what's the problem?" Agnes looked at her and began trembling. Those guys at the bunker are after us, and they have Peter, and they are threatening him. We need to get word to Joe."

Don heard everything. He was expecting something like this. He knew that the bunker people were ramping up their violence and creating fear in the locals. He walked over to the door. "Agnes, come in. Sit down. Explain what happened."

Agnes explained what her husband had told her. She was weeping by this time. "I'm afraid for our lives."

"I understand. We need to do something. These people are getting more and more belligerent. They really want to take over our town."

"Can you get word to Joe? My husband thinks they're trying to kill Joe. Peter is caught in the middle, so we'll all need to be very careful."

Don had mixed feelings. He had known Joe since he had been a teacher at the local school, but he didn't really trust him. He was an outsider, although a Yooper, but he was not from here. Don had always been a bit leery of outsiders, but this time, he knew he had to help. He thought that Joe had left the area a while ago, and he wasn't even sure he could find him, but Agnes gave him what he needed to find Joe.

Don reassured Agnes, and then he jumped in his truck and roared off.

Poplar

Meanwhile the barber was headed for Poplar to make sure no one was following his wife. As he turned into Matt's family's driveway, he noticed in his mirrors the same vehicle that had stopped at his shop earlier in the day with his son and that trainer, Wallace. He no sooner got out of his truck, when they pulled up behind him.

Wallace jumped out and confronted the barber. "This is where he is?"

The barber knew what he meant. "Who are you talking about?"

"That guy we're hunting, Joe."

"He's not here. I'm just visiting some friends."

"Why are you not doing what we told you to do?"

"I am. I'm trying to find out where he is. That's what you told me to do."

"We'll see about that."

The barber's son exited the vehicle along with three other burly looking military dudes. Peter spoke to Wallace. "I told you he was just investigating. Why don't you believe me?"

"I don't trust anyone. I'm thinking that Joe is right here."

Peter shook his head, and the barber did the same.

Wallace said, "Well, let's take a look." He and the three troops didn't even bother to knock. They just threw the door open and bolted inside. There was an old woman sitting at a table drinking a cup of something, coffee maybe. She screamed.

Wallace went straight for her and said, "Where is he?"

"Where is who?"

"That ex-teacher, Joe."

"Who? No one by that name lives here. I'm all alone since my son left."

"And who is your son?"

"Just a man trying to find work." She knew enough not to give away that her son was Matt. She knew he was on the run and hiding.

Wallace and the two men ransacked the place and found nothing. After several minutes, Wallace admitted they had nothing. "All right. I believe you. We'll get out of your way."

"Who's going to clean up the mess you made?"

"You are. And if you know what's good for you, if you hear about that guy Joe, let me know right away. You can call the barber."

Peter was standing near his father. The barber looked at him and then at Wallace. "I told you I was here to get information for you. Now you messed that up good. Nice going. How the hell do you expect me to find out anything if you keep harassing the local people? Just let me do the job you gave me."

"Okay, but you better do it quickly." With that the four men turned and left. Peter gave his father a nod as he exited the door.

Chapter 31

The hideout

It took Don a while to find the hideout. He knew the area, but he did not know the roads because they were difficult to find, and he had never been this deep into the woods on this side of town. He hoped he would not get lost. He wasn't even sure what the place would look like when he got there, so he was a bit nervous. Plus, he did not entirely trust Joe, and who else might be with him.

He was so nervous that he was talking to himself. "What if they take me for one of their enemies?"

Joe, Ron, and their wives were both sitting down quietly deciding what they should do next. The consensus was to join forces with Ann and Loretta, but where would they meet? They just needed a plan. They were on the verge of calling them again when they heard a vehicle.

Shanice looked out the window and told the others it was a truck. She could not make out who was in it. Joe stood, grabbed a weapon, and told the others to get armed just in case. He walked to the window. He watched Don get out of his truck and head straight for the door.

"You can relax. It's Don, the Mayor. What the hell is he doing here? Something is up for sure, and it can't be good."

Don was apprehensive. Should he even knock? He did not have a weapon, and he knew he was on foreign ground here. He looked in all directions and did not see anyone, and then he raised his hand to knock as the door was opened in front of him.

The hideout

"Don, what brings you here?" Joe asked.

"I've got some information for you. First, we need to talk. I know I haven't always had your best interests at heart, but right now we'll need to work together. That group from the bunker is getting more and more powerful and violent. I know it must have been you guys who attacked the place. I was staying out of things, thinking it would not affect our little town, but that has changed. The barber's wife, Agnes, came to me and said that they are looking to take you guys out. They are also turning our town into something it has never been. What the hell is going on?"

"Don, come on in and sit down. We'll tell you all about it. If you have an open mind, you'll see the real picture of what's happening."

"Yes, but you need to hurry. Agnes says that the barber is in real trouble with these guys. She fears for his life. They are after you, and their son, Peter, is caught in the middle."

The story was a long one. Don was not quick to buy in for some time. He had his own beliefs about the country and what was going on. What made him begin to understand was when both Joe and Ron agreed that the country was at risk of being run by people outside of the U.S.

Joe informed Don about what he knew. "The committee, as we can tell, is made up of several individuals who are not citizens. In fact, many are leaders of foreign countries, some billionaires, some people who just want to see the U.S. taken down."

Don was surprised. "You mean the people out at the bunker take orders from foreigners?"

"Well, they're not all foreigners. Some are citizens who want to take over any way they can. They see democracy as too slow to change. That it cannot keep up with a changing world. They feel that the democratic organizations cannot function for the people."

Ron added, "Others feel that corporations have taken over and are running the country."

"We have people here who believe the same. Some who want the country to change, but these people want to take over. They see us as a bully in the world order, so they want to make sure that we lose our standing as a moral force in the world."

Don was not clear. "Exactly what do you mean?"

"Well, they feel we push people around and want to control them. There's some truth to that, but they see us as the big bully and use us as a scapegoat."

Don was pensive. "We have enough problems right here at home. Nobody can get along anymore. Families are divided because of politics. No one compromises."

Ron agreed. "True. The fringes of the left and right seem to control each side. There's no middle road anymore. There is, but no one listens. They only hear the loud screams from those almost out of control who yell the loudest, or those who have the wildest conspiracy theories."

"But, Don, the problem is this outside force. They continue to drive a wedge between groups and make them seem like they are divided by a huge chasm. That's what they want. Keep everyone apart. Keep them arguing."

"I can see what you mean."

"Don, we don't have the same views, but one thing we do have is this belief in our country. We need to pull together to preserve it. We have more in common than we know."

"I agree, Joe. How can we fight these people? You said they are powerful and rich. We don't have the resources to fight them."

"We do if we can stick together. We need to convince people who are not on their payroll that they are the enemy."

"I'm in, Joe. What can I do?"

"First, we need to know how we can help the barber right now. What else can you tell us?"

Don sat quietly and then he began. "I'm not sure, but we need to hurry though if they're going to hurt the barber and his family."

Ron said, "I guess we need to somehow beat these guys at their own game. How can we fight them?"

Don answered. "How? We need to save our people and our homes, and we somehow need to turn the town against them'"

"Not just the town, Don. The country. They're in all the states. We need to get a lot of people on board in the country, or we won't be able to stop them. I like your idea, but we need to figure out what their plan is for eliminating us."

Don was unsure. "How will you ever find that out?"

"We have ways. Thanks for the information. We'll keep you informed as we work on this. I'm not sure we can beat these guys, but we must try. We know they're after Charlie, Matt, and Tommy. Now us, for sure. It's Bates who knows we're alive, and he's the one after us. We took him down, so now he wants revenge. For a long time, they thought that we had been eliminated, so we've been able to quietly work against them."

They talked for a short time and then Don said he had to leave, so they decided on how they would handle the situation with the barber and Peter. They shook hands, and Don gave them his word that he would work with them to bring these guys down. He really had no idea what he was getting himself into.

Lansing

Ann and her husband had had it. They were sick and tired of what had transpired over the last few years. Ann knew she had to fight to get her job back, but she knew she could not do it in her current office. There were too many people she could not trust. She and her husband had been very frugal, and they had enough funds to last a while. Her husband worked from home, so that was not a problem either. Together they decided to organize and fight back. Ann would take the time she had to become an active obstacle to the people trying to take down the country.

Ann spoke to her husband. "I'm calling Loretta. We decided that we would let each other know. She's ready to do something too, and she still has her job, but she could be an inside conspirator with us. Maybe she could even find out more about the local group who is doing this to us."

"Yes, but we need to organize more people. What about Aaron and Jerry?"

"Aaron is working at the same office with Loretta, and Jerry is on medical leave, but they are helping her."

"So, what is our next step?"

"We meet with Joe when he calls. He'll fill us in on details. Then we begin to enlist people we can trust."

Colewin

Peter was driving Wallace and the three other troop members. His mind was buzzing. He was thinking about what would happen if Wallace was not satisfied. *What could he do to protect his family?*

"Peter, what the hell is wrong with you? I've been talking to you, and it's like you aren't even here."

"What? What did you say?"

"I said, take the next left. We're heading back to the bunker until we get some information from your father. I've already told Bates we're headed back."

"All right. Will do."

Peter drove until he reached the next road, and he took a left heading back to the bunker. Once again, his mind was on his family, not what he was doing. He could only hope that everything would somehow work out.

"You better hope your father comes up with something soon. We need this. Bates is angry, and the boss has given him a new position of authority. He wants these guys, and he wants them now."

"I hear you."

Peter drove, but his mind was not on the road.

Chapter 32

The bunker

Peter returned to the bunker with the others. Wallace had talked the entire way back. Peter had learned a lot in the short ride. It was getting to be late afternoon and most troops were in the mess hall. Peter knew he had to take time to let his father know what he had learned. He texted.

At the bunker. Word has it, Bates wants to take out Joe and Ron with a drone. We have a lot of them, and they are dangerous. Gotta go.

Peter heard someone, and he put his phone back as quickly as he could. It was just a couple of guys coming from the mess hall. "Hey, Peter, you're going to miss chow if you don't hurry."

"Yeah, I've been to Colewin with Wallace. He has me running all over the place. I guess I better get moving."

"Grub is good tonight. The cooks are gettin' better here."

"That sounds good."

Colewin

The barber received the text, and he knew he had to get the message to Joe, but, once again, he thought he was being followed. As he drove home, he kept muttering to himself. "How will I get this information to Joe? I can't send Agnes again. We can't have Don running all over the place either. I hope he was able to warn Joe."

The barber pulled into his place. His wife was back. He jumped out of the truck and ran to the door. Agnes met him. She told him that she was able to reach Don, and that he agreed to go to Joe. "I'm not sure how it went, of course, but knowing Don, he probably got the message to Joe."

"I hope. I have more news now. Peter sent this." He showed the text to Agnes.

"What does that mean?"

"It means that they have a way to hurt people from the sky when they least expect it. And from what I know, these things are accurate and lethal."

"I'm going to have to take a chance and drive out to Joe's place. Again, I don't want to text or call about what Peter said, just in case."

"Not alone. I'm going with you."

"No, you stay here in case we need you to do something else. Who knows what Peter might say next?"

"All right, but take your phone and let me know that you're okay."

"Gotcha."

The hideout

Joe knew he should call Ann and Loretta. Together, they had to decide on what to do, but they were all waiting for word from Peter.

Joette said, "We need to take care of this mess first. What are those bunker people planning? We need to find out."

Ron shook his head back and forth. "Until Peter finds out, we're in the dark."

"I agree. We can't guess, but maybe we should try to figure out what they might do. They haven't been able to find our place, but it's only a matter of time."

Don drove back to Colewin, and on the way he passed a truck going very fast. "Was that the barber?" He could not be sure, but he wanted to get back to town, so he kept moving and wondering what was up.

The barber saw Don's truck and had the same thoughts. He kept the pedal to the floor and moved as fast as he could. He was breathing heavily. When he arrived at Joe's hideout, he jumped out of the truck and ran to the door. He was out of breath from the short jaunt, but he pounded on the door and yelled for Joe. He had trouble catching his breath, but he yelled again.

Ron answered the door. "Come in, come in. What's up?"

The barber took a deep breath, trying to get his wind back.

"My son, Peter, has news!"

Joe jumped off the couch, and Joette and Shanice both turned and stood at the kitchen table. They could see the barber was shaken.

Joe walked to the barber and told him to take a seat at the table. He dragged himself over and sat. "Try to relax."

"Sure, sure."

"Take a deep breath. There's no hurry. We're safe here."

"I know. I'm just afraid for all of us. My son included. That guy, Bates, has this jackass trainer, Wallace, out scouting the area. They went back to the bunker, and Peter said that Wallace and Bates are planning a drone attack on you guys, and who knows who else?"

"Does he know when?"

"As soon as he finds out where you guys are hiding. The guy is looking for revenge. I can't understand why they could not keep him in jail."

"Nothing we can do about that, but we do need to protect everyone we can. We must find out as much as we can—and then act on the information."

The barber said, "I'll let you know what I find out, but I don't want to put my son in jeopardy in any way."

Ron thought that they might have some time, so he suggested that they plan to leave the hideout if need be. "We can find a place that's safe. Maybe it'll be a long way from here."

Joe agreed. "We've spent too much time here trying to do something. Maybe it's time to move on."

"But what about us?" the barber asked.

"We'll need to be sure everyone is safe, but I'm not sure how to do that. Since the attack on the bunker, they have reinforced it with personnel and weapons, including helicopters and now drones."

"This town will not survive with them around. How will we?"

"As we were telling Don, we need to organize, but we need to find people who believe as we do. Most of the individuals who helped during the attack are in hiding or scattered around keeping a low profile. No one wants to be identified as working against them."

Ron moved to the table and took a seat next to the barber. "You can see what happened to Charlie, Matt, and Tommy. They're after them because they're sure they were in on the attack."

The barber agreed. "I can see that."

"They know we were in on it, so I guess we're next."

Joe sat across from Ron and next to the barber. Joette and Shanice were standing, leaning on the counter. Joette said, "Our time here has to end, but how will the locals be safe?"

"Like I said. We need to organize. Not just here, but in every state, but we need to start here."

The barber moaned.

Joe said, "You go and don't do anything suspicious. Keep us abreast of what your son does and says, and we'll work on a plan. If he spots any drones being prepared, we should know. We'll have to move quickly."

Chapter 33

The bunker

Bates and Wallace were in a conversation about the people they wanted to take out. Bates was really into revenge. "We have Charlie. Looks like he's not going anywhere too soon. I think we can figure out where that Tommy kid is once we take care of Joe. We need to do some investigating to find out where Matt is. He was definitely in on this."

Wallace said, "I think we can get answers soon to the whereabouts of these people. We need to focus on this Joe guy. He seems to be the one everyone is protecting, but I have an idea that we can work this out. That kid, Peter, is from there. We should let him do more investigating. He's local. People will open up to him."

Bates was firm in his assessment. "I agree. Start tomorrow again and just in case, get the drones ready. Have three always ready to go, and have three in the air at all times. If we spot them, we're ready, and if they happen to shoot one down, we'll have backups. They won't expect that."

"Good plan. However, you should send a reconnaissance drone when you first try. We'll keep the drone at treetop level. It'll be easy to shoot down, but it could get us valuable pictures. They probably don't have the capability to jam or control our drones, but we need to consider that they might. If they can, they could turn them on us."

"Good to know."

"I'll have our people come up with a decent plan of attack as soon as we find out where they are."

Bates had an epiphany. "Wait. I have an idea. Why can't we have our drone people fly them around the area looking for the people we want to eliminate? We could have them in the air in no time, and we might be able to find them faster than the local guys. The community has been tight-lipped about anything we want to find out. This could be our way of keeping an eye on everyone and everything!"

"That could be risky."

"Yes, but it could also be very successful. When could we start?"

"We could begin right away. I would have to notify the technicians who run the things, then we would be ready to go."

"Let's do it!"

Wallace smiled. "We're on it."

The hideout

Joe and Ron talked late into the night. "We tried to take out the boss in 2019, we were almost killed twice by these people, we attacked the bunker to try to bring this to an end, and we captured one of their key logistics people. Yet, we have not even put a dent in their organization."

Ron agreed. "They are even stronger now at the bunker than they were, and we're all scattered around the countryside. They have weapons that we can't fight against. They are just too powerful."

"They are all over now. They have grown bigger than they were a few years ago. We can't keep this a local fight anymore. We need to organize as we've said."

"How do we do that?"

"We begin by calling Ann and Loretta."

"It's too late now, but in the morning, we are on the phone to them. Hopefully, they have a way to get us all organized."

Morning

Joe was the first to rise. He did not sleep much after his talk with Ron. They both knew that what they had done so far to knock this group down, only strengthened them. Ann and Loretta were in the same predicament. It was 7:00 a.m., and Joe was restless. He wanted to call right away, but he decided to wait a bit.

Joette was the next one to rise. "You're up early."

"Couldn't sleep. I need to call Ann and get something started, or this thing is going to be completely out of hand, if it isn't already."

"It sure seems like it. The more information we get, the more we learn about other parts of the country being in the same kind of predicament as we are in here."

"They are. All the research we have points to a serious situation."

Joette sat next to Joe. "Do you want some breakfast?"

"I'm just going to have a bowl of cereal for now."

"You sure? That's all?"

"Yep."

Then Ron walked into the room. He was followed by Shanice. "You make a call yet?"

"Not yet. Hope to call by 8:00 a.m."

"We really need to get something going to save this country. My son said that the chatter is very strong and very frequent these days. Your son has found the same thing. They are organizing for some kind of coup, they think."

"I'm sure."

The four of them talked about what they might do, and at 8:00 a.m. sharp, Joe picked up his phone and called Ann.

"Hello, Ann here."

"Ann, this is Joe."

"I've been waiting for your call."

The bunker

Joe wasn't the only one up early. At 6:00 a.m., Wallace had four of his drone operators up, and they were getting four drones ready for action. They were just small ones that would do some reconnaissance, but they were very effective and had expensive cameras that could identify a person, especially if the person was looking up at them.

"The idea is to fly one in each direction using Colewin as the center, back and forth, looking for anything that looks suspicious, especially anything that looks like someone is trying to hide something. Each one of you should man one drone, and keep an eye on what is sent back. When you have anything that looks suspicious, let me know immediately."

"We can do that."

"When you find anything, then we'll send the armed drones and level the place."

"Won't that get us into some trouble with the law and with the local people?"

"We have that covered with the sheriff. The local people won't do anything because they're afraid of us, and we can handle them."

"Whatever you say. You're the boss."

"No, I'm not the boss, but I have the okay to do this, so let's get on it."

Chapter 34

The hideout

The conversation was long overdue. Joe and Ann had been in contact with each other, but they had never been able to plan anything. Loretta had been in on it too, but with all that had happened over the last few months, she and Ann had to lay low. Loretta and Ann did have the governor's ear, yet they knew there were others in the capitol who might not be on their side.

"Joe, what are you thinking?"

"We've come to the conclusion that we have to begin to join forces to fight these guys. They have become too powerful for just a small group to contend with. They have grown much bigger than we ever thought and since they are in every state, we need to fight them everywhere. We're not sure how to do that."

Ann said, "We had the same thoughts. We have begun to organize people whom we know believe like we do. We have a small network, but we can expand it quite a bit with some help. We just need to make sure everyone has the same goal as we do."

"To preserve the union."

"Yes, these people have no intention of keeping our democracy. We know they want to take over the government any way they can."

Joe was considering everything he knew about the group. "We know that they have a key leader. You know who I mean. We tried to take him out a few years ago."

"Oh, I'm aware of that, and I've filled in Loretta. He's the leader for sure, and we have learned that he's going to make a run at the presidency as an independent. Not sure how that will go, but I know they have money to back him up, so who knows."

"That is a problem."

"It is, for more than one reason. We know he'll use any tactics to get what he wants. They've already set up groups in each state to help with the election."

Joe was surprised. "How do you know that?"

"We have people all over working against these guys. I've been in contact with agents across the country who are with us, but they too are not sure who to trust, so we have to take it slowly and move cautiously."

"You mean there might be people in the agency who are with this group?"

"Not might be—there are. We know that for sure."

"Man, this is worse than we thought. When we began fighting these guys, we thought this bunker was the only stronghold they had, then we found out about several others. We've known for a while that the boss had aspirations of running for the presidency, but we didn't believe he had much of a chance, not anymore."

Ann had her phone on speaker, and Joe heard Loretta. "We need to meet to organize ourselves here in Michigan. Then we can think of what we can do to get a network going around the country."

"That's exactly what we need to do, organize to fight back and to knock this guy out of the political arena."

"No, we probably need to find out who is bankrolling this group. We know they have a committee that meets a few times a year, and they are really in charge. Although this boss has a lot of power, without the financial support, he has nothing, so our goal will be to hit the committee in some way. We need to either break them up or eliminate them, but it won't be easy."

"Where do we start?"

Ann knew they would have their hands full attempting to destroy this organization, but she felt that it had to happen right away. "We need to get all of our information consolidated. You have someone working online searching for information, right?"

"Yes, both Ron's son and my son have been on them for a long time now. They have as much information as anyone. You must have access to some type of electronic surveillance, probably better than what we have."

"We do, but we need to know where the people stand before we can have them searching for information. Remember, this is the government. We'll have to jump through some hoops, or we'll need to find out for sure whom we can trust."

"We can meet anytime. Any ideas where it might be best?"

Ann was certain where she wanted to meet. "We think we need to get out of here for a while. We have the governor working on finding out what she can. She has a few people she can trust. We need to just wait it out until she can give us some solid information about people."

"All right, but I would not meet around here. We have a problem with the bunker right now. They are surveilling the area with drones looking for people who attacked the bunker, and they're willing to just take them out."

"That doesn't sound good. You need to get out of there."

"How about we meet where our sons are right now? They're both in the U.P., not going to say exactly where, but you know where Ron and I and our wives hid during the pandemic? It's close to there."

"I know where that is. Let's meet in that town."

"Great. We'll pack up and head there. We cannot stay here anymore. I don't like leaving all our friends behind, but we have no choice. We'll have to let the key people here know that we and not abandoning them, but only trying to figure out how to help."

"Let's say one week from today."

"Let's say ten days. We need time to close this place down and notify everyone."

"Ten days it is."

Chapter 35

The bunker

When the drones were ready, Bates was informed. They would be in the sky in no time. He was happy, but he was not celebrating until he could take out anyone who had anything to do with the attack on the base. He had Charlie, and they had a lead on Tommy. They needed to find Matt, and anyone else who was in on the attack. Otherwise, he was willing to just eliminate the entire area if he had to. However, Bates was preoccupied with the two men who had taken him captive after the attack. Joe and Ron were on his radar, and he was laser-focused on them.

"You have to make sure you get these guys before you go after anyone else. I don't care what you have to do, just get them and then prove to me that they're dead. I won't sleep soundly again until they're gone."

The trainer was convinced. "We'll get them. This time they won't have a chance."

"Good. They've messed up our mission too many times. The boss has given me the reins of this operation, but to move forward, I need these guys eliminated. They're the only ones who have made our lives miserable. Everywhere else we're in control, and we haven't had any trouble like here. We end this now!"

Bates watched as the four drones were sent aloft, each with specific directions of what area to search. The men in control were going to practice this first day, and then they would be ready to search for real. Each man had orders on exactly how and where he would operate for the next week. Bates was sure that a week would not be necessary. He had a few locals who were helping, and he had a feeling this was going to go well.

Colewin

Don was in town ready to head to the Sportsman's Bar and Pizzeria for lunch. He left the town hall and walked down the street to the bar. As he was walking, he noticed something in the sky. *It was one of those small drones that kids played with these days*, he thought. Then he remembered what the barber had told him about drones, and Don forgot about his lunch.

Don ran back to the town hall, dropped into his chair, looked around the room, and then picked up his phone. He called the barber. "Hey, this is me, Don. What did you say the other day about some drones?"

"We shouldn't be talking on phones. Can you run down to my shop? I'm not busy right now, and we can talk."

"I'll be there in a few minutes."

Don half walked and half ran to the barber's shop. All the while he was talking to himself. He thought he was going crazy. He reached the barber's place and threw the door open, but the barber had someone in his chair.

"Hey, Don, how's it going? You're next. Have a seat. It won't be long."

The man in the barber's chair looked familiar to Don, but he couldn't place him. He thought, *I know everyone in this town. Who the hell is that* guy? *He* must *be an outsider? Is he from the bunker? What is he doing in town? Those guys don't come here for haircuts.* Don picked up a magazine and pretended to read an article. His mind was all over the place. He feared for his small town and the people in it.

After about ten minutes, then the barber said, "There you go. All finished."

This brought Don back to his senses. He looked up and, as the man paid the barber, he dropped the magazine. The man said, "Thank you. See you next time."

"Have a good day," the barber responded.

When he left, Don walked over and sat in the barber's chair. The barber said, "Just a minute," and he moved toward the door and locked it.

"Who the hell was that guy?"

"I'm not sure. I've never seen him before. Said he used to live in Poplar, but I know most everyone in Poplar, and he ain't one of 'em. So, what's up, Don?"

"I saw one of those drones flying low over our town. Wonderin' if that's what your son was talking about. I mean, have they started checking out the area to take out certain people?"

"My son thinks that they're after Joe and Ron, and that they're the main reason for the drones, but he also said that the Bates guy wants revenge for the attack on his base, so he's afraid that we're all possible targets because they don't have a clue who was really involved."

"I've stayed out of this stuff long enough. You have any idea how many people from Colewin might be involved, and how vulnerable we might all be?"

"I can't answer your questions, but I don't trust those guys. I think you better get out to Joe and Ron and their wives and tell them to be on the lookout. This is serious shit. You know they load munitions on those things. They could destroy a place in no time—and who would know what happened?"

As Don and the barber talked, several people in town and in the countryside saw drones too. They were just over the tree tops.

Many people thought they were just kids playing with these new-fangled toys. Anyway, what harm could they do?

While the drones were in the sky, Peter and one other local were sent to town again with Wallace to search some areas that were not well-known by the bunker people. They had previously searched the ridge area where a lot had happened since Wyatt had killed Tommy's Uncle George there. They had found nothing new. They had also searched the area where Charlie had begun to dig a tunnel, but it was still abandoned. They had searched the area around Charlie's place and had been through Poplar, too. Now, they wanted to search between Poplar and Colewin, an area that was thick with trees and not much else.

Don and the barber were not sure what exactly to do. They knew heading to Joe's again might lead to someone following them, especially a drone. A call was shaky too because they thought their phones might be compromised. Yet, they had to get word to Joe about what was happening.

Hideout

However, Joe and Ron were already on it. They knew if there was the possibility of drones that they had to do something. Ron had an idea. "Joe, if these guys figure out where we are, they're going to send a drone to wipe us out."

Joe looked up and nodded. "I agree."

"That means we need to get out of the area. We planned to meet with Ann in ten days. Why not go early and just leave every-thing as it is here. Let them think we're hiding. If they destroy the place like I think they might, they won't be able to find anyone anyway."

"Good point, Ron."

Shanice and Joette were listening, and they were thinking the same thing. Joette was the first to speak up. "Let's get out of this place, now. We have nothing keeping us here anymore, except the bunker, and that place is a fortress with more people than ever. Why not join our sons and their families?"

Shanice said, "We've done what we could here. We need to join forces with Ann and Loretta and figure out how to destroy this organization."

"All right. I guess we should plan to get out of here. Let's leave a couple of vehicles and most of our things, so it looks like we're here. We'll take one vehicle and everything we can fit into it, and that'll have to do."

Ron approved. "I'll leave a few things around outside to make it look like this place is inhabited. It's not going to take a long time to find our hideout if they have drones searching the area. I say let's move right away."

"We'll need to let someone know, so they won't think we abandoned our friends."

Joette said, "Before we leave, we can let the barber know, and we can tell him where we're going, but only him. He'll let the right people know what's up."

"For sure. That's what we'll do."

Ron decided to set up the area like it was still being used, and so he drove the four wheelers out of the shed and parked them in front of the building. He also opened the shed door to make it look like someone was in there. The two cars they were leaving were parked next to each other on the side of the house. "Man, I hate to leave those cars. What a loss," Ron said as he walked away from the shed.

As Ron was heading to the house, he heard it. He looked up and right over his head was a drone. "Damn it," he shouted as he ran toward the house.

The bunker

Wallace received word immediately that one of the drone operators had found something interesting, a cabin that had not previously been on their radar, and a man that fit the description of one of the men they were looking for.

Wallace went to Bates and had the pictures uploaded to his system.

"That's him! That's one of the guys who had interrogated me and sent me to prison. Get on that spot right now. Send in the armed drones!"

"Are you sure?"

"Yes, I'm sure. Don't hesitate. You can see he looked up and saw your drone. If he is suspicious at all, he'll be out of there in no time."

Wallace had the armed drones up and in the sky in less than five minutes. He yelled at his technician. "Get these things to that same spot and destroy anything and everything there. Send two more drones if necessary."

The technician responded, "Two will not be necessary. This one has enough firepower to take out a city block."

"How long will it take to get there?"

"As the eagle flies, maybe five minutes. It won't be long."

"Good, take out anything you see."

Chapter 36

The hideout

The hideout had been a good place for the two couples to spend some time while trying to take down the bunker. It was far off the beaten path, and few people would ever go in that direction, possibly some loggers. That's how they had found the place. Charlie had been logging there and found the clearing in the woods. He knew it would be a good place for some of his people to hide, if need be. When Joe needed a place, Charlie knew right away. It was far enough away from both Colewin and Poplar that no one would just wander in, yet it was accessible on some roads that loggers had made. It was the perfect spot, *until the drones found it.*

Ron ran for the cabin. He knew what he had seen, and he thought that was the end, but the drone circled and left. He threw himself in through the door and screamed at everyone, "We need to get out of here right now. Don't hesitate! A drone just flew overhead. I thought we were toast, but it left. I'm sure they're coming back with some type of firepower. We need to leave now!"

The three people in the cabin just froze in place. Joe was the first to react. "What? What did you see?"

"A small drone. I'm sure it had a camera. I thought they were going to take us out right then."

"All right. Let's jump in the truck and get out of here now," Joe yelled to them.

"Don't hesitate, or take anything. Just leave."

Joette and Shanice looked at each other and began grabbing anything they thought they should. Joe said again, "Just leave."

Ron had the keys for the crew cab, and he was already in the truck. He cranked it and backed it out and pulled in front of the cabin door. The others ran and jumped in. Ron hit the accelerator and tore a long patch of dirt into the air as the truck swerved and shimmied and roared out of the clearing.

They had gone about a quarter mile when the first explosion rocked the truck. Joe turned and looked, but another explosion sent trees, wood, and dirt into the air where the cabin had been.

The truck shook again. And then another explosion, much closer, threw something through the back window of the truck. It broke the glass and flew between Joe and Joette in the back seat, and it hit the front window and cracked it. Ron could not hold the truck on the road, and it swerved and crashed into the side of a small tree. All four passengers were thrown forward as the air bags inflated.

The bunker

Bates and Wallace had four drones in the sky over the hideout. One was used only for observation so they could see what was happening. It was much higher in the sky, so the pictures were not as clear as the ones the first drone had gotten, but they were able to spot the vehicles thrown near some downed trees and torn apart from the explosion. They were destroyed as was the rest of what was left of the cabin on the second explosion.

Bates was determined to get anyone who might be there. He gave the order to keep bombing all around the area just in case. There were several explosions. He had the drones move down the road that led out of the clearing in case anyone was heading out. The explosions rocked the area for some time until Bates was happy with the results.

"I think we got anyone who might have been there." As Wallace looked at the screen, smoke and fire were all he could see from what had been a cabin and some out buildings. There was a huge crater in the center of the clearing, and wreckage was strewn all over the place.

Bates eyes were wide with hate. He looked like a madman, and he was laughing and yelling. "Hit it a few more times around the tree line, and get that road leading out again."

The truck

The four people in the truck were all pinned right away by the air bags; then they deflated. Shanice's nose looked like it might be broken by the air bag since she was bleeding profusely. Joe and Joette in the back seat were all right but shaken when another explosion sent rocks and trees in their direction, and then another explosion that tore a huge crater in the road behind them. The truck was peppered with dirt, stones, and wood. It was sitting with the back end up and the cab sunk in a depression on the side of the road. Rocks and wood hit the truck, shaking it sideways and sending it deeper into the side of the road. They were off the road, which provided some tree cover, so the truck was hidden.

When things calmed down a bit, Joe asked, "Is everyone all right?" Shanice and Joette answered, but Ron did not. He had been knocked unconscious by some material that had flown through his window. "We need to get out of here and walk away in case they come back and begin again."

Shanice was the first to exit. She was still bleeding, and aside from looking shaken, she was able to help Joette out of her seat. Joe's door was jammed, so he had to slide across and exit the right back door. When the three were out of the truck, they tried to get to Ron, but his door was also jammed, and he was not responding.

They would have to get him out through the passenger's side, if they could.

The bunker

Once Wallace saw the destruction, he knew that if anyone was anywhere around it, they were gone. He smiled as he turned to Bates and said, "Well, that does it. They're toast."

"It looks like it, but I'm not taking any chances. Get a group together, at least twenty troops, and get over there and inspect the area. If you see anyone, take them out."

"You sure? That place is a mess."

"I'm sure!"

Wallce got twenty of his best troops crammed into one of the military trucks, and they were off.

Colewin and Poplar

Explosions like the ones that took place that afternoon, could be heard in both Colewin and Poplar. Some people thought it was the end of the world, some thought it might be an earthquake since the ground around Poplar shook. Others thought it was just those militia dudes playing war again. They had heard a lot over the years, and it just kept getting louder and louder.

The barber, on the other hand, had a good idea what it was. The barber finished with a customer, locked his shop, and was heading to the town hall. Before he left, Don called. "What the hell was that?"

"I have no idea, but I can guess it was what we feared. I wonder if Joe and Ron and their wives are all right."

Don said, "We need go there and check on them. Maybe send an ambulance."

"I agree. Can you get that going? I'll grab my truck and pick you up at the ambulance garage."

"Okay, I'm outside of the Sportsman's right now, I'll get the ambulance on this. Be careful, but hurry."

The truck

Joe thought he might try to help push Ron from the driver's side as their wives pulled, so he tried to crawl around the truck to get there. He was able to, but the door was pushed up against the tree they had scraped, and he could not get at the door or window. Joe climbed into the back seat and released Ron's seat belt. He reached down and moved the seat back as far as he could. He was able to lean Ron almost forty-five degrees. Then Shanice grabbed ahold of him and pulled as Joe lifted. It took some time, but they were able to get him out. He was bleeding badly.

Joe turned to Joette and Shanice. "We have to hide or get out of here. If that drone comes back and begins again, we won't have any protection. I have a blanket in the back. Let's put Ron on it and walk along the road and get as far away as we can."

Shanice looked at Joe with disbelief. "Joe, Ron is over two hundred pounds. How are we going to pull him?"

"I'm not sure, but we have to try something."

Then they heard a vehicle approaching. They panicked. Joette yelled, "Who could that be? We need to hide."

"Let's all move to the other side of the road away from the truck. We can drag Ron that far."

When all three pitched in, they were able to get Ron into the woods and under an evergreen tree. They waited.

A military vehicle

The truck driver was unsure of exactly where they were headed, and he took them down several dead-end roads until he thought he found the one that led to the hideout. "I'm sure this is the one. Look at the smoke," Wallace said.

"It could be. Let's be ready in case anyone is out here. I don't want us to be caught unprepared," the driver added.

"Good point. Stop the truck."

"What?"

"Let's get these guys in the back prepared. We can have a few troops follow us on foot. We'll drive slowly so we'll be ready. Everyone, get prepared. Be locked and loaded."

Chapter 37

Colewin

The barber hustled to his shop and got his truck, but before he picked up Don, he went home and got a chain saw, some chains, a winch, some medical supplies, and blankets just in case. His phone rang as he was jumping into his truck.

"Hey, this is Don. The ambulance is on a run to the Petoskey hospital. I guess there was some kind of emergency in Naubinway, so they're not available."

"I just threw some medical supplies in my truck. Can you get anything? Maybe bandages or something to clean wounds just in case. Although after that second explosion, I don't have much hope."

"Don't say that. Let's just hurry. People are beginning to gather outside around here. They'll be nosy, and I'm sure they'll want to check out the area. And what if the sheriff shows up?"

"Pick me up at the town hall. There's an emergency medical kit there, and a defibrillator we might as well take."

The barber pulled up to the town hall. Don had a large bag of supplies. "I grabbed some food, and I'll get some water too, just in case. He threw the bag in the back and went back into the town hall and came out with a case of water and threw that in. "There, let's go!"

The barber's truck squealed out as he pulled away from the town hall. Several people stared at him as it was so out of character.

They drove as fast as they could. They knew just where they were going. When they arrived at the road where the hideout was, they saw a truck turning down one of the logging trails.

The barber fumed, "That's a military vehicle full of troops."

"Yeah, but it's headed down the wrong road. That's an old logging trail. We need to beat them to the hideout, or what's left of it, or they'll make sure no one comes out of there."

They passed the logging road and saw the truck moving down the logging trail as they sped by.

"The hideout road isn't far now. Slow down a bit."

The barber hit the brakes and said, "Right." The turn into the road wasn't difficult to see. It had been camouflaged, but now it was clearly open. "The road is wide open. They're going to find this next. We need to hurry. They won't leave so much as a cockroach alive if they find anything."

The military vehicle

The truck rambled on until it hit a dead end. Wallace could see that this was not the road. Yet, he had his troops out scouring the area to see if there was a hidden road somewhere. "Forget it and get back in the truck. This can't be the road."

The troops jumped into the truck, and the driver backed up to turn around when he hit a dip in the ground and became stuck. The driver yelled, "Everyone out. You need to help us get out of here and quickly."

All twenty of the troops and Wallace jumped out. They tried pushing forward, but to no avail. They pushed backward and the truck jumped quickly and bounded onto solid ground, but it also landed on the foot of one of the troops. He yelled, "Son of a bitch!"

They stopped and attended to the troop, but it wasn't as bad as it sounded. He limped around for a few minutes, and then said

he was all right. They pushed again and the truck moved forward
a bit, then back again, and forward until they had the truck free.
The driver turned it to face the road and they were off.

The hideout

The barber turned onto the dirt road to the hideout and drove as
fast as he could. It took him a few minutes and then he saw the
truck. He knew it was Joe's.

Don echoed his thoughts, "That's the crew cab I saw at Joe's
place."

"That's his truck all right."

They pulled up alongside the vehicle and looked around. Don
yelled, "A drone. Three o'clock."

The barber left the road and drove under a tree. "I see it. It's
moving off to the north. Is that one armed?"

"I sure as hell don't know," Don said.

As they left the truck and walked up to the crew cab, they
heard a voice. It was Joe.

He greeted both Don and the barber.

Don asked, "Are you guys all right? That truck looks like it
has seen better days."

Joette and Shanice walked out from behind the trees. Shanice
said, "Ron is hurt. We need to get him help right away."

The barber immediately went to the truck and got the medical
supplies that they picked up. He gave them to Shanice and Joette,
who went to help Ron.

Don said, "We need to get you out of here right away. There's
a truck full of troops heading this way, and the drones are still in
the sky."

"We've seen them, and we've been trying to stay hidden."

"Let's get your truck out of here if we can. Otherwise, they're
going to know you made it out—and that'll be bad."

The barber moved his truck behind the crew cab, and Don got the chains they had brought and hooked them to both trucks. It didn't take much to pull the truck out. Joe jumped in and started it. It roared to life. He tried driving it forward, and it was good.

The three men then went to where the women had Ron. They cleaned the truck's bed of all the debris, made a bed from the pile of blankets that the barber had brought, lifted Ron, and placed him there. Joe had to clear the glass from the broken back window, get rid of the air bags, and knock out the rest of the glass from the side window. A small hole in the windshield on the passenger's side created a spider pattern on both the driver and passenger's side, but Joe could see well enough to drive, and even with the side and back windows out, and a huge dent in the door, it was drivable.

The barber yelled to Joe, "Wait until the drone is out of sight, and then take the next road. Stay on that. It's paved and you won't leave a dust trail. Stay on that road to U.S.-2. You'll have a lot of tree cover."

"Thanks!"

Don added, "You'll need to take your truck to the Manistique Hospital. We'll head back to the road and wait for the party to begin." Don knew that in no time, besides the troops in the truck, many people would be out checking on what happened.

After cleaning more glass off the seats, Joe and the rest were off to Manistique. Don and the barber drove out of the hideout road to the road where the troops would soon be, and they waited.

The military vehicle

Wallace decided to call Bates and have the drones tear up the area again before he went in. He wanted to make sure no one came out alive. "Say, Bates, have those drone operators send more drones and have them drop some more explosives along the road to that cabin, and light up the cabin area again in case anyone happened to survive. We'll sit at the end of the road and wait."

"I'll check with the tech guys who are running those things. We have one drone moving back and forth over the area, and, so far, we have found nothing moving."

They sent another armed drone. It didn't take long before the place was lit up again with explosions. Don and the barber pulled away from the road and headed back toward Colewin. They moved far enough to avoid the explosions and debris. They turned and watched from a distance when the military vehicle edged up beside them.

Wallace got out and walked to the barber's truck. "What are you boys doing out here?"

Don looked at him and just shook his head. "What do you think? I'm the mayor of this town, and I would like to know what in hell is going on. There will be all kinds of people here in no time checking this out. What are you doing here?"

"Checking it out just like you are."

"Yeah, I bet. What's with all the armed troops?"

"Just a precaution. You know. Best to be careful."

A drone came close to the road, and they watched as it moved back and forth around the area, then it sped off into the trees near the road where the barber and Don had just been.

"You controlling those things?" the barber asked.

"You talking to me? I'm not controlling anything."

"Then who is?" Don said.

"Not sure what you're talking about. We're just here to check this stuff out."

"Sure you are. A bunch of military guys in a truck and military drones flying over dropping explosives, and you have nothing to do with it."

"Nope."

Wallace walked back to his truck and told the driver to move forward to the road up ahead. He wanted to see if there would be any chance of anyone making it out of there. They drove close and looked. The last drones had taken out the road and there was no way they were driving in. "Okay, everyone out. As soon as we get the all clear, we're moving into the area on foot." Wallace called Bates and told him what was up and to stop with the drones, but to keep one eye in the sky.

On the way to Manistique

Joe was not sure if he had escaped without anyone following him. When he reached highway M-117, he had a clear view of the road behind him, and he could not see any cars racing to catch up. He kept the speed at fifty-five, any faster and the fender rattled too much, and too much debris flew around the cab. He wanted to go faster, but he knew he couldn't.

Shanice had called ahead and informed the hospital that they had a man who had been seriously hurt in a car accident. That is all she let them know. "Ron, can you hear me?" Shanice kept trying to keep Ron awake, but it was a chore.

Joette kept as calm as she could to help Shanice deal with the situation. She knew Ron was serious. "He'll be all right. I'm sure of it," she said, but she really wasn't sure.

Shanice was worried. "He's lost a lot of blood, and he seems unconscious at times. He hasn't said a word since the accident."

Joe kept the speed up, and they reached the hospital safely forty minutes later without any other problems. Joe pulled into the emergency entrance, and they were met by a team that gently took Ron onto a stretcher and hurried him into the hospital ER. Joe looked at Shanice and Joette. They were a sight. Both had blood all over their faces and their clothes were dirty and bloody. Joe asked, "Are you both all right?"

Joette answered, "I'm okay. I hurt, but not too badly."

Shanice, who was hurrying into the hospital after Ron, just said, "I'm fine."

They followed her into a waiting room where a nurse said, "I think all three of you should get checked. Were you all in the same accident?"

Joette answered, "Yes."

The nurse took them in and had all three examined. They had a lot of cuts and bruises, but they were all good, except for their concern for Ron. Joette thought Shanice might have a broken nose, and she spoke to a nurse about it, but it was just a bad bleed.

After quite some time, a doctor came out and talked to them. She asked if anyone was related, and Shanice told her that she was Ron's wife. She took Shanice aside and spoke to her. "Your husband has a compound fracture of the left arm and a bad ankle. He has lost a lot of blood as a result, but we were able to stop the bleeding and ready the arm as best we could for a specialist. It's a bad break, so I suggest you take him to Marquette."

"How will we get him there?"

"We can air lift him. We have a helicopter for such emergencies."

Joette gave Shanice a hug and said, "We can drive there. Can Shanice ride with her husband?"

"I'm not sure there will be room, but I'll check."

As it turned out, Shanice rode with Ron, and Joe and Joette took what was left of the truck and drove the ninety miles to Marquette. It was not a very comfortable journey, but they made it.

Chapter 38

Colewin

Back in Colewin, the fire department had arrived at the scene, but they also noticed that they could not get to where the fire was. They could see a lot of smoke, and they were concerned. The DNR had also been contacted, and they had equipment there not long after the fire department. They saw the military truck and asked if the troops could help to extinguish the fires. Wallace was happy to assist them.

It took several hours, but the DNR, with the help of the fire department and the troops, were able to snuff the flames.

Don and the barber talked to the DNR about the damage and the explosions. They had no answers. Sheriff Daryl came along shortly after they were all back on the road getting ready to leave. "Looks like some kids playing with dynamite again. We have to stop that."

Don looked at him and shook his head. The barber just spit out of his window, turned the truck around, and drove off.

Marquette

Joe and Joette met Shanice at the regional hospital in Marquette. As soon as they saw her, Joe went right to her and said, "We should have left Colewin a long time ago. I'm so sorry. Ron and I were hoping to make sure everyone who helped us was safe after our attack on the bunker. I also didn't want to abandon anyone."

"You shouldn't worry about Ron and me. We were fine with staying there, but we are happy to be getting someplace where we're not looking over our shoulder each day. This move will help all of us."

"It's just too bad it was at Ron's expense."

"He should be fine. The doctor said that the surgery went well, but he will be in a cast for some time."

Joette said, "Why don't we all get something to eat and rest a little. There must be someplace we can eat in the hospital."

Joe was wondering what he could have done differently. "I should have gotten ahold of Ann or Loretta sooner and set something up as soon as they started going after our people. We might have avoided some of this. And Charlie? What will happen to him?"

Joette tried to stay positive. "No sense looking back. We're meeting with them next week, so we can see what we can pull together to end this mess."

Colewin

As the barber drove toward town, he and Don talked about what had just happened and whether Joe, Ron, Joette, and Shanice had made it to the hospital in time. They were concerned about Ron.

"Man, he lost a lot of blood. His arm looked terrible. I sure hope they had time."

"That's for sure, Don. We did a good job to get them out of there before the troops came or a drone spotted them. I sure am going to miss those guys. They've been a big part of helping us get rid of that bunker. We didn't succeed, but we sure messed them up for a while."

"Glad we never found anything after the fire was out. Looks like there weren't any people around anywhere near that place. It's a long way from anything out here."

The barber was sure. "I think it was only the four. They had a lot of people staying there after they attacked the bunker, but most of those people are back to their normal lives—if there is anything that's normal anymore."

"That's for sure."

"This is going to change this area without Joe around."

The military vehicle

Wallace was happy with the results. He saw what was left of the building and vehicles that had been at the hideout. His men had helped the DNR put out the biggest fires, and they had searched for any sign of life, but they could not find anything. They did find some blood on the trail heading in to the site, but it wasn't much. If anyone had been in the cabin, Wallace knew they could not have survived. He called Bates as they readied to head back. "Bates, we were able to get into the area and check it out. We helped the DNR put out some fires, and we searched for quite a while. We're heading back right now."

"Did you see any evidence that the people had been eliminated?"

"We checked out as much as we could, but there were so many craters from the explosions that it made it difficult to really find anything. The spot where the cabin was supposed to be was just a big hole in the ground. Big trees were thrown around like matchwood. There wasn't much left."

"You didn't find any bodies?"

"We saw some blood in spots, but there was no telling what it was. I'm telling you the place was destroyed. We found two vehicles, or that is, we found some parts of what must have been two vehicles, but they were so mangled that we could not even make out what type they were. No one could have survived."

"But you did not find any evidence of bodies?"

"No."

"Then they escaped."

"How do you figure that?"

"Because I know these people. They are very resourceful, and I'm not going to say they are dead until I see a body. There had to be something. There had to be four people there when you include their wives, so you should have found something."

"Well, when we got there that barber and the mayor were sitting in their truck watching the fires. Maybe they had something to do with this. Maybe they helped them escape."

"Now we're getting somewhere. We need to question those two. Maybe we can go into Colewin and find them and get some answers. We could put some pressure on them."

"I'm not sure that's the answer. These people stick together, and that could be a problem."

"We're going to eventually have close to five hundred troops here. We'll have almost as many people as there are in Colewin. They won't be able to resist."

Chapter 39

Ishpeming

The next week, Ron had been given the okay to leave the hospital. He was wheeled out into a new crew cab that Joe had gotten after trading in the old one. He didn't get much for it since it had several issues. He wanted to repair the old one, but it had too many bad memories, so he just let it go.

Ann and Loretta had arrived, and they brought along Ann's family, so they could all get away from Lansing for a while. Ann, of course, was no longer with the FBI, and Loretta had only a few days before she had to return to work. Jerry and Aaron arrived a day later. Jerry was still recovering from wounds he had received while working to free Ann. Aaron had taken his vacation time to help Jerry in his recovery.

They were all excited to be getting a plan to address this group that seemed to be growing stronger by the day. Word from Colewin was that another two hundred and fifty troops had arrived at the bunker. They had prepared for more troops and had several more barracks built over the last few months. One could only wonder what was going to happen next.

Joe and Ann set a meeting for the next day, so Jerry and Aaron would be there, along with Ron and Loretta. The first meeting was just those six people. They found an old, very large house where Ann and her family would stay with Loretta. Three stories high, the top floor was a large attic. Jerry and Aaron were going to stay there until they realized that Jerry would not make it up all the stairs, so they gave Jerry the very spacious living room.

They met in that living room. Ann spoke, "We have a huge task ahead of us. We need to build a network as large as or larger than the people we are going to try to take down. We have all suffered at their hands, and there is no way to tell what is going to happen next, but it cannot be good for the republic."

Loretta chimed in. "I'm sick and tired of them being able to control the narrative. I have no idea how we've survived to this point. A lot of it has been luck. We have all been hurt, some of us physically, so we need to be emphatic about what we're going to do, and it's going to come with a lot of sacrifice."

Unruffled, Ron offered these words. "I don't care what we do, but I'm committing the rest of my life, or whatever it takes, to destroy their organization."

Joe agreed and said, "We won't be able to do this with so few people. We are going to need groups in every state and every city. How do we go about doing that? On top of needing those people, we somehow need to vet all of them if we're going to include them. Well, we won't have to vet all of them, but someone will have to in each state, so it's going to be important to choose people who can lead, and who aren't afraid of repercussions because there will be many."

"Joe, I have already spoken with some agents I know around the country, people I know that I can trust. We have several on board, but we have a long way to go."

"Ann, that's good to hear! Ron and I have many contacts from our years in the military, and our exploits working for the FBI and CIA. We've begun to contact some people, only those we know would be of similar minds."

Aaron spoke up for the first time. "We'll need some type of online surveillance. The FBI has a lot, but will we be able to find some tech people who will assist us?"

Ron said, "We have both my and Joe's son searching the web for any information. They are good, but they don't have the capability of the government, so we have some help, but I agree we will need a lot more."

Joe asked, "What are you thinking, Ann? I know you have been through hell the past year, and you've said that you have some ideas."

"Yes, this organization is very large, and through some investigations before my boss had me incarcerated, I realized that we can't just hit small groups around the country and hope to make a difference. Joe and Ron, you have tried to take down the base in Colewin, but your own admission is that it made very little difference, so we need to look at the bigger picture."

"Meaning?"

"We need to find out where these people are getting their financing. It's the cash flow that's keeping them afloat. Without the money, they couldn't do some of the things they have. As you said earlier, they have weapons galore and bases and troops all over the country. That's not cheap."

"For sure. Are you saying we should go after the leader again? We tried that once, and it didn't work so well."

"I'm not saying that. What I know we must do is go after the large committee. We learned that the organization meets a few times a year. Sometimes they have online meetings, but they also meet once a year in person. We need to find out when and where they meet, and then we need to do something big to end the flow of money."

"We'll probably still need to keep investigating these bases and their leadership."

"Of course, Joe. That's a given. As a matter of fact, we must do that to make sure they are not focused on what we're planning."

"I get it, but that's a big order. How in the world do we compete with billionaires and heads of state?"

"I guess that's why we're here."

Ishpeming, late evening

The discussion went on late into the night. At 11:00 p.m. Joette and Shanice showed up with food for everyone, and several bottles of wine. The discussion stopped while they set up a table where they could all eat. Joette had made Joe and Ron's favorite—spaghetti and meatballs, salad, and wine. They gathered all the family members, including Ann's husband and her adult children who had come along. They sat down for a very late supper. The talk drifted to the food and drink as everyone enjoyed both.

Ann addressed Joette and Shanice. "Thank you very much for all the work you put in getting this ready. It's delicious."

"No problem. Shanice and I enjoy cooking and working together, so we had a lot of fun. It wasn't all work since we shared a bottle of Italian red wine."

Shanice laughed. "We had so much fun."

When the meal was completed, everyone pitched in to clean and take care of the dishes. Then they decided to rest and meet again the next day.

Joe, Ron, and their wives headed out to his brother James' cabin that was south of Ishpeming. They had previously stayed at the cabin north of Ishpeming during the pandemic. It belonged to another of Joe's brothers who seldom used it, but he kept it for family to enjoy, but right now Tommy, Wendy, and her parents were staying there.

The next day

The next day the meeting was held in the same place where Ann was staying. This time everyone was invited, including Tommy. It was a reunion of sorts for Tommy and Wendy. They had not seen people from Colewin for some time. They knew several and had met Ann, but they had never met some of the others, yet it was good to be among friends.

Ann led the meeting as everyone had agreed she would be the leader of this effort. She had the best background to know just how to approach this problem, and everyone listened to her. "Welcome to everyone. I am happy to see we have so many individuals who are willing to take part in this effort. I want to make it clear before we start that this organization is going to be involved in some serious situations, and you should know it could mean you might have to put your life on the line, or, if these people succeed, we could all go to prison. Not a happy thought."

Joe added. "Ann is right. This is serious, but we need to make sure everyone is in for the long haul. If you have any doubts, now is the time to speak up."

Tommy spoke up. "After what has happened in the last few years, the way I see it, there's no other option. We either do this or go down anyway. They are after us for protecting our community, and they will use any methods to be successful, so there's no choice."

A lot of people agreed and everyone gave a promise to move forward and do what had to be done to save the country and their way of life.

"First things first. We have got to make a list of people we believe think like us, and who would be willing to join. We need to fan out to the entire country on this. We cannot just keep it local. Joette and Jerry have decided to keep records. If you can know for sure that a person thinks like us, contact them and ask for their help. Tell them what you must, but if you have any doubts about anyone, don't include them."

The meeting continued for a couple of hours. Everyone understood the chance they were taking. They realized that they would have to devote a lot of time to this group, and they knew it would impact their lives and livelihoods, but everyone was on board. After much discussion about which political leaders could be contacted, they came up with a few names. They had three governors that they felt they could trust, but they knew that there were people around them who might not be on board, so Loretta decided to make as many contacts as she could in person. Everyone else would just contact people they knew.

Loretta had to head back shortly after the weekend as did Aaron, but Jerry was still recovering, and he felt the U.P. would be a good place to continue his work. Ron was also still rehabbing his arm, and he and Jerry agreed to go to the same therapist. Ann and her husband decided to rent the home where they were staying. She did not want to head back to Lansing until they had things moving in the right direction. They set up a headquarters for the duration of their stay, and everyone agreed it would be the permanent headquarters there.

Chapter 40

Months later, March 2023

It took a lot of time to contact people around the country, but with both Ann's and Loretta's connections in the FBI, and Joe's in the FBI and CIA, and Ron's in the military, things began to come together. The others had communicated with people they knew, and by this time, they had forty states with small groups that were involved. They had no contacts in ten states, but they were working on them. The interesting part was that others had also learned of this radical organization in their states, and they were concerned before even being notified. It looked like they had a contingent of left, right, and center-thinking people—all with the same goal.

Ann was the leader, and the key people in each state reported to her. She made a chart of who and where her people were, as they did for the insurgent organization's troops that they discovered were at various places around the country. Ann had information from Joe about the bunker in the U.P. She also identified the sites where troops were amassed, and they had confirmed what Joe had said about troops in every state.

"Joe, this is concerning. We have groups of these military troops all over the country. They seem to be planning something in each state. So far, we have found small groups of around one hundred to two hundred, and they are training constantly."

"Ann, Ron and I have followed their trucks from the U.P. to several states around the Midwest. We know they send troops all over the country, so this is not a surprise. The seven bases we have found each send people to surrounding states. We think that the bunker in the U.P. where Bates is must be the one directing a lot of the traffic."

"And we know that the U.P. has well over four hundred troops now. What's the plan?"

Joe said, "Who knows, but we should keep an eye on the leader. That guy we tried to take out a while back is a key player in this. We know he aspires to the U.S. presidency. Maybe stopping him should be our goal."

Ann had other thoughts. "Yes, yet I still believe that if we hit the organization's funding partners and stop the flow of money, we can kill this group."

"Well, maybe we should focus on both. I could head up a group to try to destroy his run for the presidency. If he is successful, what a mess this country would be. He let us know what his goals were a few years ago—and they were not good."

"Then let's do both. Joe, you head up a group that will try to destroy his run for the presidency, and we can still focus on hitting the main organization some way to stop the flow of cash."

Joe knew what the old boss was like. *He has no conscience, and he wants to be supreme ruler for life. If he ever gets into the White House, we will never get him out.* Joe recalled what the man had said when he and Ron tried to take him out, and it wasn't pretty. *If he succeeds, there will be no chance to take him down then. He will have all the power and money behind him, plus he will be Commander-in-Chief!*

The bunker

It had been months since Bates had Joe and Ron's hideout destroyed, and they had heard nothing of the people they had tried to take out. He spoke to Wallace, "Maybe we got them this time.

There hasn't been a word or any sightings of those two since we destroyed their hideout."

"I told you the place was a mess. The only people we found that survived were the ones on the road, and we've harassed them for months with no luck. That barber and the mayor were the two we found, and we've had troops in town checking on their movements. Nothing. They know nothing," Wallace said.

"Well, that's good to hear."

"What are our next steps?"

"Wallace, we will just keep up the planning and back the boss when he makes his move. He is working on getting on the ballot in 2024. The organization is spending all kinds of funds on building groups in each state to help with the election. He also has groups around the country that we are training to infiltrate election places. We are going to blame the harassment on both the right and the left. They already have enough trouble as they try to keep people from voting and accusing each other of crazy things, so this will not be difficult, and no one will realize that it is us who are taking over slowly."

"It's a great plan. Is there anything you want us to do? Our troops are trained and ready for anything you can throw at them."

"No, we need them to just sit tight until the boss says to move. Then they will have their hands full. Your group is going to take down the governor of Michigan. We have people inside who know the place and will keep us informed of the best way. Don't say anything to the troops. They don't need to know until the time is right."

"All right. We'll just keep training. Can we allow some of the guys to go to town and have a beer? They're getting a bit restless."

"We can. Just don't send too many. You could allow them to head to St. Ignace, too. Just give them a curfew. If they don't follow your rules, you know what to do. We won't stand for any insubordination."

North Ishpeming

Tommy had been in hiding for some time, so his meetings with Joe were great because he could move around a little. He felt better, and he decided to contact Wayne and Cathy to come and stay with him for a while. Tommy knew they were in Marquette, about thirty minutes from where he was. He had been in contact with them, but they had never gotten together since Tommy had gone into hiding. He had heard that Wayne had completed his therapy and was doing much better. To be on the safe side, he had one of Joe's relatives send a message to Wayne.

It wasn't long before Wayne and Cathy were on their way. Wayne pulled onto the road to where Tommy and Wendy were staying. He drove up to the front of the cabin and parked the car. Tommy and Wendy came flying out to see them. "How in the world are you guys?"

Cathy answered, "We're doing great. We love where we have been staying, and Wayne has completed his therapy, but we miss everyone."

Tommy gave Wayne and Cathy a big hug, and Wendy did the same. Cathy said, "Come in you guys! It's so great to see you."

They talked for a long time, and the topic of Charlie and Matt came up. Tommy said, "I can't stand that we aren't able to help those guys. Matt's in hiding and Charlie is locked up."

Wayne was visibly upset. "It's worse than that. Charlie had been in a coma. Something happened a while ago when he was in jail, and Charlie ended up in some hospital. Last I heard he was in rough shape. I guess he's a bit better, but he's still in some lockup. Grace has been traveling back and forth to see him. She said he is not the same person."

Wendy choked on her words, but then said, "That's horrible!"

"I agree. I want to do something about those people. We need to get revenge!"

"Right, Wayne. You know we eliminated the three guys that we thought were responsible for your injury."

"I know. I just want revenge on that whole group for coming to our home town and making it a place where we can't ever live peacefully."

"You need to join up with our group, Wayne. Joe and his FBI friend, Ann, have organized a group that is growing around the country. We don't have the resources of the bunker people, but the people we have are loyal and want to try to bring calm and peace back to this country."

"Is that even possible?" Cathy said.

"If we don't try, then no. These people are going to attack every part of our lives. They want power, and they'll do anything to get it."

"We're in, Tommy."

Chapter 41

Lansing

All Loretta had been doing was contacting people around the country. She had the governor doing the same thing. Together, they had reached out to other governors whom they knew would be on board with them. When Loretta was not working her regular job, she was one hundred percent in on contacting people.

She had Aaron doing the same. They were at her home when Loretta got an idea. "Aaron, both Joe and Ann think we need to hit the people payrolling these troops they have around the country." Ann had said something about getting at the organization, and Loretta wanted in. She was one of the few women trained as a Green Beret. She was smart, and had an uncanny ability with weapons.

"I want to infiltrate these guys."

Aaron looked at her. "Which guys?"

"The organization."

"But they don't take women. We haven't found one female in their entire organization."

"Maybe not, but these are rich guys, right?"

"From what we have learned, they are very rich."

"And they party, right?"

"I would guess they do. From all accounts, Ann and Joe have said that they have found elaborate meetings in remote places."

"My guess is that they bring in some women."

"I don't know."

"Sure, you do. Isn't that what rich guys do? They like to party, and what better way than to have a bunch of females…ah…chaperones?"

"I'd say that would be risky. You could get yourself killed."

"Yes, but I'm smarter than they are, and I know some other women who would jump at the chance to help me."

"I'm not sure, but whatever you plan, you should clear it with Ann and Joe."

"I will. Ann told me that she and Joe had divided the work, and she's working on what I want to do. That's how I got the idea."

"All I can say is…good luck with that."

"I'll contact Ann, and then I'll begin to build my group. This is going to be fun."

Kincheloe Michigan Correctional Facility and Colewin, months later, summer 2023

Charlie was not in good shape. When he was tazed, his heart stopped for a short time, and he developed some heart issues. He also was now subject to seizures. When Charlie was awake and feeling somewhat healthy, he would just fume. His wife visited him often, but for a man who had been extremely healthy and strong, he was not the same—and he was just plain angry.

Charlie had been transferred to the Chippewa Correctional Facility where he was housed in a level IV security area, but he was treated like an even-higher-risk prisoner, and so he was allowed only one hour a day outside. For someone who spent most of his life outdoors, this was the most troubling for Charlie, and he knew he had to get out soon, or he would go crazy. Several months had passed since he was first incarcerated, and no one was able to help him.

Charlie's wife had been in touch with a lawyer, but he was not able to do much. She decided to talk to Don again since he had helped her as much as he could since Charlie's problems began. He was out of options too. He did tell her that she should try to contact the governor.

"How in the world do I do that? I have no idea how I could contact her, and I don't have money to get my lawyer again. I spent all of our savings, the little we had."

"Let me work on that for you."

Don had some contacts at the governor's office, but they were little help. He was beginning to think that Charlie would never get out of jail. It had been some time since he had heard from Joe, so he decided to see if he could contact him. He knew that Joe had connections, and that was his next move. He did some digging and checked with the barber who had a way to contact Tommy. They found Joe! When he was able to get ahold of him, Joe filled him in about what was going on.

Don said, "We would be happy to join up with your crew. We can work here to make sure nothing changes. I'll enlist as many people as I can."

Joe said, "I'll have Ann and Loretta work on trying to get Charlie out, but since he has been sent to that correctional facility, I don't know."

"Thanks for the help. I'll let Charlie's wife know.

1,500 miles away

"It is official. I am on the ballot in forty-nine of the fifty states. I only need to finalize Hawaii, and we will be all set." The old boss was very happy and could not wait to tell the new boss. He had people on the ground in all fifty states, and they were working, not only on getting the old boss on the ballots in each state, but also becoming poll workers. This was a strategy the old boss thought was important.

The old boss also had the committee that oversees his and the new boss's positions to add millions of dollars to investigating how the internet and AI might be used to sway the election. If not only through conspiracy theories and lies about the other candidates, but also if they could break into the voting machines and change the outcome.

The people he had working on this were many, and they were working feverishly to come up with something doable. One of the most outrageous plans he had was assigning individuals to polling places where, if they were not the poll workers, they would intimidate the voters. His most devious plan was to have a few of the voters who queue up on election day sprayed with bullets, to make the rest scatter.

He thought he could also use the mail service to intercept ballots in areas both heavily left or right and then destroy the ballots. At the same time, he would pit right and left against each other and send out false information showing that one side or the other was at fault.

The whole system would have to work well enough to give him the votes to win, although that would not be necessary since he would have his people in charge in each state and at the federal level. They had worked for years getting their people in place, and soon they would be ready. He kept thinking that if the event was effective as planned, the election wouldn't even matter.

His only concern was the military. He had many low-level troops on his side, but he could not get enough of the more important generals to join. If he could not get the people he needed, it would be difficult to take over if the U.S. military got involved against his troops.

The new boss knew of all the preparations for the elections, but he thought it was too far off. "Do you think we have too much going on and too much of a delay until the election?"

"No, I know the timing is just about right. It will put both of us in the White House, and we will have all the power and control that we will need."

Chapter 42

Ishpeming, Michigan, summer 2023

Joe got word from his people who were keeping track of the election that the old boss was now a candidate. They said he was running as an independent, so his chances would be slim, and they thought that was a good thing. They were getting information on how he was planning to influence the election by interfering around the country. They also realized that there was a lot of interference already—and that would be a problem, which might give him a chance.

Joe and Ron were working on a plan to infiltrate as soon as the old boss was set up somewhere. They found he had a headquarters somewhere in Florida. They thought it might be Tampa since that was where he used to reside, and sure enough, Joe's people located the headquarters.

"We need to get someone in there right away. We have people down there who are capable. Let's discuss this with Ann. She might have a plan."

Later that day

They met with their entire team in Ishpeming, and Ann had several suggestions. Wayne was included now, and he said he would like to volunteer. "I want to go there or somewhere and be a part of taking these people down."

Joe turned and looked at Wayne and shook his head. "Wayne, you would be out of place down there, and besides, you have that revenge factor, and that might be a bit much to overcome if you saw this guy. You know what I mean, right?"

"I understand, but I need to do something to help destroy this organization. What better way?"

Ann said, "I'm not sure, but we have people in Florida who are very capable. I'll contact them to see if they can infiltrate. They have quite a large group there who are eager to get involved. Let's not send people from here. We might need you in some other capacity."

"Well, then what can I do here? I'm tired of waiting and doing nothing."

Tommy agreed and said they needed to have a more active role. They wanted to do as much as they could. "Wayne and I want something more. We can't return to Colewin because of the trouble we are in, and we don't have much to do but target practice and get ready to fight if need be."

Joe looked at Ann, and both were concerned. Wayne and Tommy were adamant in their positions. Ann saw the look in their eyes. They were so determined to do something. She stood up from her seat at the table and said, "Let's take a look at everything, and maybe we can get you guys involved. This is tricky because we have this organization doing awful things, but the left and right have their own problems, and we don't know what some of them might be doing to mess up the election. Remember what happened in 2021. That wasn't this group, so there are people out there who want to win no matter what. We're really trying to make this election safer, and to help people who want a country that can have peaceful transitions of power like we have had since this country began."

Joe and Ron agreed.

Lansing

Loretta had spent a lot of time with Aaron trying to find where the next meeting of the people funding the organization might be. She had some FBI agents and a few CIA people doing some real surveillance. She had them check with Joe's and Ron's sons who had been doing surveillance on the group for a long time. They gave them all the information they had and together were able to break into what the group thought was their secure site.

Loretta and Aaron were meeting in Lansing to arrange the information they had found. Their key contact said, "We have the place and the date of the next meeting, but you might want to wait for the meeting that will take place at the end of 2023 or the beginning of 2024 because that one will have most of the players present. This next one will have a lot of people online."

"Are you saying the majority will meet in person?"

"Yes, by the sound of it, it will be like a fun get-together for them. I say fun, but I mean they will use it to adjust strategy. You get what I mean?"

"Yes, and that is exactly what we've been waiting for. Tell us more."

"We don't have much more. It's going to take some time to find out all the details, but we'll keep you posted."

"That sounds good. Talk to you then."

Aaron turned to Loretta and said, "That sounds exactly like what you had in mind. How are you going to figure out how to infiltrate?"

"I'm not sure yet, but I have some ideas. Let's go over everything we know about the past meetings these guys have had, and maybe we can figure a way in."

"Hope you're right."

1,500 miles away

The new boss thought that more had to be done to help the old boss's campaign. His first thought was to make his opponents look bad. "It's time to send some conspiracy theories out there about the left and the right. They are fighting each other like a couple of badgers. I can even sense some sound effects. Let's put something out there that will cause some real disaster."

"What are you thinking, boss?"

"I'm not real sure yet, but we need to get something that will cause some bad press. Like having some of the representatives in congress on both sides argue with each other over some political fodder."

"Any ideas there?"

"Not yet. The old boss doesn't like this approach, so we can't let him know we are doing this."

"Is this going to get us into some deep trouble with him? If so, I don't want to get my people involved."

"You won't have to worry. He will have no idea where it is coming from, and, anyway, they are constantly doing this to each other."

"I guess you're right. I can't believe how they treat each other even when they are supposed to be getting along a little. They argue and scream at each other. No wonder they can't get anything done in this country."

"I agree. It's a great tactic though if we make them look and sound bad."

"I think they have already accomplished that."

The new boss laughed and patted his second-in-command on the back. "Good one!"

"Can we get some of those people who are working on the campaign to come up with something?"

"It might be good to check with them since they work with this stuff every day."

Chapter 43

North of Ishpeming

Tommy and Wayne were angry. They wanted to do something to avenge these guys. They returned to Tommy's hiding place and sat at the table with their wives brainstorming what they could do to get their town back to what it used to be.

Wayne spoke up, "We can't go back to Colewin and just start bombing the base because Peter is still there, but that's what I would like to do."

"I get it, Wayne. We could take out the whole group, and I wouldn't care a bit. It might get us back to normal."

Wendy leaned in. "You guys are talking crazy. You can't do that and you know it. We have to work with Joe and Ann and hope that they can end this."

Wayne pounded his fist on the table and scared everyone. "End it. It's been going on for years, and even after we attacked their base and caught a key player, nothing changed. It actually got worse."

Cathy looked frightened. "Wayne, settle down. There isn't much we can do right now."

"Yes, there is. Tommy and I have been talking, and we think we should head to Tampa and take that guy out. Joe and Ron tried a while ago, but they didn't have any success. No one would find us or even know that we were there, and we could get the hell out of there in a hurry. We'd have a lot of planning to do, but we could do it and get away with it."

Cathy gasped. "Oh, my gosh, Wayne. You have gone over the edge."

Wendy stood up with tears in her eyes. "You guys cannot do this. You need to talk to Joe and Ron. They know more about these guys than you two ever will, and this isn't like going into the woods and hunting. You'll have cops, body guards, and who knows who else just waiting for something like this. This guy is going to be on the presidential ballot, according to Ann, and that means he'll have all kinds of reporters and whatnot around. You just need to think a little."

Tommy sat back on his chair and looked at Wendy. Her tears were real and were running down her face. "We'll talk to Joe and Ron. If they say it's too difficult, then we back off, but we're going to do something."

Wayne was not happy, but he respected Tommy and Wendy. He turned to his wife and said, "You guys are probably right. What would we do in a city? We know a lot about Colewin and the woods, but we're not city slickers."

1,500 miles away

The old boss met via video with some of the key players in the organization. "It is agreed then. We won't have much of anything to do if we can get inside the heads of the left and right. We'll keep them fighting each other. The worse it gets, the better it gets for us. We'll play the 'can't get anything done in Washington because of all the lifelong politicians' thing. That always gets a reaction from the public, and we'll be able to show that we aren't like that."

One of the key leaders of the organization said, "We have many resources that we can provide. We also have people in high places who can help to keep this festering. If the two sides keep up with their inuendoes and infighting, we can have our people make it worse by keeping the vitriol going."

The old boss agreed. "That will be a great help. I need the people I have on the ground getting this off and running. I'm way behind in the polls, but we can make up some of that. A third-party victory is going to be difficult, so we need to do everything that we can to make the event a success."

"And we will," the leader said.

"By the way, our key man organizing our assets says that everything for the event is now in place in every state. All he needs to do is give the word and each will unfold as we planned."

"You're sure all the states are prepared?"

"That's what he says."

Another person on the call spoke up, "This guy we have. Can we trust him? How long has he worked with you?"

"Bates is the one we always had, except for the time he was incarcerated."

"How do you know that won't happen again?"

"He was taken during the attack on the bunker in the Upper Peninsula. We have increased the number of troops there so that will not happen again."

The same person said, "The Upper Peninsula? Where is that?"

"It's a part of the state of Michigan. It is very remote, and it is right next to Canada. We have had assets move between the two countries. It has been great. They are so remote, no one messes with them. Well, except for those local guys who did a while ago, but so far nothing since we have increased the number of troops."

"Hopefully, you are right."

The leader spoke again. "Will we have any trouble taking over in each state? Do you have any contingency plans if something goes wrong?"

The old boss said, "Nothing will go wrong. You have my word."

The leader was excited. "So, we can take over each state before the election, and then we will have control of the ballot boxes, right?"

"That's the plan. We have people in places to take control of the polls, not all of them, but we'll be in charge in most."

"That's a well-designed plan!"

"It should work."

Colewin

Charlie's wife was sitting at home wondering what to do next. She had been to the Kincheloe Correctional Facility to see Charlie, and he was not doing well. As she prepared a sandwich for lunch, the phone rang. It was Joe.

"Hello."

"Hello, is this Grace?"

"Yes."

"This is Joe. Charlie is going to be released tomorrow. The governor cleared Charlie, Tommy, and Matt. Loretta, a friend of ours in Lansing, has been working with the governor, and they finally got pictures to her, and she said it was not them. You need to have someone take you there tomorrow."

"Charlie's not doing well. He's very sick."

"Maybe this will heal him when he hears the news."

"I hope so. They had him in solitary confinement. Can you believe that?"

"I can believe anything these days. Can Don help you get there?"

"I'm sure he will. I'll check with him right away."

Joe ended the call, and Grace immediately called Don."

"Hello, Don."

"Hey, how you doing Grace?"

"They're freeing Charlie. Can you take me there tomorrow morning?"

"Really! I can't believe it! Sure. What time do you want to leave?"

"I'll check and see when he'll be released. I'll get back to you."

"All right. I'll wait for your call," Don said.

North of Ishpeming

Tommy got the word not long after Joe called Grace.

Joe gave Tommy the good news. "You're free. The governor has cleared the three of you."

"Do Charlie and Matt know?"

"Grace knows that Charlie will be released tomorrow. We can't find Matt."

"I think I might have a clue where he could have gone to hide."

"Really?" Joe asked.

"If we're free now, that means I can head back to Colewin, right?"

"You can if you want to, but I suggest you wait here a while and work with us. That'll make sure that Sheriff Daryl received the word—and doesn't harass you."

"You're probably right."

"Glad for the good news for you and the others. See you to-morrow."

"Right. Thank you!"

Tommy turned to the others in the room. Wendy, Wayne, and Cathy were all sitting around having a beer and sharing a pizza. Tommy gave them the good news.

"Does that mean you'll be heading back to Colewin?" Wayne asked.

"Sure does, but not for a few days. Joe thinks we should stay here for a while until everyone back home gets the word."

Wendy said, "That's a good idea. We can relax for a while and enjoy this place. It was nice of Joe's brother to allow us to stay here."

Wayne had a smile on his face—but he looked angry at the same time. "When we get back, we'll have to contact Charlie to see if we can get ahold of Matt. I'm sure they both have some ideas about getting even." He grabbed a piece of pizza and chomped hard on it; then smiled again.

Cathy squirmed and looked scared. "I don't like that look on your face, Wayne. What are you thinking?"

"Oh, nothing. Just happy to be heading back to Colewin soon."

"But what about my job in Marquette?"

"You need to keep that and stay here for a bit. I'll head back and just check things out, see Charlie, and then come back here."

Chapter 44

Ishpeming

Ann contacted Loretta to get an update after they had talked about the men who were freed. Ann had a lot to report. "In the last few months, we have placed a few people inside the campaign of the old boss. We have also learned about their strategies that they will use to try to swing this election. One of them is to keep the in-fighting going between the two major parties. I can see that allowing the two parties to fight will be easy."

Loretta said, "I agree, and now we need to begin to create some type of interference. The election will be enough trouble with all the fighting that is going on within and outside of the government. How we approach our plan to keep this country from going the way of any radicals is going to be difficult."

Ann put the phone on speaker so Joe and Ron could listen to the conversation. "We can intercede though, but it will mean involving several players whom we have not contacted yet. What is your idea? I know you want to hit the committee. Has that been coming together?"

Loretta reported on what she knew. "We not only have the governor's ear, but she has contacted the President—and he is all in. This is the best situation for us. He is also leery about spreading the word related to what he's doing since he has some people around him who are questionable, but the plan is to have me lead a group wherever it might take us."

"Sounds great! Joe, are you listening?"

"I heard every word. Now we need to improve our plan. There are three prongs to this. One is what we are doing to help ensure an honest and fair election and destroying this group's candidate, the old boss. Another is what Loretta is doing. We need to destroy the money flowing to this organization. The third is that we need to get rid of Bates at the bunker. He is the key to their organization. He moves everyone around and sends out all the encrypted information for the group. These are big orders."

"Three pronged. I see what you're saying, and you're correct. We seem to have the first two going well. How do we get rid of Bates and shut down their key communications center?"

Joe turned to Ron. "Ron, do you think you could head up a group to help Wayne and Tommy? They want to destroy the bunker. Not like what we did in the past. I mean Wayne is really into doing something crazy, and they will need someone to keep them from doing something stupid. You have the knowledge, but if you do go there, you'll have to stay out of sight since they think we were taken out. You can stay a week or two and then return."

"I could do my best."

"Just get them started and make sure they have a sound plan. You can let me know what you think, and if you believe their plan will work. You don't have to stay there once they are organized."

As they spoke there was a knock on the door. Ann walked to the door and opened it. It was Tommy and Wayne.

Wayne stomped in and walked right to Joe; Tommy followed. Wayne spoke immediately. "We're headed to Colewin when you give us the word. We want to help. What can we do?"

Joe looked at Ron and shrugged his shoulders in disbelief. "If you really want to know, we were just discussing Colewin and the bunker. We need to do something to get rid of Bates."

Tommy said, "We're in."

Ron walked over to Joe and said, "Let's see what we can do."

Colewin, fall 2023

It had been months, a long time for anyone locked up, but finally, Don and Grace rescued Charlie from the Kincheloe Correctional Facility. He looked terrible. He was pale and bent over, and he did not look happy. After his release, they helped him into the truck and returned to Colewin. It took about an hour, and when they arrived, Charlie went right into his home without a word. Don spoke to Grace who thanked him, and then left.

Grace knew that Charlie needed rest and sustenance to get back to himself if that was even possible. When she walked in, he was sitting at the kitchen table with his head down resting on his forearms. He was exhausted. Grace did not say a word, but she put a hot cup of coffee in front of him and started a meal. He needed to eat.

Charlie raised his head and said, "I'm gonna get those guys, and I'm gonna kill Daryl for what he's done to me. I don't care what happens after that."

Grace's eyes were wide with fear. "Now just relax a bit, and we can talk about all of that later. You need to rest and get some nourishment before you go all crazy with revenge."

"Have you heard from Matt? Is he still hiding? Does he even know we are off the hook?"

"I don't know any of that, but Don will come by tomorrow, and you two can discuss that."

"I know where Matt is hiding. I mean I think I know. Are Joe and Ron around?"

"They haven't been heard from since their place was destroyed."

"Destroyed?"

"I guess someone used explosives there. Don said they destroyed everything. You remember where they were, right?"

"Yes, the new hideout. Is it completely gone?"

"Don knows more about it. He can speak to you tomorrow and tell you the whole story. I only know bits and pieces. It happened a while ago."

"Those bastards. It was the bunker people, I'm sure."

Grace was able to get Charlie to eat, and then he settled in for a nap. It lasted the whole night. Grace sat at the table thinking while she drank coffee and nibbled on some cookies she had made for Charlie. She was not happy, and she knew that Charlie would do something to try to get even, but she knew he needed help. She vowed whatever he decided, she was going to help him—or die trying.

Chapter 45

Ishpeming to Colewin

Ron decided to get moving right away. He told Wayne and Tommy to be ready to leave in the morning. They arrived at 6:00 a.m. as planned. Wendy and Cathy were staying behind for the time being. They would take a ride on the weekend and visit them.

Wayne and Tommy planned to stay at Wendy's parents' home until they could get a better place to hide out and plan their assault. Tommy decided—for obvious reasons—to avoid his old cabin that he and his uncle had built. Ron would stay with them. They gathered what they felt they would need, and after Ron said good-bye to Shanice, Joe, and Joette, they all turned and left in Tommy's truck.

It wasn't a long drive, a bit over two hours, but the three hardly said a word. It was as if they were communicating telepathically. They made one pit stop in Munising, and then drove straight to Colewin.

Wayne's first move was to visit with Don to find out what he knew about what was going on around Colewin. He had to get caught up on everything since he and Tommy had been away. Ron was not a permanent resident like they had been, so he let them lead the way to find out what they could. He knew he had to stay out of sight, so no one would learn that he and Joe had survived, so he constantly stayed in the background whenever they were in town.

Don was in the townhall going over some paperwork when the three walked in.

"Hey, Don, how are you doing?"

"Well, I'll be darned. Wayne, how are you? It's been a while. How are you doing?"

"I'm doing well. It's been a long rehab for me, but I'm a lot better. Hoping to return here permanently if we can come back to some peace and quiet."

"I hear ya. It's been crazy here. I just helped Grace get Charlie yesterday. He's not doing so well, and he's angry. Wants revenge."

Tommy said hello, and then asked what he meant by "not doing well."

"I just mean it's not the same old Charlie. He's pale and skinny, and all he can talk about is destroying the bunker and getting revenge on Daryl. That's not healthy."

"It sounds good to me," Wayne added.

"What?"

"I mean getting rid of the bunker. Revenge. I agree with Charlie."

Ron walked in quietly behind Tommy, trying to stay out of sight. He looked at Tommy and shrugged. He knew what Wayne meant. He had felt the same way when Bates had him and Joe sent away to be eliminated. Luckily, they had survived.

Ron said, "Let's go and check on Charlie and see how we can help. That's why we're here anyway. Enough of this just doing things half-assed. Let's get them and end their reign here at Colewin."

"Spoken like a true leader," Wayne said.

When Don looked at Ron, he could not believe his eyes. "Good to see you! You survived after that horrible injury and that explosion out there a while ago? How's the arm?"

"Sure did. Arm's good now."

"How's Joe?"

"He's fine and so are our wives. All is good."

"Well, that's good news. What now?"

Tommy turned to Don and said, "Well, we have an idea. Can we count on you to help us?"

Don stood up and threw his paperwork on his desk. "You're damn right you can count on me, and anyone else I can round up to help. People around here are sick and tired of this mess."

Ron was startled, but at the same time relieved. "Okay, I guess we should go and talk to Charlie. He still has access to a lot of munitions and firearms. I guess he'll be all in. It's time to plan the end of that place."

Ishpeming

Joe felt like he had lost his right-hand man when Ron left, but he still had Joette, Shanice, Ann, and Jerry. Plus, he had his son and Ron's son still working on finding information on the web. Cathy and Wendy said they would help as did Paul and Sarah. He knew they had to keep working to destroy the old boss's campaign.

They met the next day after the three men had left. They were all enthusiastic about coming up with a plan to take down the political activities of the old boss.

Ann had an idea. They met at Ann's place and set up a table with materials they might need. They already had some of her thoughts in motion. They had someone in the main office of the old boss, but so far there was not much to report. They felt that the person would have more information as the days rolled into active campaigning.

Ann began. "Can we come up with something to make this guy look like the evil man he is?"

"We have access to people who can make commercials to sow some doubt into his character."

Jerry said, "Do you mean like the left and right are doing to each other right now?"

"Yes, they're using AI to produce false scenes with the opposition saying things that have never happened. It makes me wonder if this whole election is going to be a choice of the lesser of several evils. Do you see what I mean?"

Joe nodded and agreed. "What's happening is as bad as anything that might come from the event, but we need to take care of that first. The old boss is bad news, and this democracy will not hold together with him in power. He wants to be supreme head for life, and his message says it all. He would dismantle our democracy."

Joette said, "We know all of that. We've rehashed it many times, but we still need to do what his team is doing to destroy this guy. Can we have our people make commercials with his plans to turn this country into a monarchy—with him as king?"

Ann agreed right away. She said that she already had people working on spots that will be aired once the campaigns are in full swing. "Not only do we have people on the ground in his campaign, but I also have agents working with some AI techs. They are making some incriminating commercials. The problem is, as we've said, that both major parties are doing the same thing. They are all beating each other up with lies and innuendos. It seems to me that this election will be the nastiest in our history. We may not be happy with any candidate."

Joe wasn't sure what to say, but he responded. "Yet, we must do something to stop this guy. The rest of it will work itself out. I have great faith in the American voters if they can get their votes to count. Most people are somewhere in the middle of all this, and that will eventually show up."

Jerry sat quietly until this last information. "Then what should we do right now to help? Maybe we should just send someone to take him out like Wayne and Tommy wanted to do. That would make quick work of the event."

This got Joe a bit riled since he had first-hand experience with the old boss and saw what happened when the new boss had been in charge for a while. "No, then the new boss would just step in and take his place. He is ruthless too, and I wouldn't trust him at all. I'm not as concerned about the election as I am the event."

"More reason to just take both of them out!"

Chapter 46

Lansing, a few weeks later

Loretta had been granted a leave. Her plan had come together the past few weeks, and Loretta was happy with it. She knew she would be in the center—and be a target if things went awry, but she was all in.

The person running the sting, a Navy captain, was versed in this type of activity and he said, "We have investigated several scenarios, and none seem to work. We will not be able to get people on the island any other way. They have very tight security. Your idea has a lot of merit, and we have been able to solidify much of the plan. As you suggested, you will be part of a group run by a famous person who sells high-priced girls to very rich men. We are going to arrest her people, and she will have to look for new help. That's where you will come in. This committee works exclusively with this person, and she will not want to disappoint them. You will have to go to California to be trained and to fit into our group as soon as possible, so when the committee meets, you will be ready."

Loretta said, "Who else will be involved, and what will I be trained to do?"

The captain answered. "Plenty, and by the way, this is going to take some time…months to prepare. We have a group of Navy SEALs who will assist you, but they will not be able to do much. They will find out where and when the group will meet, but they will only be able to help you escape the island. They can't go in guns blazing because some of these people are leaders of other countries, some are just very rich men, and some are political figures from the U.S. The President made it clear that we cannot be involved militarily unless they do something first."

"Holy shit!" Loretta was surprised even though she knew the plan had to involve something like this. "When do we begin?"

"Tomorrow. You will be given the information later today. Someone will deliver a package to you. You will sign for it and then read everything. Do not share any of it with anyone, even your family. If you decide not to do it, then let us know right away by texting me the word—NO."

"And if I'm in?"

"Do nothing. Just show up at the airport with the ticket you will receive."

"Roger."

1,500 miles away
"When do you think we should give the go ahead for our troops to take over all the state capitols? We need to go early in the campaign prior to the election, but it can't be too early."

The new boss was trying to get the old boss to pin down a date when they could take over the Capitol Building and the governorships in each state. They already had a few governors on board, but they needed to have most states under control, so they could dictate policy as they neared the election. It would be messy because no one would know exactly what would happen, and they needed to corral the entire legislature in each state, so the plan had to unfold when they were in session. If need be, murder was not out of the question.

The old boss said, "I've been thinking that it needs to take place about three months before the election. We'll need to be entrenched in each state, so we have a chance to affect the election."

"You think that is soon enough?" the new boss asked.

"I am hoping that it is. I have had some of our more dedicated people working on this. They seem to think that it will work."

"Great. Also, we need to make sure the payments to the troops are on time. Some of them are getting impatient. Last month the payments were a week late, causing a lot of grumbling."

"We could not help that. It's been a problem getting everyone paid. Most have some form of electronic deposit that we set up, but some demanded cash, and delivering all that cash to the right places and on time…. You can't imagine the problems we have run into."

"I can't. It must be troublesome getting it to every state on time, and it's important to keep the troops happy. Some of these guys are here *only for the money.*"

"I know that, and once I am in charge, we can dump these troops. We will not need them anymore."

"Who will we keep on the payroll?" the new boss asked.

"We have a list of the people in each state who are committed to our cause. They will be the ones who will continue to get paid. The rest can go home."

"Won't that be a problem?"

"Not when we are in charge. Anyone who is out of line can be taken care of. Right?"

"For sure. I like how you think. How is your campaign going? We don't see much change where we are."

The old boss said, "Not much luck so far. We are way behind in the polls, so I guess what we have planned for the state capitols will have to work for us. The campaign has kind of stalled out. Maybe I can get it moving at the next debate. I was lucky to get involved. No one wanted me on the same stage because they said I was an independent, but I was able to win over a few people and here I am."

"Do we even need the election? Won't the event take care of everything?"

"Yes. It could. The event could be all we need, but we always need a backup plan."

Chapter 47

The bunker

Bates had been working late for many days. He was moving troops around and making sure all was going smoothly for the event to take place on time. He had the boss's full backing now, and he was making more money than he had ever made. He had the reins of the organization, and without him, no one knew where all the troops had been stationed and how many were at each place. He was feeling very good about himself. Even though he was tired, he felt like he had made it.

His top trainer wandered to the bunker and pounded on the door, but Bates saw him on his monitor. "When are these guys going to learn that I can't hear the pounding?" He walked over to the door and threw it open. "What do you want now?"

"Nothing in particular. I'm just bored with these guys and what we've been doing day in and day out. The good thing is we haven't had any trouble from the locals."

"I know. We finally got rid of the trouble makers, and I guess we did a really good job. Haven't heard anything from Joe or his buddy for months. I'm sure we got them, or we scared them off for good," Bates said.

"The locals are like lambs right now. Scared of their own shadows. Haven't had any problems."

"Good. This is the way this place was supposed to be from the beginning. It's well-hidden and no one should have bothered us here. If that teacher, Joe, hadn't gotten inquisitive, I bet even Wyatt would have been all right."

"Who?"

"Never mind. Just someone who used to be here. We had some good times carousing and tearing up the place."

"Sounds like fun."

"It was, but he was a little off if you know what I mean. I could never get a real handle on where he was headed. I think his tours in the military messed him up. No, I know they messed him up."

"Anything we need to do that can change some of this boredom?" the trainer asked.

"Not really. All is quiet, and everything is in place for the event. It won't be long now and you'll all have some major action."

"That sounds better. This place gives me the creeps. Nothing here. No one around. I'm not used to this type of living."

"Say, I've been here for years and I'm not complaining. Just do your job and be happy the money keeps rolling in like it does."

"I guess. It's just too quiet. I've always been cautious when things get this quiet."

"Well, I'm glad. We've had enough action here for a lifetime. Enjoy the time while you can. I've got work to do, so you can head out," Bates said.

"All right. Got to get back to these idiots and see what I can have them do to keep them occupied."

Colewin

Ron, Tommy, and Wayne left the town hall and drove straight to Charlie's place. Don said he would pick up the barber and head out as soon as he could. Ron wasn't sure what Tommy and Wayne had in mind, and he wanted to check on Charlie to see if he was in any shape to help if they were going to do something big.

They drove through Colewin and then took a left heading toward Charlie's place. The talk on the way was about how they could assist Charlie and get him back on his feet. Wayne was very upset as they drove. Tommy kept trying to keep him cool, but he had little luck. Ron thought this was not a good situation. People who are this angry make mistakes because they act irrationally at times. He had to keep a lid on these guys.

When they arrived at Charlie's, they saw Grace walking around in the front yard like someone lost. Her head jerked up when she heard the truck.

They pulled up next to the front door, and they all jumped out. Wayne was the first to speak. "Grace, how are you doing?"

"Wayne? I haven't seen you in a coon's age. What you doin' here? And Tommy? And is that the man who used to hang with Joe? I thought he was dead."

Ron spoke, "No, I'm still here."

"Well, good for you."

Tommy asked, "Is Charlie here, and is he okay?"

"He's here, but I can't say he's all right. He looks pale and weak, and all he can talk about is takin' down the bunker, come hell or high water."

Wayne gave Grace a hug and added, "He has the right idea, and we are here to help him."

Tommy said, "Well, we want to help Charlie, but taking down the bunker might be more than what we can all handle. Can we talk to Charlie?"

"Sure. He'll be happy to see someone besides me. Come in. I have coffee on if you'd like?"

Ron answered, "Sounds good."

Later...

Don left the town hall and headed right to the barber shop. He jumped out of his truck and ran to the door. The barber was finishing up on a customer when he entered. The man walked past Don and said, "Hello, Don," and then left the shop.

Don went right up to the barber and spoke quietly in his ear. "I got some news for you. Tommy, Wayne, and Ron are back here in town."

"What? You mean Joe's friend, Ron?"

"Yep."

"Then he made it?"

"Yes, and I think they're here once and for all to take care of the bunker."

"What about Joe?"

"He isn't here, but I guess he's working someplace else to help take these guys down."

"That sounds good, but you know my son, Peter, is still out there. I want to get him out if I can."

"I'm sure he'll be a big part of this. Can you call it a day and head out to Charlie's place with me?"

"I guess. It hasn't been that busy anyway."

"I got my truck out front," the mayor said.

"Follow me home. I'll change and get some things together and then I'll jump in with you. I figure Charlie and Grace need everything since he hasn't worked for a while, and I know that Grace was struggling for some time now."

"All right."

Don pulled up to the barber's home, and they filled the truck with food, some clothes, and beer. "Let's head out, Don. I'm not sure what they need, but this should help. Hope Charlie can recover from this crap."

"I agree. We must do something about Daryl, too. He's made a mess of things around here," Don said.

"For sure. He's not even from here."

"Sticks his nose into everything."

Chapter 48

Ishpeming

Joe and Ann were working day and night to figure out the best way to accomplish all three tasks. The main concern was timing. What should be accomplished first? Will what they do slow down or destroy the event, or are they just going to expend a lot of energy for nothing, and still lose to these revolutionaries?

"If Ron can help Tommy and Wayne to slow down the base and take out Bates, that should happen as soon as possible. He's the logistics person, and he moves people around and sets all activities in motion based on the old boss's plan—which we don't really know. The problem is with winter coming, they might have to wait. Ron said that Charlie needs rest too."

Ann thought what they were trying to do would probably not work without losing some lives on both sides, so she was doubtful about the success, but she was on board. "You said you have a man inside, right?"

"We do. The barber's son. He has given us a lot of good information over the past year."

"Then I say do something as soon as you can, and get Ron back here where he will be safe. If you have to wait until spring, then Ron shouldn't spend the winter there."

"That's my thought."

Ann was pensive. "We'll continue to upset the campaign since we have people inside there too, but that will take time. Loretta says that she is ready to do her part. She is taking a leave of absence from work. She's on her way to learn what she will be doing, and who will be helping her. There is a plan to eliminate the committee members, but they can't send in the military or any munitions—too many important people. It would look like the U.S. was taking out heads of state."

"Well, the commercials you have your people running seem to be having an effect. There hasn't been a change in the polls. Their man is dead last."

"My one fear is that he's going to do something drastic unless we move quickly on these other two. If he does what we believe he has planned, going after the state governors and legislatures, that will be a serious escalation."

"Have we notified all the governors?"

Ann was not very positive about their recent contacts. "Many say that we sound like a bunch of people running scared. Some have said it's just a conspiracy theory. We do have people on board. We'll see what we can do."

"If Bates is out of the picture, then it will slow down the event on the state capitols."

"If…" Ann was not confident.

1,500 miles away

The old boss was on a rant. His poll numbers had not changed, and he knew that there were forces out there working against him. "We need to vet our workers around the country. Something is going on. I should have had a bit of a bump this month. We might have to move up the event and get control of the states. Then I can swoop in and just take over."

His campaign manager was dubious, "But how does that work? You can't just take over."

"If we have all fifty states in our hip pocket, we can control the election. That is my hope. We'll pump millions of dollars into the effort, pay people off, destroy ballots, change ballots, and eliminate candidates. It'll work," the old boss said.

"That sounds a bit wild! If we can do all of that, who will control the military? What if they come after us?"

"We'll take care of the people in charge. I have plans to take down the Pentagon. Our best troops have deployed rockets, helicopters, tanks, and we even have a few jets—all gathered in strategic positions to take the place down. They'll never know what hit them."

"Really? Is that possible? I hope it all works," said the campaign manager.

"We just have to make sure that our man Bates is on time with everything. He's the key. If something happens to him, we have no backup, so we need to have him work with someone else so we don't get caught without a logistics guy. He gives all the signals when to begin. He's connected to everyone."

"I'll get on that. That's a great idea. We can't have just one man with all the knowledge of the timing. I'll send word to back up Bates in all ways."

Colewin

The barber and Don arrived at Charlie's with the supplies. They exited the truck, took out the food, and carried it to the door. Don knocked. Grace answered and welcomed them in. She was thankful for the food. "We've been limited. Haven't had much. We're out of money."

Don was shocked to see Charlie. He didn't even look like himself. "Don't you worry none. We got this, Grace. We're gonna take care of you two."

Wayne, Tommy, and Ron were all huddled around Charlie. Charlie was telling them what he had gone through. He was not happy. Don and the barber said hello and sat on chairs that Grace quietly brought out for them.

"Good to see you, Charlie," the barber said.

"Good to see you too. I've been telling these three about my experience. I want revenge."

"We can help," Don said. "What do you need?"

"Nothin'. I got the plan, and it's gonna work. I've had a long time to think about it. I'll need Peter's help, but I have everythin' I need, now that I'm not tryin' to get the bunker back. Now I just want to destroy it, and all the people in it."

Ron looked at Don and the barber, who were wide-eyed. This didn't sound like Charlie. Ron spoke. "His plan is good. It will work if we can get Peter to do a few things inside. His whole idea has to do with taking down the bunker, but not attacking like we did the last time. It'll be more subtle—at first."

Charlie said, "I want to see the end of that place. I want nothin' to be left when we're finished."

"Is that possible?" the barber asked.

Ron repeated. "Like I said, the plan is very good, but we need to get on it right away before they reinforce the place anymore, and we need a plan to get Peter out. I might have one. Let's talk it out and see what we can do."

Wayne and Tommy agreed. They were totally on board. Wayne said, "I like the plan, and I'm ready to start right now. Let's not wait."

Ron said, "I spoke with Joe earlier, and he said it's important if we're going to do something that it happens right away. He said it had something to do with the election and the committee that provides all the finances for this group."

Wayne laughed. "Then let's get at it."

Chapter 49

Much later

The best laid plans, as they say. It took more time to plan their effort to take down the bunker. Winter set in, and they knew they had to wait until the snow was gone. It was good though because it also gave Charlie time to heal—and to improve their strategy. Tommy and Wayne also were gathering explosive material for Charlie. Ron had returned after spending time with Shanice in Ishpeming.

The spring had been warm, the snow melted, and the roads had dried out, so it was time.

The plan was simple. Each week a semi rolled off U.S.-2 and dropped supplies for the troops. This had been going on for a long time since they had so many men at the base now, and they did not like using the local towns for supplies. When the trucks rolled in, three or four trucks would head to the drop-off place, load the supplies, and head back to the base.

Charlie's plan was to take one of his trucks, an identical one to the army vehicles they used. He would drive it out and park it up the road from where the supplies were being loaded. When they were finished, he would drive his truck right behind the last one and in through the gate. The trucks were then parked near the armory.

Charlie's truck would be filled with explosive material, a combination of ammonium nitrate and fuel oil, and he wanted to park it as close as he could between the bunker and the armory where it would do the most damage.

"Won't they know we're an extra truck?"

Charlie wasn't concerned. "Not really. Peter will take care of that. He'll be the guy opening and closing the gate. He'll have control of that situation. There'll be four guards, two in each tower by the gate. Peter will be one of them. The others won't even know the difference."

"But then how do we get out?" Wayne asked.

Charlie had an answer. "That's where Peter comes in. Since he is on guard duty that day, he's gonna take out one of the guards for us. He don't think that will be a problem. He'll have a pistol with a silencer—we'll have to get it to him somehow—and when it's dark, he'll take out the first guard, and then we can help with the other two. We'll also have silencers. Once inside, the one problem will be that we'll have to stay hidden 'til dark. He says he has a spot for us to lay low behind the armory."

Wayne was concerned. "Will we have any backup?"

"Don't worry. Matt has contacted me, and he's in. He will be in the woods with some of his buddies, and if anythin' goes wrong, they'll have enough fire power to back us up. If there's no problem, we're gonna walk through the gate and down the hill where Tommy, the barber, and Ron will be ready with four wheelers. If all goes well, we'll hop on the four wheelers and be gone."

"It's too bad we can't take the guards out like we did when we attacked the bunker, but they have prepared for that, and they stay behind barriers now. What about the truck? How does that work?"

Charlie was confident. "We'll set a timer before we go, and it'll go off twenty minutes after. We gotta get the hell outta there 'cause there'll be enough explosives to take out a city block."

The bunker

Bates was sitting at his computers working on the final steps for the beginning of the event. He was sure all was in place. He also had several groups in place to upset the campaigns of anyone else running against his man, but word had come in that an incident had taken place at one of the leading candidates' headquarters. His campaign office had been ransacked and several of his workers were hurt. No one was killed, but there was an investigation into who was behind this attack.

This made Bates wonder. Did some of his people move at the wrong time without the old boss's approval, or did the new boss jump the gun? He decided to contact his key people to see if one of their groups had acted independently. "So, what do you know? Was it one of our groups going solo?"

"I can't speak to that, but I've been in contact with the new boss, and he has no knowledge of any movements by our teams. He also checked with the old boss, and no one in his camp has any idea what happened."

"We did not go early then?"

"No way. Who would have given a command to attack at this time? We need to wait until the time is right to begin our harassment."

"That's correct." Bates was puzzled. He thought, *Are there other groups using violence who might help us out in this? There must be.* "All right, let's have some of our people check into this and find out what happened. Not sure what we should do if it wasn't our people. Let's hope whoever is doing this can help our man get into the White House."

Ishpeming

Ann was mystified. She had just been on the phone with the governor of Michigan, and she informed her that there had been some break-ins at several campaign headquarters. She was sure this was the beginning of what Ann and Loretta had said would happen. The governor had been in touch with the President, and he and his advisors thought the same thing. They were convinced that the event would take place, and they thought this was the beginning.

Ann turned to Joe and told him what she had just learned. Joe was shocked. "There's no evidence that they were going to begin this early. From what we know, the event is not scheduled for some time yet. This can't be it."

"What else could it be? Somebody ransacked several campaign headquarters."

"Do you know which ones?"

"They haven't put out any information about that yet. We have people looking into who was hit and what happened. The President has several agencies on it too."

"That's good. We need to check with the tech people and see what they know. If the event has started, we need to act quicker. That means that the bunker people will be heading out, and Loretta will be late to do her thing."

"Agreed. Call Ron to see if he knows anything about changes at the bunker. I'll get ahold of Loretta. She's in California somewhere training with Army Rangers and Navy SEALs. She might know if their plan is still in place. That might tell us something."

Joe was on it as quickly as he could. He picked up his phone and risked calling Ron. They had decided they would call as few times as possible since the bunker people had been using their cell signals to pinpoint them in the past. "Hello, Ron?"

"Joe?"

"Yeah, had to make a quick call. There's some news that someone messed up several campaign headquarters across the country, and we're wondering if there has been any movement at the bunker."

"They've been under surveillance by Charlie's people—Matt included, and there has been no change. Peter verifies that each day."

"That's interesting. We can't figure what is going on. We thought it might be the beginning of the event, but if the troops in Colewin have not moved, then this probably isn't that."

"No, no movement here, but who's to say they might not. If anything changes, I'll let you know."

"Great. We should keep this short. Talk to you soon." Joe turned to Ann who was on the phone and relayed the information when she looked his way. She nodded since she hadn't ended the call with Loretta.

Joe's next call was to his son who was working with Ron's son and several tech people trying to glean as much information as they could from the internet. Ron's son picked up the phone. "Hey, Joe, what's up?"

"Have you gotten any information about the event lately? We've had some strange happenings at campaign headquarters, and we're wondering if the event has started."

"We haven't heard anything except what we gave you a few days ago. It's supposed to start in each state, but it'll be at each state capital, not campaign headquarters as we understand it."

"Okay, if you see any changes, can you let us know right away?"

"Sure will. We'll be in touch."

"Talk to you then."

1,500 miles away

The old boss was dumbfounded. He had spoken to several of his key people, and what Bates had told him was true. Someone had torn apart the offices at several campaign headquarters, and it was not his people. He had everyone check in each state and none of his people were freelancing. "What does this mean?" His call to the new boss had verified everything that Bates had said, and it proved they were not involved. He thought, *Someone was helping his plan to make a mess of this election. Good for them. As long as we can keep a lid on it and direct it toward the other candidates.*

He turned to his group of leaders. "We need to keep this going. It'll really help our plans. We'll look like liberators when we come in and save the day in each state. We'll put armed guards at each polling place. That'll make us the heroes. This will give momentum heading into the event when we will get to control who votes and how the votes are tabulated in each state."

The old boss knew this wasn't a for-sure thing, but he felt that given the opportunity, they could make the most of it. He took a deep breath and was almost levitating with joy. He added, "People will think we are there to stop the violence, and we will be, but it will play into our hands. The event as we have planned it is even more important now, and it looks like it will be easier than we thought."

Chapter 50

California, training base, June 1, 2024

Loretta had been in training for months. She had learned to use all kinds of weapons, and she was trained in demolition using C-4 and other explosives. She trained with several different types. The idea was not to leave any trace of U.S. interference, so using some explosives at the site would point toward the U.S., and the President did not want that, but Loretta had to know how to use them just in case. The training was grueling for her, not having been involved for several years, but she passed, and now the actual mission was a go.

Loretta wondered when she would be deployed, but she knew that it depended on the committee's meeting time somewhere near the Philippines. She knew it would be a quick in-and- out mission based on what she had learned. Her bosses were military people who would direct every move.

Alone, she was trying to get some rest. She seemed to always be in a state of heightened anxiety, and she was trying to calm her nerves. She knew the mission could go awry, and she might find herself in a real mess. She heard footfalls on the steps to the barracks. In walked her commanding officer, a woman a lot like herself who would have taken Loretta's place except for an injury she had sustained several months earlier. Her ACL had snapped in training, and she was still rehabbing. "Loretta, it's time. Word has come down that everything is set to go. The enemy is scheduled to meet soon, and we have gotten you attached to the madam who will be providing services for these creeps."

"I'm ready. What's the timetable for leaving? You will head out to L.A. this evening where you will meet with the woman who will take you and several others. It will be on a private jet, and you will head directly to the resort area where they are meeting. The clothes you already tried on are ready. I'd say get moving, so you don't miss your plane to L.A. After you land, you will be on your own until the planned destruction."

"Are there still the same SEALs who will assist, or has that changed?"

"No, nothing has changed. It's the same ones. The ones who trained with you."

"Then, as planned. Everything as we trained, correct?"

"Roger. As you trained."

Loretta stood to get ready. The sergeant left Loretta so she could prepare and be ready to leave. Loretta's heart was pounding, more than usual. She knew she had to change and get into the dress of a civilian woman. She showered, did her hair as they had planned, spent a little extra time on her makeup, dressed, and left for the hanger where all was ready for her. She did not look like the same person who had been trying to relax an hour ago. She walked out of the barracks, and there was a vehicle ready to take her to the plane. It would be about a thirty-minute ride, so she sat back and closed her eyes.

Colewin

According to Ron, the time had come. He knew that Joe and Ann wanted the bunker to be the first move to make sure that Bates would be neutralized, a nice way to say "killed." Bates still had the key job of moving people around and arranging times and places for the event. Ron knew that the time had finally come to act.

"Ron, what do we need yet in order to pull this off?" Tommy was concerned. He did not want to leave anything to chance. He knew that Wayne and Charlie were in one hundred percent. They were a little overboard during the winter months because they wanted to begin right away. Since Matt had come back, the three of them had only one thing on their minds—revenge, quick and thorough.

Ron had to rein them in as best he could. They could not afford for anyone to go ballistic during the mission. They needed to keep their heads and do exactly as they had planned. "We need to get all our equipment checked and make sure the plan is fool proof. Charlie wants to drive the truck into the bunker. I don't know if that's a good idea. Wayne wants to go with him, and he also wants to drive the truck. We do need two people, but I worry about them."

"They'll be good. I've talked to Wayne, and he understands how important it is to keep his wits about him, and besides Matt, he's the only one who can talk sense to Charlie."

Ron bit his lower lip and shrugged. He didn't feel confident in the two men despite Tommy's words. "I'll go along with their plan, but we need to have a strategy to get them out quickly. Remember, Peter will be there, and he needs to get out, too."

Tommy was also concerned. "As long as we can eliminate the guards without any problems, then we'll succeed. That to me is the one problem that could set us back. We need to make sure Peter is prepared."

"Don't forget. Matt will be in the woods with Shanice and some of his buddies, and they will provide covering fire for the escape. He said, if there is a problem, they'll let 'em have it, and then they will get the hell out of there through the woods."

"But will we be successful getting the silencer to Peter? Peter said that he doesn't have guard duty on the hill where we plan to put the weapon. He can't just waltz out there and walk up the trail to the hill."

"That is really the one problem we have."

"We need to figure that out first. You know what? If Peter gets us through the gate with the other trucks, we can just hand him the weapon. It should be simple."

Ron was dubious. "That sounds almost too easy."

Ishpeming and a campaign office

Ann received a call from one of her people who was imbedded in one of the campaigns. It wasn't a very affirming call. Ann thought the person had some information on how they were succeeding.

"Ann?"

"This is Ann."

"Say, last night our office was ransacked. We were watching it as you said, and several men with masks broke in and just tore the place apart. This will set us back. We were just beginning to get information for you."

"Could you tell who these people were?"

"No, but they weren't dressed in military outfits. I mean they had on camouflage, but they didn't look like they had a plan. They just all worked kind of independently. You know, like they didn't have a real leader. They yelled things about January 6, 2021—and how this was payback."

"That doesn't sound like what we expected from the event, but who knows for sure."

"They spray-painted obscenities on the walls, tore up all the literature and signs, smashed the computers, and even lit a fire. When they left, we were able to put out the fire, so it didn't get too far along, but it could have burned the place down."

"Damn! That's serious stuff. If you learn anything else about them, let us know."

"You know we will. This must be the other major party. Who else would do this?"

Ann said, "We don't know yet, but the president has people on it, and they'll figure it out."

"Should we keep working on this campaign?"

"Yes, stay there and keep reporting to me. I'll let you know if we find out anything."

Ann turned to Joe. She was shaking her head. "Joe, I just can't figure this out. Are these the people who are planning the event? Is it the event?"

"From what I have figured out, these are not the people we are working to take down, and it is going to make a real mess if it keeps up. How can we fight two fronts? We have the old boss and his people, and in my mind, we have these others who are just raising havoc. It's not the bunker people. They are too organized."

"I tend to agree. We need to inform our people that this is going on, and the people who are doing it are a group of vigilantes. They are out to make a mess of this election, if it isn't already."

"This election is going to be a problem all around. If we can get through it successfully, and elect our next president without this interference, we'll be lucky."

"It's curious who might be involved. We need to get some information from the people who are investigating for the President."

1,500 miles away

The old boss had an idea that he realized would help propel him in the polls and put a damper on the other's campaigns. All he had to do was put some doubt in people's minds. He turned to his trusted assistants. "I have an idea that will assist us in our efforts to hamper the other campaigns. The destruction at campaign headquarters has been to *only one campaign*. If we can somehow retaliate with the others, it'll look like some type of war going on between parties."

"What are you saying, boss?"

"All we need to do is create more havoc in this election. Make it look like everyone is out to ruin it or destroy the other side. We need to have our people attack several of the other campaign headquarters and make a mess of them. We will have our people hit them in several states, and they will have to do something to make sure they know it is the other major campaign who did it."

"Not sure we follow you, sir."

"Make it look like the other side is retaliating against what has happened at the other headquarters. We need to do it quickly though, so there will not be a lot of security there. I'm thinking tonight. Get the word out in six or seven states, and have our people make it quick. We cannot get caught, but if someone is, then they need to deny that they belong to us. They will need to say they are just people who did not like what happened to the other campaign headquarters."

The assistant turned to the other people in the room. He looked doubtful. "We can do that. I'm not sure how quickly we can get the word out to everyone."

The old boss was excited. "Just get the information to Bates in the U.P. He'll do the rest. He knows about each group and where they are. Do it now! Move. Let's see what happens."

"We can do that, but how do we make it look like it was the other campaign?"

"Check with Bates. He always has good ideas. He will come up with something."

"For sure. I'll have the tech people get ahold of Bates, and I'll get the message out."

"I can't wait for the results."

Chapter 51

Fifteen minutes later

The assistant was on the phone with Bates not long after the old boss gave him the task. "So, you understand what needs to be done, and it needs to be completed tonight."

Bates was sitting at his desk in the bunker. He was listening intently, but he wasn't sure what he was hearing was accurate. "You're saying we have to get this together for tonight, and we need to make it look like they are retaliating in some way."

"That's it. Can you get it together right away?"

"I can do anything the old boss wants. I'll get this going, but what can we do to make sure the group that is hit will know it is their opposition?"

"That's your problem. Boss says you can do it."

"And I can. What would piss me off if it happened to me? It's easy. Whoever is involved will write the words in big letters on the wall— 'retaliation' in really large letters."

"That's it?"

"That's all they will need to do. Let me get this to the groups that will make the greatest impact. I know just the spots. Don't worry. I've got this."

"If you say so. Let the old boss know when it is all set."

"Sure. I just have several messages to send. I can send the same thing to each group."

Bates worked rapidly for about an hour, thinking of which groups would be most effective in which cities. When he was ready, he sent a secured message to several leaders in seven cities. He made sure to tell them to dress in civilian clothes and not to carry any ID. He ended the message with these words: make sure that they write "retaliation" in very large letters on the wall or on the building after the troops have trashed the place, or it might not work as well.

Bates finished and sent a message to the old boss.

It's all taken care of. Done. Should be news tonight or early in the morning.

The boss was relieved. He knew Bates would handle it, and he thought, *Now, to just wait until it all is on the news.* Then he abruptly said, "Well, this is exciting!"

A military base in northern California

As it turned out, Loretta was driven to a private airfield, where she met with the madam who would be her boss. She knew the woman was given a pass by the government to complete this task. If she worked it without incident, she would be off the hook. This did not give Loretta much confidence in her. She knew that if this woman got into a jam, she could flip and not return to the states.

As she boarded the airplane, she recognized it from a fleet of private jets, but she did not know which one for sure. As she stepped inside, she noticed how tall and wide it was. It was much nicer than the planes she had ever flown in. Once inside, she also met the other women who would be going along. This diverse group of women were friendly and cheerful. It was just another job to them, and they would get to travel overseas. Exciting!

Loretta spent a few minutes gabbing with the other women, and then she was escorted to her seat. As soon as she made herself comfortable, the madam came and plunked down right next to her. "I don't know much about you, but I'm telling you, you will have to be careful. The people who hire us are scary, terrible people, and they have all kinds of security, so you need to be vigilant."

"Why do you work for these people if they're so terrible?"

"They pay extremely well. It's all about the money. They're good to my girls as long as they're submissive and polite—which by the way you will be too."

"That could be a problem."

"No, it cannot be. Just behave and do your job. I assume everything has been explained to you. I mean what you must do."

"Oh, yes, I know what to do."

At that point the madam rose, looked at Loretta, turned as if to leave, then turned back and said, "You had better be good. Don't mess this up for me and my girls, or else you could meet with an untimely accident."

Loretta was not the type to take that kind of admonishment and threat, but as she turned to respond, the madam walked away. Loretta's stomach turned over as she squeezed her fists, ready to lash out, but she knew that her job was not going to take much time, so she inhaled slowly and exhaled long as she sat back in her seat and wondered if the madam would survive.

Hopefully, the women would be safe, but who knows when it is all over what the result might be. She just trusted that she would escape. As she sat back and tried to relax, she heard the plane roar, and then it began to taxi down the runway. She lowered herself into her seat, closed her eyes, and dropped into a restless sleep.

Somewhere on the West Coast

On the tarmac, a long way from where Loretta had just lifted into the air on a long journey, another plane was preparing for a long trip of its own. As a matter of fact, it was headed to the same place. The SEALs were going to work on this clandestine operation. Their goal was to leave no trace of their participation. They knew they had a lot riding on the success—and that they had one person they needed to rescue. They had trained with her, and their task was to get her home safely, but she was taking on a task that might end up…well, not good.

The leader of the team said, "It all hinges on whether she can accomplish her mission without your help. We have studied the island, and we have found a way to cause a catastrophic fire using the air conditioners they have installed.

"We have studied the ins and outs of these air conditioners, and we know that if not properly installed, they can cause fires. The buildings on this island have been outfitted with them for the people who will be meeting there. For the local people, they are recent additions to their lifestyle. They really don't need air conditioning, but they have been told it would be good for the older inhabitants. Probably not true in all cases." The officer projected a picture onto a white screen.

One member of the team asked, "Are you saying that the building we are looking at has recently added air conditioning?"

"Our only intelligence is from our satellite photos. We have ascertained that, yes, someone is installing AC in a big way in several buildings. Some of the larger structures have had conditioning for years, but not all."

"So, this is why she has been studying different air conditioners?"

"Yes, and she is going to use her knowledge of them to cause a catastrophe on the island, which has poor fire protection, but only if she can get into the structure they will use for their meetings. She won't know until she's on the island and can identify which building will be for meetings. However, only three or four are possible, and all have added air conditioning in the last few months.

"This should be easy for her if those are the units they installed."

"Yes, three structures have six stories, the rest are much smaller, but they all have these air conditioners. We think it will be one of the six story buildings."

"I bet they already have a problem with fires. Look at that mess."

"Yep."

The leader of the group was going over the plan one more time before they embarked on a journey they did not know where, but they understood their task, and how they had to accomplish it. They were to fly and meet a carrier in the South China Sea. It was really a routine operation for them, but it did have its risks. They understood that the security at the site was very good, and they had trained to avoid any confrontations with these people. They had to do this as quietly and quickly as they could.

The leader said, "Once we drop you, you'll be on your own. You won't have any special devices, except for what you used in training. You will be armed. The agent on the island knows what she had to do. When she is successful, she will give the signal, and you will proceed. This must look like an accident, and you cannot get involved unless something goes awry. You cannot be seen, nor can you leave anything that would point to the U.S. being involved. Just get her out safely."

"We'll drop you at this point on the map. It'll be a bit of a journey from the carrier to the island."

Chapter 52

Colewin, June

The problem of the silencer was still a concern. Since Peter would not have guard duty on the hill for some time, and his chance of just wandering up the hill was slim to none, getting Peter the silencer that way was out of the question, so Ron decided that he would go with the plan to have Wayne or Charlie hand him the silencer when they drive through the gate. It had to work.

Ron was being cautious. He did not want anything to go wrong. He knew how meticulously they had planned for the original attack on the base. He wanted to be as precise on this one. "I know you can't just throw it over the fence and hope he finds it, and handing it to him at the last minute is risky, but it's plausible, or we need to come up with something better."

Charlie was concerned. "Then we need another plan to eliminate the guards. We can't do what we did the last time. They have prepared for another attack."

Tommy and Wayne were brainstorming to work out a way to get the silencer to Peter when Tommy said, "Why do we need to do that? Can't we just have him take out the guy quietly, say using a knife? The walls in each tower are much higher now. No one would see him do something like that. The other two guards would not even see anything or hear anything, if he does it quickly."

Ron was thinking out loud. "No, we have decided that we will just have Charlie hand him the weapon."

"We'll have to check with Peter."

Wayne was insistent. "No, Peter has to do it! He could just slice his throat from behind. Grab him and use a blade to cut him. That would work. He's gonna kill him anyway!"

Everyone just turned and looked at Wayne. This was just brutal to all of them, but they knew that some people were going to die before this thing was over, and it might be a whole lot of troops at the bunker. It certainly would include Bates, and anyone near the bunker or armory.

Charlie was insistent on the plan working. "Let's ask Peter what he thinks."

Ron turned to the others and said, "Let's not have Peter do anything except make sure he can get us through the gate with the truck. He said handing him the silencer would not be a problem. If we can get the truck in, we're good. It's going to be late anyway, and it'll be getting dark, so let's just plan that way."

Charlie agreed. "I guess that could work."

"Let's check with Peter and make sure we can pull this off."

Ishpeming

Joe and Ann were very busy keeping track of each situation they were monitoring. They had just gotten word that several of the campaigns had been hit again, but this time it was the other party. "What in the hell is going on?" Joe asked Ann.

"I'm not sure. But our people have investigated, and they're not sure what is happening. The word *retaliation* was written in large letters at each site. What is that supposed to mean? Is it the event unfolding, or is this just someone reacting to the attacks on the other campaign? The word *retaliation* sure makes me think that."

"I've been checking with our tech people, and they said that they can't tell who the group was that ransacked the sites last night. There were some videos from some of the sites, and it looked like a group of men, but they were not dressed in military outfits, nor did they have weapons. They just broke in and tore the places apart, wrote on the walls, and then left. That doesn't sound like the event has started, nor does it look like the people we have been following."

It wasn't long after that Ann received a message from her tech people, and they had a much different take. "Well, the message I received from the people we have working online is that it was Bates from the bunker who gave the orders. I'm sure he was ordered to send the troops in. They surmised that they want to keep the harassment going between the two major parties, so it will give them a boost."

"For sure. That changes everything. They want to make it look like each party is attacking the other. That could give another party a chance to make a run at this. They would look a lot safer to people."

"What a mess. I also received a note that Loretta's plane is not headed where they thought it was. They were not even sure where it was for a while, but they have it tracked now."

"How could that happen? Where could it be going?"

"The people in charge know they are headed somewhere in the South China Sea, probably a small island where they have prepared for the conference."

Joe clenched his fists and made a horrible sound at the same time. "What the … Does that mean that they don't have a clue how to eliminate these guys? I mean the plan they had involved some SEALs. They even had the building chosen where the committee would meet. Are the SEALs going to be able to help, or is she on her own?"

Ann just shook her head. This was not what anyone had anticipated. "I know. I'm worried about Loretta. She's really in a bad situation. Their security is so good that they might even be able to figure out that Loretta is one of us—FBI—I mean. This was all supposed to happen the first or second night, and she would have been out of there. Now who knows?"

"She's in danger. What can we do?"

"I'll check in with the team in charge and see if they have this under control."

Joe realized that they were in no position to help Loretta where they were, and they had to head to D.C. to meet with people who were working with the president who was trying to find out as much as he could about the event. "We will have to keep in touch with them on our trip. Joette will be going too. Shanice had left for Colewin with Ron. She was worried about him and their plan, and she had a lot of military training and felt she could help."

"All right. Let's plan to leave early in the morning. We have tickets out of the local airport. We'll have one short layover, and then we have a direct trip to D.C. Jerry will be in charge here while we're gone."

"Good. I'll let Joette know. We'll be ready."

Colewin, June

The day had come. It was time to make sure that everything was in place. Matt had gotten three of his friends together and along with Shanice, they were going to hide in the woods opposite the gates as others had done when they had attacked the bunker previously. This time, however, they would not have clear shots at the guards, but they could back up Charlie and Wayne who would be in the truck, and they could provide firepower if needed.

Everyone knew what had to be accomplished. Ron, Tommy, and the barber had driven four-wheelers to a spot a mile from the road to the bunker. They would hide out until dark. Then they would as quietly as possible, head to a spot just below the bunker gates, and wait.

Peter and another guard were on duty in the left tower as Matt's people faced the gates. Two other guards were in the right tower.

Charlie and Wayne had loaded the truck with as many explosive devices as they could. Charlie knew it was enough to completely take out the bunker. Ron had worked on that part of the plan, selecting the right materials, and he felt that there was enough for overkill, but they wanted to be sure. Charlie and Wayne were parked in a clearing, not far from where the semi would enter with the supplies. They were close, but they were hidden.

They watched the semi pull in, and not long after, two trucks just like the one Charlie was driving, entered the clearing where the semi was. They would have to make several trips to empty all the supplies.

Troops were helping to load the trucks, and when they were finished, the trucks drove away. They sat and watched as more trucks came back several times. It turned out there were more than two trucks. Charlie and Wayne thought there must have been at least six that made the trip down and back. It took some time, but they finally emptied the semi and the last trucks headed back.

Charlie moved right in position to follow the last truck. Up the hill, slowly like a turtle, moving deliberately but with a goal. The trucks reached the gate and drove through. Charlie followed. Peter was right there to let them in. He was close to the truck as Charlie handed him a silencer. He grabbed it and stuck it inside his Kevlar vest, and then he closed the gate. Charlie pulled up next to the armory. The bunker was on his right not far away.

Bates was inside the bunker, watching the trucks roll in. He had positioned cameras around the perimeter, so he could watch movement outside. He noticed a truck pull up near the bunker and armory. "What the hell are those guys doing? I told them never to park a truck where it blocks my view of the area. Stupid idiots."

Peter locked the gates and returned to his post. It was already dark. The lights on the tower came on, and they lit up the area around the gates. Matt saw the lights turn on and motioned to his people to be careful. It was a lot brighter than they thought it would be. Apparently, Bates had the lighting improved since the last attack.

Charlie saw the lights too and turned to Wayne. "I didn't expect that much light!"

Wayne looked at him and said, "I know." He looked worried. Then Charlie saw someone walking toward him. It wasn't Peter. He looked up in the tower, and Peter gave the signal that he was ready. It was time to move.

Charlie opened the door and Wayne did the same on the other side. They had their silencers out ready to help Peter take out the other two guards. As Charlie turned to head to the tower, someone said, "What are you doing? You know you can't park that truck there."

It was Bates.

Chapter 53

Somewhere on an island in the Pacific

The plane carrying Loretta and the other girls landed on an island more than fifteen hours later. As she peered through the window, she saw nothing familiar. Loretta did not recognize anything from the pictures she had been shown during her training. The plane taxied to a stop and the door opened.

The madam stood and said, "Everyone on your best behavior. Do nothing stupid, and leave anything that might be considered a weapon or any contraband—like drugs, etc.—on the plane. We'll be here for the week, and your work will begin tonight. Treat everyone with respect. The security here is extremely tight, and you don't want to end up on the wrong side of these guys, or you'll never get home. On the other hand, you are going to make a lot of money if you can be sweet and friendly."

There was no response from anyone, just abject obedience. It was just a job, but they were nervous.

Loretta stood and hit her head on the overhead bin. "Ouch," she blurted out. "Where exactly are we?"

"None of anyone's business until the week is over. Then we head back. I'm not even sure myself where we are, but this has been the pattern for all our trips, so it isn't out of the ordinary."

"You might have told us that earlier."

"Why? Why would you need to know?"

"Just curious."

The girls all walked down the aisle to the door and down the stairs to the tarmac. There was no terminal here. There were armed guards all around. Loretta scanned the area and saw several towers with men and machine guns. She turned to the madam and said, "This isn't scary at all."

"It's not really bad, but the security is crazy here."

As they walked toward a small building, Loretta noticed numerous cameras. She thought, *Why are they watching us right now?* She saw several guards, well they looked like guards, but they were dressed like tourists in shorts, Hawaiian shirts, and sandals, but they had holsters with guns and rifles over their shoulders—AK-47s.

The women entered the building and walked through what looked like a metal detector, then another X-ray machine, and finally more cameras. Loretta turned to one of the girls and asked, "Why all the cameras?"

The girl looked shaken, but she answered, "The madam said they are facial recognition cameras. She said last time they pulled a couple of girls later in the day and sent them home, or at least she thinks they went home."

"Oh, great!"

"Why? Are you worried?"

"I'm always worried, but I just wanted to know. I guess the security is very good here."

"I'd say it is."

After they walked through the building, they were given a ride to the place where they would be staying for the week. Their luggage was taken care of for them. Once they were settled, they met other girls from other countries who had also been invited to the island. They all looked relaxed and ready for work.

They were staying in a large one-story building that opened to a long hall divided into smaller, single rooms on each side. Each

had a bed and a few amenities. There were televisions, closets, pictures on the walls, and cushy carpeting. There were name tags on
each door, and when the girls entered, they saw their luggage already there, clothes hung, or placed neatly in drawers.

Loretta opened her door, saw her clothes, walked to the bed,
plopped on it, put her face in her hands, and just shook her head.
She knew she was alone. There would not be any help. She needed
to find out as much about this place as she could, where and when
the men would meet, if it would be soon. She wanted to find out
if they would all be together as they planned, but she needed to
figure out how she would take them down by herself.

Loretta opened her door and saw that no one was around. She
looked up and down the hall before she slipped out of her room
and outside. She took some time to look at the layout of the island.
There was not much there, but what she saw was beautiful. She
saw the crystal clear blue-green water rolling onto white sandy
beaches. Lush green trees blocked her view to the west. She did
not see anyone that looked like the security people who had escorted them to their rooms, and so she figured that now was the
time to find out what she could.

She knew she had to get the layout of the place. There were
four major buildings: the one in which she and the girls stayed, a
large three-story building that looked like a hotel and possible
meeting place, another that she could not tell what might be inside,
and a fourth that looked like it was a storage building or power
plant like those she had seen once on Guam when she was in the
military. It looked like the place was also powered by several solar
panels located on the south side of the island.

Loretta was sure that the committee she was looking for must
be staying in the three-story building. The entire island and buildings were very opulent. She could only imagine what it was like

inside. She realized she could not linger, and she began to wonder if she might be missed already.

She wandered away from the building and strolled down a path leading north. When she walked down the path, she was on the fringe of a golf course. She looked around and noticed a lot of people—men—playing golf. To the east in the distance, she could see where they had landed a short time ago. The lone building the only structure to the east.

Loretta peered north and then south and had an epiphany. "I know what I am going to do!" Suddenly, she was roughly grabbed from behind on her upper arms, and someone spoke in a language she did not recognize.

Chapter 54

Marquette Sawyer Regional Airport—Heading to D.C.

They left early for their trip to D.C. The flight was at 8:25 a.m., so they had to be there about an hour earlier. They would have about seven hours before they would land at Reagan Regional Airport in D.C., which was in Virginia, about three miles from downtown Washington D.C. Joe and Joette had a seat at the front of the plane and Ann was across from them.

They were all a bit nervous, afraid of what the trip might bring. They knew they had a serious situation ahead with the election, but they hoped the president and his people would have more knowledge of what was going on, although they felt that they probably had as much information about the event as anyone, since they had been dealing with the bunker people and their personnel for years. Were they as well-informed about this as anyone? Would the president's people even have as much knowledge as they have?

When they landed, they were met by a man in a dark suit in a black SUV with tinted windows. Ann had arranged the ride. The driver spoke, "Ann, the package you ordered is on the floor."

"Thank you, Dominic. You're the best."

"No problem."

Joe looked at Ann. "You know this guy?"

"He's been a part of our organization for a long time. He and I attended the FBI Academy in Quantico at the same time. We helped each other through, and he wouldn't let some of the harassment from other trainees affect me or him. He was a rock. We lost track of each other in 2019 when he went undercover and infiltrated this group before I even knew anything about them. Right, Dominic?"

"Right." Dominic turned around and looked straight at Joe. "Ann filled me in about you guys. I met you once before. You might remember a little trip to Tampa—a limousine, an airport, some zip ties, a gag, and a guy left at a parking garage. You guys left me tied up in my vehicle."

Joe groaned, "That was you? Sorry about that. We thought you were one of them."

"As you should have. I could not blow my cover then. I'm just glad you didn't hurt me too much. I was quite nervous for a while until you left me at the airport. It took a while, but I was finally rescued by the bad guys."

Joette remembered the man. "I guess crazy situations can happen all the time, but that is almost ridiculous that we would meet up again! On the same side!"

They all had a little chuckle, but realized this was no picnic.

It was about a forty-minute ride into D.C., and then to a building in D.C. that none of them recognized. Ann gave Dominic the address she had received from her contact.

Joe wondered if their driver had taken them to the wrong place. *Were they not supposed to meet with the President?*

Ann knew right away. They were being taken to a place where no one would expect them to be, and she knew it had to do with the FBI or CIA. She turned to Joe and Joette and said, "This is not all that uncommon. We probably won't see the president. We'll be dealing with people who are in the know, and who have a direct line to the information."

Joette was disappointed. "Oh, I thought we might meet the president. I'm a bit disappointed." She was also a bit terrified. "This all looks like something out of a spy novel. Scary."

"We might get to see him, but it won't be right now. We'll have to see what they know, and if the President needs to be involved."

Joe shook his head. "We understand. Let's get this started so we can find out what they know."

Joette and Joe exited the vehicle, Ann was last to leave and grabbed her package.

They were led to a room. As they peered in, they saw that there were no windows, one door, but it was well lit. Joe realized where they were. "This is a place where we can talk, and no one will be able to hear or record what we're saying, right?"

Ann looked at him and said, "Right. It's soundproofed if that's what you mean. This is definitely FBI. I've been in these situations in the past, and this room looks very familiar."

The person who led them into the building left, and another person walked into the room. She looked very serious. She was tall and wore a very distinctive dark suit. She was FBI for sure. "We cannot have any electronic devices in here. If you have cell phones or other devices, put them in this box. They'll be right outside if you need them."

Ann was not happy with this development, but she complied. "All right, but we need them back right away when we're finished."

"And the package?"

"Just my personal items. I'll hang on to them."

"Fine, just head into the room."

"For sure, and welcome to D.C. I hope this meeting is productive. Let's get right to it. Everyone, take a seat, and I'll get a person to keep track of the conversation." She opened the door and said something and another man entered. He had what looked like an iPad. She sat and looked at everyone, turned to Ann and said, "Go ahead. What can you tell us?"

Ann began. "We have a lot of knowledge of the group that I spoke about on the phone. I assume you are the person I told."

"Yes."

After a lengthy explanation from Ann and Joe, the woman was quite convinced that bringing them there had been advantageous. She listened until they finished, and then she responded. "You want to know what we know about the events at the campaign headquarters for the two major parties?"

"Correct." Ann said.

"What we can tell you is that it seems both parties are trying to influence the election through scare tactics, and by destroying their mechanisms for gaining votes and getting information out. We have worked with both parties to try to find out who the perpetrators are, but we have found very little. We are really confused by the second series of attacks because they have gone completely dark. We have no leads except for the written message on the walls—*retaliation.*"

Ann and Joe looked at each other. Joe spoke. "We're not sure, but our thinking is that this group who wants some event to take place soon, is causing these break-ins to create havoc during the election. They hope their man, the one we spoke about, will then gain the presidency. We're not sure how they'll do this, but we have some information leading us to believe that they'll infiltrate state governments in some way to control the election from within each state."

The woman shifted awkwardly. "How do they propose to do that?"

Ann looked at her and said, "We were hoping you had some idea about how they might accomplish this. We think they're going to attack every state capitol, and then they hope to take over in each state. That's the best we can come up with based on our tech people and what we have learned."

The woman's face turned cold, and she looked at the man with the electronic devices. "We have heard about that, but we don't see how that would be possible. They would need hundreds or thousands of people to do that."

Ann, Joe, and Joette all said, "We know."

Joe added, "And they do have the personnel that they have been training for years."

"They must be the troops you have been having us investigate. We have found some, but nothing like the number they would need, and we have not found them in every state."

Joe was excited and nervous as he said, "No, you probably haven't, but they are there. We've followed several over the years, and they have bases around the country. We just didn't have the resources to check out every state."

Ann took a deep breath, and Joette just shuddered as Joe finished. Joette was not confident that the government was on top of the group they had been watching and hiding from for years. She had seen the organization's tactics when she, Joe, Ron, and Shanice had escaped from them in Tampa, a few years back. Joette could only muse: *They were ruthless! What type of rulers would they be if they won the presidency and took over state governments?*

Chapter 55

The bunker in the U.P.

Charlie did not move. He stood frozen by the truck trying to come up with something so he would not ruin the plan. He saw Wayne quietly leave the truck and hide on the other side.

When Bates looked at Charlie, he let out a sarcastic laugh. He said, "What in hell are you doing here, you sad SOB? I thought you were still in the lockup. Didn't Daryl have you put there for good?"

"I'm here to get my things. You have all my trucks, weapons, clothes, and all the stuff I had in that there bunker."

"Yeah, well Charlie, it's not yours anymore, and I told you if you came back here, it would be the end of you. Why would you come back?"

"You know why."

"Bates turned and yelled, "Guards, come here and take this man out to the range and shoot him. Then get rid of the body."

Peter was one of the men that Bates called. Peter was now near the gate where he had let the truck through. He had come down from the tower when he saw Bates. He looked up at his buddy in the tower and said, "I got this. You stay on duty. I'll be back in no time."

Bates grabbed Charlie by the arm and twisted him around until he had both arms behind his back. Charlie realized what was happening, and he just went along with it. When Peter came over, he took Charlie's hands and tied them behind his back. Bates was very happy.

"Now, take him out of here. I never want to see him again. I told him if he ever came back that it would be the end. Make sure you put a bullet in the back of his head."

"Got it. I know what to do."

Bates turned and headed back to the bunker. They watched as he opened the door and closed it behind him.

Peter whispered to Charlie. "Just go along with this. He has cameras all over the place. We'll walk until we are out of sight."

Charlie said, "Wayne's on the other side of the truck. We have silencers. Can we take these guys out and get out of here?"

"We can, but we need to be careful so Bates doesn't see us. We can dismantle a few cameras. I know where they are near the gates, and we'll be able to get out of here, but first keep moving."

Wayne heard everything. He was kneeling on the other side of the truck.

Peter said, "Wayne, stay there until we get back."

The guard who was in the tower with Peter came down to see what was going on. He walked right over to Peter who was walking Charlie into a dark area. The man followed. When he reached Peter, he said, "What's going on?" and he lifted his weapon and aimed it right at Peter.

Chapter 56

The room

There was a knock on the door. Someone leaned in and told the woman in charge that there was a message for her, and that she should come immediately. She left.

Just as the door shut, the man across the table pulled out a gun with a silencer.

Ann looked at him, and asked, "What do you want with that?"

"The three of you. You know too much. This is where nosy people find out how this will end."

He raised his weapon, but before he could do anything, two shots tore through the table and quietly entered his chest. Ann sat there without any emotion holding a pistol under the table with its own silencer. She looked at Joe and Joette. "Had to be done. I'm not sure who he was or what is going on, but we need to figure out if we can get out of here. Joe grabbed the dead man's gun. Ann handed Joette a small Glock that she pulled from her package.

"How did you get these?" Joe asked.

"My friend, Dominic. The package. I knew we would need protection because we can't trust anyone."

"Thank you for that," Joette said.

"Now we need to get out of here. I hope that our contact who was here was on the level, but who knows who is out there now. You both ready? Check your weapon, Joette, and make sure the safety is off. We may need them right away."

The three lay on the floor. Ann and Joette were behind a wall on each side of the door. Joe was lying on the floor near Joette, ready to open the door. He lifted to one knee and turned the knob on the door. He opened it slowly just a crack and looked out. He saw someone standing nearby. He motioned to Ann. She was on his right.

Joe whispered, "I see one man."

Ann whispered back, "Open the door half way."

Joe did. As he did, the man said, "Hey, you finished in there? We need to get rid of those bodies. She said to do it quickly."

Ann's eyes widened. She knew what that meant. *They were not among friends, but that woman had been her contact all along.*

She whispered again, "We need to take him out. Can you do it?"

Before Ann could get another word out, the man dropped to the floor. Joe had taken the shot.

They waited to see if anyone else would react. Nothing happened. Joe motioned that he was going to crawl forward and check out the place. Ann and Joette followed close behind. Joe reached the main room in the house, but he did not see anyone. He walked to the window, and he saw two guys hanging around a van having a smoke. "Two more. Both outside."

Ann looked at Joe and said, "We have to get rid of them. Our best bet is for the two of us to open up on them since we have silencers. Joette should be our backup just in case. I'd rather not have the noise if we can avoid it."

Joe and Ann talked and decided who would take which guy. They were a bit farther away than Ann liked, so she searched for a back door. If they could get closer, it would make for a more successful shot. She found a back window, and it opened easily. They all crawled out and around to the front of the house.

Parked in the driveway, the van was hidden from the street by some evergreen trees on one side, and a neighbor's house on the other. They knew they had to be successful right away. They walked near the edge of the house, Joe knelt on the ground next to Ann, and they fired. Direct hits. Both men went down. Ann scurried to the van, checked both men. They were gone.

Joe and Joette were right behind her. Joette said, "Well, that's not the welcome I expected here."

"That's for sure!" Ann responded.

"Now we must figure out who that woman was. You say she has been your contact? Who can we trust?"

"There's one person I can trust, for sure, and it's Dominic. I'll call him to get us out of here. He's waiting about a block away." Ann grabbed for her phone and said, "We don't have our phones!"

Joe looked around and said, "None of us have them. They could be in the house!" He moved into the building and searched the place, but he could not find any phones, but the guy he had taken out earlier, had one in his jacket pocket. He moved out to Ann and Joette. "I found this on the guy in the house."

"We found our phones in the van. Now if I can get Dominic's number right."

Ann tried, but she kept getting the wrong number, but on the third try, she reached him. "Dominic, come and get us, but be careful. This place is not what we thought."

While they waited for Dominic to arrive, they decided to hide the four bodies in the interrogation room, and they checked the van for anything that might give them a clue about these people, but they had no luck.

D.C.

Dominic drove behind the van and stopped the car. It took but a second and all three people were inside. Ann jumped in the front seat, and Dominic asked, "How did that go?"

She looked at him and said, "You don't want to know. Can you drive us someplace safe?"

Joe and Joette were in the back seat, both breathing quite heavily from all they had done. Joe asked, "Is there any safe place—and is there anyone we can trust?"

Dominic smiled. "I can relate, but you can trust me. We have a group of people who have been fighting this for a long time. They aren't what you might expect. They are people from the left and the right, but they are all in the center in their thinking. They work together to get things done. They even smile occasionally. Isn't that nice?"

Ann looked at him and said, "You're kidding, right? No one seems to work together these days."

"Well, they do, and they have been a part of our effort to stop this organization from taking over. Although we haven't had a lot of success, we have the president's attention now, and he's working with us."

Ann was a bit dejected, and her words mirrored her thinking. "This is unbelievable. How can this even happen? We have been watching this grow for years, and it's as if no one really cares. So many people just want to destroy this country and what it represents."

Joe added. "We have come a long way to get information to the president and his people. We thought we were meeting with them this morning."

Dominic was unsure of what they were referring to. "You mean the meeting you had with that group of people?"

"Yes. It was bad!" Ann proceeded to tell Dominic the entire story, and he was baffled.

"Wow," he said, "That's why we don't trust anyone unless we have thoroughly vetted the person. You cannot trust anyone in this town. We can trust the President, but we are not sure of the people around him. How did you get mixed up with these people today?"

Ann was somewhat confused herself. "We've been in touch with this woman for quite some time. At least we think it was this woman. I'm not sure anymore that she really was my contact."

Joe spoke up from the back seat. "Whoever that was, and whoever she had employed, they were not afraid to get rid of us, so this tells me that they have knowledge of the key people in D.C., and they must also have knowledge of the event. I wonder if we could find this woman again?"

They drove on in silence. No one said much more as Dominic drove across the city to a place that he felt was safe, and where they could spend some time with people who thought like they did.

Chapter 57

The bunker

When Wayne saw what was happening, he moved slowly from the side of the truck to the back. He had his silencer pointed right at the back of the guard when a shot rang out and whizzed past Wayne's ear. He quickly moved to a spot that the shooter could not see. It was one of the guards from the right tower who had shot at them. When the shot rang out, Wayne wasted no time and let the guard on the ground have it.

Peter cut Charlie free, and the three of them took cover. "There's going to be a whole lotta troops coming out of the barracks in one minute. We need to get out of here, but first we need to get by the two guards that are left."

"We need that M-16 that the guard had. Can you reach it Charlie?"

"Got it."

"All three of us need to fill that tower with holes," Peter yelled, "and get the hell out of here."

They did. Charlie fired the M-16 while Wayne and Peter emptied their silencers. Charlie pulled two more clips from the dead guard, and they all ran for cover near the bunker door. Charlie could see one of the guards, and he fired and the guy fell to the ground.

Peter heard noise and turned and saw troops heading their way. They did not have much time. "We need to just take a chance and get out of here."

Charlie looked like a man possessed, crazy with revenge. "You guys go for it. I'll cover you. Hurry, there's no time."

"But Charlie, you have to get out too," Wayne said.

"I will, but you guys go now. Right now!"

Wayne and Peter looked at each other.

Wayne choked out, "We can make it to the gate. Then we'll cover you, and you run for it."

"Sounds good. Go ahead."

Wayne and Peter ran for the gate. The guard in the right tower did not have a good view of them as they moved under the tower and to the gate. They turned and shot up into the tower. Wayne yelled, "Now, Charlie."

Charlie made his move, but before he could get to the tower, hundreds of rounds filled the air around him. He dropped to the ground.

Wayne said, "Get up, Charlie. Get up. Come on." Wayne aimed his gun, and took his last shot. He was empty. He had used up both clips.

The guard in the tower began shooting at Charlie, and peppered the area around Peter and Wayne. Charlie kept firing at the troops who were heading their way from the barracks.

Bates saw what was happening, but he could only see Charlie. He wondered why he was there, and if he was dead. He froze when he looked at the other computer screens and saw a fire-fight erupting. He signaled a red alert, and a siren pierced the air.

Peter yelled, "We have to leave him, or we're all dead."

"No, I can't. I need to save him."

"How?"

"Let's go up the other tower and see if they have anything up there to hold off those other troops."

Before Peter could say anything, Wayne was halfway up the tower. Peter fired at the guard in the right tower hoping to distract him. The guard was firing at Charlie, and he was not looking at Wayne.

Wayne reached the top and looked around. The only thing he could find was one M-16 that Peter must have left up there, but then he saw a cache of grenades, about six. Wayne was able to grab the rifle, and he shot toward the guard. Then he took a grenade and yelled, "Peter, get back farther!"

Peter heard and knew exactly what was coming. He ran as fast as he could when a huge explosion took out the right tower. Material flew everywhere. It also damaged the left tower where Wayne was. It was leaning toward the road, and Wayne had to steady himself. Wayne was able to stand and get his bearings. Then he fired rounds toward the troops and screamed for Charlie to move, but Charlie was down.

Wayne decided to heave a grenade toward the troops. He yelled to Peter, "Get down again, I'm gonna throw one at the troops to see if I can free Charlie." Peter could not hear anything because of the explosion, but he saw what Wayne was going to do.

Peter waved and yelled, "No, Wayne! What if the truck gets hit?" Then he sprinted to Charlie.

But Wayne could not hear. Wayne looked around. The other tower was destroyed, and the guard was nowhere to be seen. His ears were ringing and driving him crazy. Debris was everywhere, but he wasn't hurt. Wayne knew he had to throw the grenade as far as he could. He did not want to hit the truck. That would ruin everything and kill his friends.

He released the grenade and realized that the truck was in a bad spot.

Chapter 58

The island

Loretta had not seen anyone around, especially the security people, but when she turned around, there were three of them. *Where had they come from?*

The man who had her arm kept talking, but Loretta had no idea what he was saying. He was very frightening, and he looked like he could kill her with one hand. He was very large, and his hand wrapped around her arm like it was a little pretzel and would crunch any minute.

She whimpered, hoping to get some sympathy, but no chance. The man yelled at the two other security people who turned and walked away. He dragged her back to the building where she had her room, and he threw her in head first. Her body slammed to the floor. He radioed, and soon another security person arrived. He spoke broken English.

"What doing outside?"

"Just taking a walk. It's beautiful here."

"No walking. Stay in room only unless called. You get?"

"Yes, I understand."

"Next time…" and he put his finger on his neck and ran it across. Then he left.

1,500 miles away

The new boss had been excited about the news he had just gotten. He spoke to the men who delivered it. "We have accomplished something with our plan to destroy campaign headquarters. Both sides have come out blaming the other side. This is great. We could have the event anytime now." He pulled his cell out of his pocket and called the old boss.

"Hello."

"Boss, what you said is happening. We have both sides fighting about their campaign headquarters. We won't have to do much more to cause trouble. We can just walk in and take over and keep them arguing and not concentrating on you. The less they bring us up, the more we can move in."

"Everything seems to be working. Now we need to get control of the states' elections. We should probably move soon. Get Bates involved and have him move the troops this weekend. Have them in place by Monday, and then we'll move on the capitols."

"I'll get to him tonight and have him do that. It'll take a few days to move everyone in place, so we should probably move tomorrow morning. That will give us the time we need. The troops in the U.P. have a longer trip than anyone else. They will have to travel more than twelve hours to be in place with the others. If we send them in the morning, they should be there by 10:00 p.m. at the latest."

"We won't move until everyone is in place. Everything must happen at the same time, so have Bates synchronize the whole thing with the leaders. This could lead to everyone blaming the right and the left, just like we planned."

"Will we move on the U.S. Capitol Building at the exact same time?"

"Of course! That needs to be quick, and we need to overwhelm the guards there. The attack in 2021 was almost successful, and we have more troops than they had, and our troops will all be armed. We also have several people inside who can coordinate our movements so we don't try to attack a place that is too heavily fortified. Bates should have all that information for you."

"The people I have with me here are ready to help get this going, so I will get everything ready. I will call you when we are ready, and we will be able to watch on television."

Chapter 59

The bunker

Wayne had looked long and hard when he decided to throw the grenade, and it went far to his left away from the truck, Peter, and Charlie. His aim was good and the grenade went almost exactly where he wanted it to go. The blast was tremendous—more than he had figured. It stopped the troops in their tracks and knocked many to the ground. The concussion was powerful and threw trees, rocks, dirt, and anything not tied down.

Peter had jumped on top of Charlie and rolled for some cover. They were both splattered with rubble, and both were cut and covered with dirt. Neither one could hear a thing as the concussion knocked out their hearing. Peter's ears were ringing as he tried to talk to Charlie, but Charlie could not hear a thing. Peter pointed to the gate, and he helped Charlie maneuver toward it. Wayne came down and helped them through the gate and down the hill.

Ron had heard the explosions and had the machines move closer to the gate. They were about fifty yards away when they saw them. They were half walking and half dragging Charlie. They all looked like they were tattered and broken, but they kept moving.

As Ron slowed his machine, he saw troops heading through the gate. He yelled to Wayne, but, of course, he couldn't hear a thing. Ron, Tommy, and the barber lifted their weapons and started shooting at the men running out of the gate. That gave the others some cover as they moved toward the four-wheelers, and, as they did, shooting erupted from the woods opposite the gate. It was Matt and his people.

Matt had his group hold their fire until the three were out of harm's way. Their tracer bullets filled the air with what looked like a hail storm in the night, and they shot out the last of the lights. This forced the troops back into the gates where they tried to find cover. Several fell as they retreated.

Chapter 60

The island

Loretta sat on her bed trying to calm her nerves. She knew she had no help, and she was confined to her room. How would anyone find this place? She knew she had very capable people who were probably looking for her, but she needed to act as quickly as she could. The whole idea was to mess up this organization, so they could not operate effectively and, as a result, eliminate the possibility of the event happening.

She paced back and forth in her room, looked around for anything that might help her, but there was very little. She understood that she might have to just go through a week of hell to save herself if she couldn't figure out something. She had an idea on her walk, but now since she was being watched, that might not work.

Security detail on the island

The security people were running checks on the girls who had come to the island to make sure they did not miss anything. The facial recognition team was comparing the pictures they had with a huge database they had been given by one of their leaders. When Loretta's picture came up, there was an immediate problem. It identified her as an FBI agent.

They notified their boss. When he arrived, they had completed the assessment of all the people who had flown in. They sent for the madam before they made any moves. They had her interrogated by some very good people who knew exactly what to do. They played the "good cop-bad cop" tactic, and it worked to perfection. Before they were finished, the madam had told them everything she knew, which wasn't much, except that it was enough. They were happy with her information, and they let her leave with one of the security guards, but she never returned to her room. She knew what was coming and tried to fight, but it was useless.

Their next move was to detain Loretta and interrogate her to find out what she knew about them and this operation. The man who had earlier found her and reported her outside of her room, was sent to get Loretta.

Loretta knew that getting caught on the outside of her room was not going to go well. She had to get out of this place as soon as she could. Her only thought was to hide somewhere on the island until the SEALs could figure out where she was, but that might take some time. She knew she could not hide in her room or in the building. She had to get out again, even if it meant that she might get caught.

She opened her door and peered out. She did not see anyone. She moved quietly through the building and went to the madam's room. She opened the door, but she was not there. She walked back to the end of the building near her room and opened the door to make sure no one was there. She cracked the door enough to peek out, and she saw the madam being walked away by a security guard, and she looked like she was trying to fight him off, but he kept pushing her forward.

She also saw the guard who had grabbed her earlier walking toward the building. She needed to hide quickly or somehow take this big guy down, but how? She looked around and then ran back to her room and found something that she thought would work. Her idea was to place something right in front of the door, so he would trip and fall, and then she was going to smash his head with the base of a metal lamp from her room. Would that work?

She took clothes, some books, some other items they had placed in her room, and she put them all about three feet in front of the door. Then she grabbed the heavy lamp and held it in both hands. It was very heavy. Loretta deliberated. *She would have to get him to look straight ahead. What would get his attention?*

She knew he was upset with her when she had left her room earlier, so would she be enough to get his attention? She had to take a chance and stand in the middle of the hall when he entered, so he would not look down. *How could she keep his eyes focused straight ahead, so he would not see what was on the floor?*

She knew standing there would get his attention. *He'll be incensed to see me out of my room again. He was livid the last time, so, yes, if I'm standing there, he'll look at me, not the floor. If this did not work, she was dead, but then, she was dead anyway by the looks of things.*

Everything she had gathered was in front of the door, and she stood there like a rigid statue, except that it was perspiring profusely. Then the door opened.

Chapter 61

The hill below the bunker

Ron got off his four-wheeler and helped Wayne and Peter lift Charlie onto Ron's machine. Charlie could not really hold himself up. He had blood everywhere. His clothes were soaked through. Ron directed Wayne and Peter to the other machines, and he put Charlie in front of him on the four-wheeler and sat behind. Ron was able to grab the handlebars and turn the machine and head down the hill.

All three machines made a quick exit. Ron was the slowest as he tried to balance Charlie and drive down the hill. The troops on the hill retreated and gained cover and began shooting in their direction, but it mostly went over their heads. Charlie kept leaning to one side, and Ron had all he could do to keep the machine on the road.

They moved quickly until they reached the road to turn right toward Colewin. All three were moving down the road when mortars and then other rockets began to fly from the base. Ron looked and he could see a helicopter to his right. He thought they should all seek shelter, but then they would just blast the area and kill all of them. They had to try to shoot at the copter. It looked like a version of the Huey helicopter that they had used when he was in Vietnam. They were armed with rockets as well as door gunners operating machine guns at each door and probably a .50 caliber machine gun at the front.

At the same time, Matt heard the helicopter fire up, and he knew what was going to happen, so he had his people move out. They ran south on a trail that they had made for just such an escape. They all reached a truck they had hidden on the side of the road, loaded up and drove south as two rockets roared down on the place they had been. They were far enough away that it did not affect them, and Matt continued to drive south passing the road to Colewin and heading toward U.S.-2 where the semi had unloaded.

Ron, on the other hand, was wondering how he and the others could evade this thing. Once he spotted the helicopter, he knew they would fire rockets at them. He was sure of that, and then he heard the rockets tear through Matt's position. He hoped they were all right. The next explosion happened to their left, and it blew Ron and Charlie off their machine and into the woods.

Ron was shaken and banged up. Where was Charlie? What happened to the machine? He looked around and saw the four-wheeler on its side in front of a tree it must have hit. He was able to crawl to his knees and find Charlie. He dragged him deeper into the woods. He looked ahead and the other machines were nowhere to be seen. He could only hope the helicopter had lost them and would not come back.

He heard the chopper moving away, so he dashed out to the machine. He was able to right it, but a lot of fuel had leaked out. He got it started and moved it over to Charlie. He did not look good at all. He lifted him onto the machine when he heard another explosion ahead of them. One of his lights was out, and he decided to turn off the others, and he smashed the tail lights on the machine, so there would be no light visible from the air as he drove and braked. What would be the best move now for him and Charlie?

Ron yelled into Charlie's ear, "Can you hold on to the handlebars?" Charlie did not respond. He did not ever open his eyes. Ron decided to move forward with Charlie, hoping he would be able to stay on. Then Charlie fell over the handlebars. Ron gasped, "This might work!" And he drove on.

Tommy was leading and stopped to look back, but he could not see anything. It was so dark, and the curves in the road added to his problem. He knew he should not stop long, but he was worried about Ron and Charlie. The barber pulled up and stopped too.

Tommy and the barber had kept ahead of the helicopter, but they knew they had to lose the thing. Tommy motioned to move on, but he stopped again and motioned to the barber to stop. "Have you seen Ron?"

"I really can't see a thing. I hope he's all right."

"Should we head back to look?"

"Not sure that's a good idea right now."

"We need to do something to lose this helicopter. We need to shut down anything that might be visible from the air. Maybe if we lose them, we can double back to help. When we reach the road up ahead, there's a turn we can make that'll take us deep into the woods, and it leads to the ridge where my uncle was murdered. If we get there, we can ditch the machines and hide out near the creek, and we can follow it to Colewin. It's dense there, so they won't see us on foot."

The barber, Peter, and Wayne agreed right away. Wayne knew the area, and he thought it would work. They looked around to see if Ron was anywhere to be seen before they left the road, but they could see nothing. They knew that he and Charlie might have been hit, and if they were going to get out of there, they had to leave now. None of them liked the idea, but they knew that was the only alternative right now. Once the helicopter was out of the way, they would go back and look for them.

The bunker

Bates had watched the whole attack until his screens went blank and everything turned dark. He knew they had hit the generator. He walked into the tunnel and hit the auxiliary power, and he had lights again, but he did not have any cameras or light outside. His computers powered on though, and he knew he had to get a message to the boss. He quickly sent an encrypted message.

> Boss, we have been hit again. There is an attack on the bunker. If we are going to get a message out, we should do it now. The event can still happen, and I should be safe in the bunker to coordinate things, but they are on to us, and we should act now.

Bates received a quick reply.

> You are right. We need to act immediately in case anything happens to the bunker. Have you informed the other places of the plan? If you have, then call the event for tomorrow before first light, and coordinate everything. Since the others know of the plan, send anything else they will need in case something happens there. Do it now!

Bates got the message and was sending information as fast as he could. He knew he did not have much time.

Chapter 62

On the trail

The four men reached the creek that Tommy had identified earlier, but before they left their machines behind, Tommy said, "The truck should have exploded by now. Why haven't we heard anything? It should have been a massive explosion."

The barber turned to Wayne. "Did you set the timer?"

"I did. I set it for twenty minutes."

"Are you sure?" Peter asked.

"Yes. Twenty minutes. It said twenty minutes on the timer."

Tommy winced. "What did you see when you set it?"

"I saw the twenty, plus some zeros."

"It's been longer than twenty minutes."

"I think you set it for twenty hours, Wayne."

They heard the helicopter again and ditched the machines, and they began their trek through the woods to the creek and on to Colewin when Tommy stopped. "I'm going to go back and look for Ron and Charlie. They could be hurt and need help. You guys continue to follow the creek, and when you come to a bend in the creek, head north through the woods and you'll walk right into Colewin. Don't stop until you can get some help. Keep a phone handy, Wayne. I'll check in with you."

"No, if you go, I'm going with you."

"I'm going alone. It'll be faster, and I know the area even at night. You get to safety and then get more help, and in the daylight, come to find me if I'm not back."

The barber said, "That's crazy. You could get killed."

"I'll be careful. Go ahead. Get to Colewin." Tommy turned and began running to his machine.

Chapter 63

The island

Loretta was standing there shaking uncontrollably, knowing if this didn't work, she'd be signing her death warrant. When the door swung open, the man looked right at Loretta—eyeball to eyeball. He was pissed! He began yelling, saying something Loretta did not understand, and he looked fierce. He took a quick step and hit the clothes she had bundled on the floor. His flip-flops got tangled and he tripped and fell forward, but he caught himself. When he tried to put his left foot back on the floor, he stepped on something that made him slip again, and he fell forward head first. When his head banged on the floor, he moaned.

Loretta did not hesitate. She had the lamp in her hands, and she walloped him several times on the back of the head until there was blood everywhere. He was not getting up. She quickly grabbed his AK-47, his large knife, his pistol, and a small flashlight and headed outside to see where the other guard might have taken the madam. She felt that wherever it was might be a safe place to hide for a bit.

When she exited, all was quiet. *Where were all the security guards?* She walked down the path where she had seen the guard take the madam, and she followed it. She walked for some time when she spotted him with her. They were near a large hole in the ground. She could only figure what that was. She sprinted as fast as she could, then stopped and crept quietly until she was behind a small bush where she could observe both the guard and the madam.

The guard had the woman on the ground, but he was not in a hurry to eliminate her. He had other plans. Too bad for him. Loretta crept slowly until she was right behind him, grabbed his hair, and slit his throat.

She turned to the madam, and with a look of disdain said, "You're welcome."

The madam looked up at Loretta and just shook her head. "I have never been that close to death even with the things I have done in my life. I haven't always been a good person, but I haven't tried to hurt anyone."

"Oh, sure, you just put girls in harm's way and made them do things for money that demeans them."

"I never forced anyone!"

Loretta stopped right there, and said, "Pick up that rifle and take his pistol. Do you know how to use them?"

"I'm not sure."

"Let me give you a quick lesson because we're going to need to get to that smaller building on the other side of the main building, and we're going to get rid of these assholes. Take those extra clips he has on him too. You have thirty rounds in the clip. That will give you about twenty more. Here's the safety. Make sure it's off. It's a bit difficult, so you need to practice right now. Here, I'll show you. Now you try it."

It took several tries, but the madam got it.

"By the way, if I'm going to be hanging out with you, what the heck is your name?"

"Just call me Gloria."

"Okay, Gloria, we're going to lay low until night. Let's find a place that will give us some protection. Also, help me drop this guy's body into that hole. Looks like they must have used this for other bodies. Man, it really stinks when you get close to it."

"I think I'm going to throw up," Gloria said. And then she did.

Once she was finished, Loretta said, "Let's move toward the shore and hide in that clump of trees. If worse comes to worst, we can head to the building near where we landed. I can't understand where all the guards are?"

"They're looking for someone or something. When they were questioning me, someone came in and told that tall, mean-looking guard that someone was on the way. They seemed to panic, and that's when he sent me with that guy."

"That explains why they're on the beaches. I wonder who they're looking for?"

They moved down to the shore and found a good spot to rest and wait until dark. Loretta's plan was a bit fuzzy even in her mind, but there was not much else to do or think about, and she hoped it would work. While they waited, she kept giving Gloria lessons on how to use the weapons she had.

Somewhere west of the Philippines on a carrier
The ship's communication officer addressed the captain, "Our guys have gotten a definite hit from one of the satellites. We are sure this is the place where they took that FBI agent."

The captain was surprised. "You're sure?"

"Positive. Look at these pictures."

"All right. Let's get as close and we can. We have support from a couple of submarines in the area that can send an SDV or two, with anywhere from two to six SEALs. They can land stealthily in the dark. That may be the only way to rescue our target. Let's get a plan together."

"What about the Green Berets we have aboard?"

"They can help, but this seems to be a job for the SEALs. They're trained for this."

"How close can we get them?"

"With the SDVs they can easily make land."

"Then we need to give the SEALs all the details they'll need. We should send the photos we have of the island and a picture of the agent."

"They know her. They've been working with her for months."

"Good. The best guess is that she will most likely be in this building if the information is correct. They should go straight there and rescue her if the escape plan does not work."

"Yes, that's what they should do!"

"Hopefully, they won't have to go on the island, but in case they do, they should not leave any telltale signs that it was us."

"Roger."

The leader of the SEALs reported the news. "Remember, the order is we can't leave any footprint on the island. We cannot let them know the U.S. Government is involved. Hopefully, we can stay off the island. If something unforeseen happens, we can assist the agent in some way to take the enemy down, but, if we cannot, then we need to extract her without leaving any footprint."

Chapter 64

The bunker

Bates was intent on getting all the information out that he could, so the event could happen as soon as possible. He and his trainers had started to clean up around the gate area. There were quite a few dead, and they had to take care of that and get the rest of the men out of the area and on to D.C.

The areas around the gate and bunker were a mess, but they were going to leave the place soon and destroy as much as they could anyway. Yet, they had to make it livable for a short time, and they needed to repair the craters around the gate. They still had a helicopter out searching for the people who had infiltrated the place. Bates was not happy. He walked out of the bunker, and he spoke to one of his trainers as they stood outside near the gates. "I hope they got those people, especially Charlie. He's been a thorn in my side since day one. I'm not sure who else was with him, but I hope they're all dead."

"Those rockets made a real mess in a few places. If they were anywhere near there, then they're dead."

"But we can't be sure."

"No."

Bates went back into the bunker and ordered the helicopter back to the base. "We need everyone here to get this place ready so we can get all the troops out of here. Then we can destroy it."

He called his trainers and said, "The word is out. The event will happen very soon. If all goes well, it will be a day from now, so get these guys prepared to leave. We need to wait until they're in place, but then it can begin."

In the woods in the U.P.

Tommy drove as fast as he could. He did not hear the helicopter anymore, but he was afraid to turn on his lights. He knew the trail well, but in the dark, it was still a challenge. Several times he felt his tires leave the road, only to crank them back again. He felt his pace was too slow, but there was nothing he could do.

Ron had driven ahead for a while until the ATV sputtered. He knew he was going to run out of gas. *Where was that helicopter?* The machine finally came to a stop. He had to lift Charlie off the machine, but Charlie could not stand. He felt for a pulse, and he found a very weak one. Ron thought he was losing him, so he decided to walk him to the side of the road, and he tried to cover him with anything he could find—dirt, needles, leaves, anything to keep him warm. Then he wondered if he should leave him and walk to get help or stay put.

Tommy kept moving forward. He wondered if Ron and Charlie might have gotten off the main road and were hiding. He turned off the side road and onto the road toward the bunker. When he looked down the road, the first thing he saw was a four-wheeler right in front of him, parked in the middle of the road. He drove to it and stopped.

Ron saw the machine come toward him. He could not make out who it was until Tommy whispered, "Is anyone here? Ron?"

Ron was relieved and answered, "Tommy?"

"Yeah, it's me."

"Right here. I have Charlie and he's not doing well. Did everyone else make it out?"

"Peter and his father and Wayne are headed to Colewin. I don't know about Matt and Shanice, or the others with them, but I heard a huge explosion from that area."

"I did too."

"Let's get you guys out of here. I'll hook a chain to your machine and pull it. You can ride and hold Charlie while I pull. Where is he?"

"He's over here, but as I said, he's not doing well."

They hooked a chain to the four-wheeler, loaded Charlie, and they began to slowly move forward. Again, they did not want to use their lights, but they were moving in the right direction and happy for that.

Ron watched as Tommy slowly drove through a trail Ron had never been on previously. He trusted Tommy, but Ron could not see much. It was very dark, and there was no moon to light things up a bit. *The woods at night here are really dark*, he kept thinking. His thoughts turned to Shanice and the other crew that had been in the woods. He had heard the explosions from the bunker area, and he was hoping they were not where Shanice was.

Ron could just make out Tommy's silhouette; he looked like the headless horseman. His head was down as he navigated the road ahead. It was a bumpy, uneven surface, and Ron had all he could do to keep Charlie on his machine. He kept hoping for this ride to end when suddenly the whole area seemed to explode. Both Tommy and Ron were thrown from their vehicles, Charlie along with them.

When Ron looked into the sky, he could see light for the first time since he had been knocked off his four-wheeler.

Tommy groaned as he rolled over and looked skyward. They all sat there and listened as several more explosions rocked the woods. It was the truck. The timer must not have been set right. Ron clicked on his watch, and it lit up. It had been about two hours since they had picked up Charlie from the bunker. Hopefully, it destroyed the bunker. Tommy looked at his machine, and it was on its side. He got up and walked back to Ron as fireworks kept going off in the distance.

"That was one hell of an explosion—surely it destroyed the bunker and everything around it. We're quite a distance from it, and it still knocked us off our machines. What the hell did Charlie put in that truck?"

"What did you say? My ears are ringing so bad, I didn't hear what you said."

Tommy yelled, "That was very loud. Where's Charlie?"

"He got blown off too. He flew over me. He's on the other side of the road. If he makes it out of here alive, he'll be very lucky." Ron's machine had been moved over to the edge of the road and was leaning on a tree. It had also been tipped sideways, and it looked like the wheels had been bent when it hit the edge of the road.

Tommy said, "Let's get out of here." They found Charlie and once again loaded him on Ron's machine. They were all bleeding and their ears were still ringing.

Tommy righted his machine, and he began to pull again. Ron's machine did not move very well, but it did move. They drove toward Colewin.

Tommy had to avoid several trees that were leaning over the road and a lot of debris that was everywhere. He was worried that a large tree might be downed and he would not be able to get around it.

Ron's main concerns now were Shanice and Matt and his people.

Chapter 65

The island

Loretta realized why she had not seen many security people. They were gathered along the shore, and they looked like they were looking for something. Every direction on the shore had guards. This was not going to be the place to stay and wait until dark. She needed to find someplace for her and Gloria to stay put for a few hours until dark. She turned to Gloria and asked, "Do you have any idea why these guys are gathered so heavily on the beach?"

Gloria looked at her and said, "How am I supposed to know? I told you they were looking for someone! I was almost killed by these people because of you. I have no idea what they're doing. I do know that they watch the waters around the island to make sure no one strays this way, so maybe someone did, and they're here looking."

Loretta instantly felt better. "I bet my people have located us, and they're heading to this island. We really need to be careful until dark. Let's find a better place to hide. Once they find the guard I killed, they'll be looking for me."

"You mean the one we threw in the hole"?

"No, the big dude."

"You killed that head guard?"

"Had to."

"Then we're dead. If they find him, we won't be able to get away, they'll have everyone after us."

"We've gotten this far. Now we just need to wait it out. If there is no contact tonight, then I'm going to continue with my instructions."

"And what are your instructions? There's not much you can do with all the security around here."

"Maybe not, but I'll have to try. It's vital for our country. These people want nothing more than to take down the U.S."

"They have the money and power, that's for sure," Gloria said.

Loretta looked around. There was a lot of vegetation all the way up to the shore, then the shore was about fifty feet to the ocean, but it could be much more, depending on the tide. She wasn't sure of the tides here, and she knew that could change things. Loretta said, "You know, we could hide right down here by the shore. I need to stay on the east side of the island because that's what we planned for extraction."

"Extraction?"

"Yes, and looking at this place, the beach in front of us seems to be the most approachable on the east side."

"How in the world are you going to find someone who is try-ing to land here at night? This island is several miles long on this side. You can clearly see that."

"Sure, but I was also trained to be rescued from a place like this, and this is the best place. I know it is."

Chapter 66

D.C.

It was getting dark in D. C, and Dominic drove for some time around the city and then out north. Joe noticed that they were almost out of D.C., somewhere on the fringe north of Georgetown. He wasn't sure where they were, but he was satisfied that they were heading someplace safe, he hoped. He was not sure of anything anymore. He was in the back seat with Joette when he said, "We should get an update from Ron about the bunker and also find out if anyone has located Loretta."

Ann heard Joe and responded, "In all the excitement I forgot that Loretta was in trouble. I wonder if she was able to put an end to the committee?"

Joe called Ron first. Ron did not answer right away, so Joe decided to see if he could reach anyone else.

Ann, in the meantime, called Jerry to find out if there was any news about Loretta. She received the same information that she had previously. "It sounds like Loretta has not been located yet. I sure hope she's all right."

Joe called Tommy, and he did not answer, so he tried Shanice. "This is Shanice."

"Shanice, Joe here. How is everything there?"

"Not the greatest. We pulled off the plan, and we're waiting at Matt's place for word about Ron, Charlie, and Tommy. Seems like they all got separated after the attack. We've all had our phones off during the attack to avoid giving our positions away, but they're back on, and we've heard from Wayne. He and Peter and his father are back and safe. Tommy is out looking for Ron and Charlie. Somehow, they all got separated. I guess they were being chased by a Huey helicopter, and it was raining machine gun fire and rockets on everyone. I just hope no one was hurt."

"Oh, man, I do too. Did they destroy the bunker in the meantime?"

"No word on that. There was a tremendous explosion, so I'm guessing, yes. We're planning a trip to search for them right now."

"Be careful, and keep me updated."

Joe hung up and shook his head. Joette asked, "Is it bad news?"

"Not sure, but Ron, Charlie, and Tommy are missing, and Shanice is not sure that the bunker is gone. For as close as we think they are to the event, this is disheartening, and I'm concerned about our people."

Dominic pulled up to a place that looked like an ordinary house, but it was very large. "This is the place. People here will know a lot about what is going on. Maybe they'll have information about your friend, Loretta, too."

He drove into an ordinary garage, but it was more than that. It was massive. They left the vehicle, and they all moved rather quickly following Dominic inside the house. The place was messy, and there were people running back and forth. Joe noticed that they were talking anxiously to each other. Dominic turned to Ann and said, "This is unusual." He asked someone, "What's going on?"

The person looked at him and said, "Who are these people?"

"They're the ones I called you about earlier. They're good."

"I hope you're right. We're in the middle of it right now."

"Joe asked, "In the middle of what?"

"The event!"

Ann and Joette both looked at Joe and then at the person who delivered the news.

Ann asked, "What do you know right now?"

The man looked at Ann and was not sure he should answer. Dominic grabbed the man by the arm and said, "It's okay. These people are good. I told you the whole story. They've been on these guys longer than anyone. What's going on?"

"Our tech people said that the event is going to start either tomorrow morning or tomorrow night, depending on their troop movements. They want everyone in place before they move. We have notified the President, and he has reinforced the capitol with all the capitol police, the National Guard, and any other local police he could find."

"What exactly do we know?"

"It's very confusing. We've gotten all kinds of information. Some indicates activity in all the states. Other evidence just specifies the U.S. Capitol. We must be vigilant everywhere. The President has notified all the governors, but some of them think his people are crazy, and that something like this could never happen."

"We need to be prepared though. What can we do?"

"Nothing right now. The President said that the "designated survivor" will be sent here. We have a secure shelter under this place. He's sending some Secret Service and other people to make sure this person is safe. The President is in a secure location too."

"Did anyone give a time for it to start?"

"No, but it's imminent. Probably soon, since they will most likely attack when it's dark."

Dominic checked his watch—2:20 p.m. "That gives them about five or six hours until dark unless it'll happen in the early morning hours." He mumbled, "Who knows?"

After hearing everything, Joe's phone rang. It was Jerry.

"Hello, Joe?"

Joe was surprised that Jerry would call him directly. "Hello, Jerry, this is Joe. What's up?"

"Joe, I'm glad I got ahold of you. We just received information that Bates has sent out the message for all leaders to be on alert for the event to begin soon. We did not get a start time, but it sounds like it is going to happen in the next few hours."

"We have the same information here in D.C. Now we need to make sure everyone is prepared to resist what is going to happen. I know that Bates and his people have several hundred troops headed to D.C. Exactly how many, we're not sure. Contact everyone and let them know what's up. Hopefully, Loretta was successful in her assignment to take down the committee. I'm assuming that the bunker was not destroyed if Bates is still sending information."

Jerry said, "Not sure. According to your son, this was sent several hours ago. So far, I haven't had any information from Ron or Shanice. They were going to contact me when the mission was completed."

"I've spoken with Shanice. She said there was no definite word on the bunker yet, but there was an enormous explosion. If you hear anything, keep me informed, and make sure everyone there is on the same page."

"We've been getting the word out here. Be careful there. Talk to you later."

"Yes, keep us informed if you hear anything."

Chapter 67

The island, earlier

Loretta realized that she would not be able to complete the mission. She was a bit despondent about it, but she knew all along that it was a possibility. Now, her only job was to safely get off this island. If her intuition was correct, and what she saw going on was preparation for someone coming ashore, then it had to be her rescuers. She and Gloria would lay low for as long as necessary. She knew that once they found the dead guards, they would be after them, so she had to make sure they did not leave any kind of trail.

Waiting for dark was nerve wracking, especially for Gloria. She became a pest. "Will you just stop fiddling with that rifle? You're driving me crazy."

"I'm nervous. I've never shot one of these things, and I've never tried to hurt anyone on purpose."

"Maybe not, but you might have to shoot someone to save your hide." As Loretta was speaking, she saw some movement on the shore. It was getting dark. She couldn't make out what it was, but she could tell that several guards were moving away from where they were and were running down the beach. "This could be it."

"What?"

"Our chance to get out of here. Follow me."

Loretta and Gloria had a good view of the beach from their hiding spot, but at dusk, neither could really see clearly. However, now Loretta knew they could move along the beach and follow the movement if they stayed in the shadows of the trees. They followed for some time when they spotted about ten of the island guards taking positions around the beach and some in the woods. Loretta knew what was coming next.

1,500 miles away

The communications guy working for the old boss unexpectedly lost the connection with Bates. He tried several times, but he had no luck. He contacted the old boss. "We have lost communications with Bates. He has everything started, but we are no longer able to reach him, and that could be a problem. We need to let the other command centers know, so they can take over."

"Do you think something has happened to him? He said they were being attacked."

"Not sure. We don't have any word. That was the last he said that they were under heavy fire again, but it was under control. He said he sent out about one hundred troops and was sending the rest soon, and that is when we lost contact."

"Then something is up. He's good at what he does, so he is either hurt or compromised in some way. Contact one of the trucks that is taking the first group to D.C. Maybe they know something."

After several minutes of attempting to get ahold of the truck by checking in with a secret code, the communications man was successful. "This is headquarters checking on your status."

"I'm here. Is this about the explosion?"

"What explosion?"

"After all the men were loaded, and we were on our way heading down U.S.-2, we were rocked by a huge blast. Seemed to come from the place we just left."

"No, could it have been the bunker?"

"Probably was. We had to stop and check everything. The blast was so bad that it almost knocked the truck over. We just loaded again, but, yeah, it came from that area."

The communications person contacted the boss again, realizing that this was a serious turn of events. "Boss, it sounds like there was an explosion at the bunker. I just spoke with the driver of the truck heading to D.C., and he said there was an enormous blast in the direction of the bunker."

The old boss said, "Then Bates could have been hurt, or worse, killed. We need to delay the event. Get the word out to all the other command centers, and do it quickly. If only one truck left, then we will be short three hundred troops."

"Right. I will, but they are going to have a lot of questions because I have no idea what Bates has set up. What should I tell them?"

"Just tell them to wait for further instructions and to delay the event until I give the word. If they have other questions, we'll have to get back to them. Make a list so we can reply later."

"All right. I hope I don't mess this up."

"You won't. Just do it right away."

Chapter 68

D. C. safehouse

Everyone at the safe house was either sending a message or receiving one. Dominic told everyone to head for the lower level where they would be safe. Joe, Joette, and Ann followed.

One of Dominic's bosses told everyone to quiet down. He had a message to pass on. "The event is about to happen. It's what we have been waiting for and planning to stop for a long time, but we are not sure where or when it will commence. The President said that the attempt to take down the committee may have failed, and they are trying to get the agent out of harm's way, but nothing is for sure. They know there has not been any damage to the island, but they haven't been watching it for long because they just found it."

Joe and Ann looked at each other. They were both concerned about Loretta, and they had hoped she could take down the committee. Ann said, "If she isn't successful, then that committee can continue what it's doing. We won't be able to stop them."

"I agree it will be difficult, but let's hope she can succeed."

A very important woman was rushed into the house and taken to the lower level away from everyone else. They took her to a room with a very secure door.

"That must be the designated survivor, don't you think?" Joe said.

Ann agreed. "Must be. A lot of secret service have arrived—and other military personnel. This is unusual."

Colewin

Tommy took a left turn and then a right. He was headed for Charlie's place where everyone was supposed to gather after the attack. He was making better time now, but there was still a lot of debris on the roads, but nothing he could not get around.

Ron was holding on to Charlie who did not seem to have any life left in him. They reached Charlie's road and drove down. As they moved closer, Ron noticed a truck in the distance. It was Matt's. He knew Shanice was with him. He hoped she was all right.

Tommy pulled up in front of the house, and jumped off the machine and helped Ron with Charlie. They carried him into the house where Charlie's wife was waiting. She motioned to take him into another room where they laid him on a bed. A few others came in to help her with Charlie. Ron and Tommy left the room, and Ron saw Shanice and immediately walked over and gave her a hug.

Chapter 69

Earlier on the island

Loretta and Gloria had waited for hours. It was about 1:00 a.m. when Loretta saw something emerge from the sea. It was quite far out, but something was there. The moonlight glanced off it as it bounced around in the water. If she had not been looking out, she would have never seen it, and it did not last long. She waited.

Then she heard popping on the shore as the guards began firing into the water. At what, she was not sure, but she was hoping it was her ride home. Loretta knew enough to keep looking out, and then she received the signal she had hoped to see. She returned three short, three long, and three short signals from the flashlight she had taken from the guard.

She knew she and Gloria would have to take out some of the guards in the woods before more moved this way, so she decided to circle behind them. She and Gloria crouched and quietly moved. It was tough to see anything.

The SEALs were close to shore, but they were quite invisible. They fired when they could and took several guards down. It didn't take long. Somehow the SEALs had eliminated every one of the guards.

Loretta and Gloria were crouched behind a bit of cover when Loretta spotted movement coming from each side of the island. It had to be more guards. She realized they had to warn the SEALs, and so she fired to the right and told Gloria to fire to the left. When they shot, they were just firing at movement, but then there was return fire. Loretta told Gloria to fire whenever she saw a flash or a tracer. They were able to take out a few, but they had given the SEALs the warning, and the SEALs took out the rest.

Loretta hoped they realized that she was the one firing from behind the enemy, but she knew that might not be possible in the dark, but the SEALs recognized that someone was helping them. Soon all the shooting stopped.

Loretta whipped out her flashlight and gave the SOS signal again. This time they saw bodies come out of the water. She grabbed Gloria and pulled her along as they moved toward the sea. They were both in awe of the SEALs—and what they had just accomplished.

1,500 miles away
The delay was causing all kinds of problems. They were trying to coordinate over fifty sites, and their key person was not available for some reason. They also had to contact the military personnel who oversaw both National Guard and regular Army troops. They would have to hold them back until the boss gave the signal that all was under control.

The old boss thought that the worst problem they could have would be that Bates was injured or killed. He knew they had other capable people, but he and Bates had worked together for several years, and he had been the one he could depend on the most. Bates also had to release the troops from the U.P. to reinforce the D.C. troops. *Had he done that?*

Yet, others were taking over, and the new boss was one of those, and he did not want to delay the event because it had been too many years in the planning. *Why delay now?*

The old boss figured he had better get in touch with him. He sent a message via his communications man.

Everything is ready. Make sure you hold back until you get the word. Bates is not responding, so this communications center will give the orders now.

The new boss responded.

We should just begin now. Everything is ready. Another day will just set us back. We're ready.

The old boss felt that he might be right, but he knew they had to make sure everyone was on the same page.

I understand, but we must act together, and I think we will be better off to wait. Bates needs to get the rest of the troops on site. Hope you understand.

That was the end of the messages. Everyone would just have to wait until the old boss gave the signal.

Somewhere in the South China Sea

Loretta and Gloria were sitting quietly on a U.S. military combat ship. They were taken off the island by the SEALs and were now comfortable aboard the ship. Loretta slouched in her seat and said, "That sure didn't work out as planned since the mission failed, although I'm glad to be safe on board."

"This whole thing is unsettling. Why did you need to try to eliminate those people?" Gloria asked.

"If you have to ask that question, you didn't deserve to be saved from that island."

As they spoke a naval officer knocked, and then entered the room. "You're to come with me."

"Who, me?" Loretta said.

"You're the agent we had on the island, correct?"

"Yes."

"Follow me."

Loretta was quizzed about what had happened on the island, and she gave the entire story. When she was finished, the officer said, "Thank you for everything, and for putting your life in jeopardy. We will get this information to the President."

Loretta was dismissed and taken back to her quarters. She and Gloria were to be transported to another ship where they would be sent to Guam and then flown back to the U.S.

Chapter 70

Underground shelter in D.C.

Joe, Ann, and Joette were resting in the underground shelter when Dominic entered and said, "You guys, the head man wants to talk to you about what you know. We have definite evidence that the event will take place soon. We thought it might happen today, but he's not positive."

Joe had been wondering if their trip to D.C. would be a bust. He had always thought that he probably knew more about the group than anyone in the country. He and Ron had been focused on them since 2019, around the time Dominic had infiltrated the group, so he must know a lot too. Together they could probably put together a complete scenario of what the old boss was planning. Sitting in a chair, Joe looked up to Dominic. "You've been in this a long time too. Can we talk to someone and tell them what we know?"

"That's the idea. We can use Ann and Joette, too. The three of you can put together what transpired in the past hours. We might be able to identify the woman who lured you here to eliminate you."

"That would be wonderful," Ann said.

Dominic led them to another room where some people from the President's cabinet were seated. The room was quite large and had a kitchen area with a table and several chairs, a refrigerator, blankets, and cots. There was a door that looked like it must lead to a bathroom. Someone had prepared this place for a long stay.

They talked for some time, and they were able to bring in some pictures, and Ann immediately recognized the woman. "That's the woman! The one who said she worked for the President."

"She works close to the President. We'll pick her up and interrogate her."

"Glad to hear that," Joe said. "You should also make sure all the governors are on board. We know that they're going to hit each capitol building."

"We've heard that, and we have notified each one. We are well protected here too as is the Capitol Building. When things begin to happen, they should be quelled in a hurry."

Joe scoffed, "Are you kidding? This won't be like 2021. These guys are trained for specific tasks—and they are well armed. When you see some semis pull into the area that will be some of the troops, and they will be heavily armed. Many of the troops are probably here already. Some will come in helicopters, some in tanks, some in Humvees."

"That really is not possible. They couldn't get those near the Capitol. We have people ready to defend all parts of the city."

"I'm just telling you what I have seen and what I know."

Ann spoke up. "Listen to him. He knows."

Joette agreed and said, "Joe has seen it all from the beginning. He's been in this with his friend Ron, and they were both in the military. They know what's going on."

"All right. We'll get the information to the President and he can forward it to the proper people. You're too apprehensive. It won't be as bad as you're saying."

"Maybe not, but I'd get the information to him quickly."

"We do everything quickly and effectively."

"You need to make sure there are no other people on the President's staff who are in on the event. You can't trust anyone."

"That's a valid point. We'll have to go directly to the President. We won't involve any other staff."

The man left, and Joe, Ann, and Joette waited with Dominic to wait to see what might happen now that they passed on their information.

Joe said, "Hopefully, the man is trustworthy."

1,500 miles away

The old boss said, "Get the plane ready, I'm going to head to D.C. now, and I will be ready to take my place in the White House when this is over." The old boss was very confident in what they had planned. He had sent out the signal to attack at 2:00 a.m. He wanted to make sure everyone was in place, and he had gotten confirmation from every leader in his small army, except Bates. They were ready.

"We'll need a flight plan. Where exactly do you want to go?"

"I'd like to land at Reagan National, then have a car ready to take me to the South Capitol Street Heliport where I have a helicopter ready to take me to the White House. It has all been arranged in advance by our people. We just need to give them a time."

"How soon do you think we will have control? Will this put you in danger?"

"Hopefully not. Our people are well trained and have everything covered. We have troops already in the White House too, so they will have that secured for us."

"Really? That's great!"

The boss continued, "It has taken time, but we finally have it all under control. We just need to finish this off. Let's say we leave here at eight. By the time we land and are in the vehicle ready to move out, it will be midnight, so let's say we can be at the heliport in fifteen minutes, maybe a little more. Then we can bide our time until we are cleared to head to the White House."

"Are you planning on arriving there before the event starts?"

"Not sure. I need to wait until I get the word from our people. They'll tell us when everything is secure, and I can land there safely. I hope Bates can get the last three or four hundred troops in place. That's the only hitch right now."

"I'll get everything ready. This should be no problem. The plane is ready to go at any time, so eight will be doable. You have some time to make changes if you need to. Just let me know," his assistant said.

"I will do that, but the plan is good and we should be able to do exactly what I said."

"Perfect."

Chapter 71

Safehouse, D.C.

Joe was very nervous, and he felt that the President's man did not really understand the seriousness of the attack. He asked Dominic, "Can we trust that guy?"

"Totally."

"I mean, he didn't seem to take this attack as seriously as he should."

"He's just the messenger. The guys who really matter are those with the President right now. He has the chairman of the joint chiefs of staff with him, according to the guy who just left, so I know they are on top of this."

"If you say so, then I feel better about the whole thing, but I'll be glad when this is over, and the President can make us all feel safe again."

Ann said, "I agree. It has just been too long, and we've been through so much because of these people."

While they were talking, a military man entered and said he needed to speak with Ann or Joe. They both looked at each other and wondered—*what now?*

"We have word from our command in the South China Sea that they have rescued someone, a woman called Loretta. There's no word on the results of her mission. She asked if we could contact you to let you know she is all right. The person who sent the message said that they did some of the debriefing on the carrier, but she is on her way back to California where she will be debriefed thoroughly." After asking if there were any questions, and not getting a response, the man turned and left.

Ann stood up and exhaled. "That is such a relief. Hopefully, she was successful." Both Joe and Joette felt the same way. They knew what the situation was, and they were glad she was on her way home.

Joe checked his watch. It was getting toward evening, and he wondered if the event would start when it was dark.

Dominic needed to join the others who were running the safehouse. He stood and said, "I'll be in the big room with the others. There's food and water in the refrigerator. Help yourself. If there's anything else you need, let me know." As he turned to leave, he looked back and with a smile said, "Sorry, I can't order out."

Everyone had a little chuckle.

Time was passing slowly, and all three were getting tired after their long ordeal. Military cots were against the wall, and Joe thought they should all get a little rest, but Ann and Joette were both too hyped to sleep, so Joe opened one cot and put it against the back wall, found some blankets, rolled one for a pillow and plopped the other over him as he immediately slipped into what would become a short nap.

Forty minutes later

Joe's eyes opened and he sat up on his cot. He looked around and Ann and Joette were feasting on sandwiches and bottled water. He asked, "How long was I asleep? Any news?"

Joette put her sandwich down and said, "You slept a little over thirty minutes. Not much has happened, but there has been a lot of scurrying around out there. We peeked out a few times, but there were so many people moving and talking we couldn't tell what was going on. Dominic said that he would let us know if anything happens."

"I guess then I'll have a sandwich too. I haven't eaten anything since this morning. Those sandwiches look good. What do you have?"

"The choices are peanut butter and jelly or bologna and mayo. Any preferences? We have a lot of canned soup and many cans of beans too. Looks like some type of military canned rations too."

"Not really high on any of that, but I guess I need to eat." Joe put his feet on the floor and rose, walked to the counter, and began making a peanut butter and jelly sandwich. He grabbed a bottled water from the fridge and sat next to Joette.

Chapter 72

Colewin

Everyone who was at Charlie's was concerned about him. He wasn't getting much better. It had been hours since he had been brought home. They knew they would have to take him to a hospital and soon.

Peter was sitting at the kitchen table with Ron, Tommy, Wayne, and Matt. Some of Matt's people were sprawled around the living room on chairs and the couch. They were all waiting for Grace to allow them to take Charlie. She walked into the room and said, "I guess we better go. He's not coming around."

Matt rose and said, "I'll take you. Let me get my truck, and we can load him in the back seat. I'll have a couple of my people go along to help with him."

Grace was happy that Matt was going to take her. She told the others, "Stay as long as you need to, and I'll let you know how it goes at the hospital."

It took some time, but they had the back seat of Matt's crew cab ready for Charlie. They loaded him and left.

As they all watched him leave, Peter's phone rang. It was the phone he had used for the past year to inform everyone about the bunker, so he was surprised when it rang. He said, "Who could this be?"

When Peter picked up the phone, he was astounded. It was his friend Michael who had joined with him a while back. He had lost track of him and Tony when they were transferred somewhere with other troops. "Hello."

"Peter? This you?"

"Yes, what's up?"

"Say, Tony and I have been transferred to D.C. with about a hundred others. Are you in a safe place where you can talk?"

"Yes, we messed up the bunker for good. Some of the troops there are surely dead. Anyway, we're at Charlie's place right now."

"Okay. What I need to let you know, in case no one else knows, is that we have been added to a group of troops who are going to take the White House. Someone needs to know. We're going to try to do our best to foil the plan, but there are only two of us. They have more than two hundred troops amassed here, and I know others are in different locations, so I'm not sure what the total number is. Can you notify anyone?"

"For sure. Joe is in D.C. right now. I can give you his number, and you can call and give him the details."

"Better be quick. We're scheduled to take over the place tonight, late. Not sure when I can call again. For safety, I have my phone on vibrate."

"Sure. Here's the number. I'll give him a heads-up first. You can call when you get a chance."

Peter gave the number to Michael, and then Peter told the others what was up. He knew that this information was critical.

Ron looked agitated. "If Joe can't get some help, this will be a real tragedy!"

D.C.

Joe's phone ran, but he did not recognize the number. He wondered if he should pick it up. He said, "I've got a call. Not sure of the number."

Joette looked at him with wide eyes. "At this point, you should pick it up."

"I guess I should." Joe lifted the phone and answered it. "Hello, who is this?"

"Joe, this is Peter. I have some interesting information to give you."

"Peter, where are you?"

"We're still at Charlie's place. They took him to the hospital."

"Oh, man, I hope he's going to be okay."

"For sure." Peter had told Michael to call Joe directly because he knew second hand information was not as accurate, but Michael could not call right away, and Peter wanted Joe to be ready for Michael's call. Peter continued. "I have some news that you need to hear."

"Go ahead."

"Michael called me. He explained that he and Tony are in D.C., and they think that the President should send as many troops as possible to guard the White House and the Capitol Building. There was even some talk that the Supreme Court Building may be under attack, and that it was going to happen this evening. I know second-hand information is not as accurate, so I told him to call you directly when he has a chance."

Joe said, "I'll inform the people here, and they'll let the President know." Before he hung up, he asked, "Would it be all right to call Michael?"

Peter said, "You can call him. He has his phone on vibrate, so if he doesn't pick up, you know he can't."

Joe thanked Peter. "Thanks. I get it." When he hung up, he found Dominic and told him what he had learned. It only took a few minutes and the place was abuzz again as it had been earlier. Joe could only hope that the information was enough for them to take care of the imminent threat.

The safehouse

Dominic's boss was on the phone before he even finished telling him the whole story. Then one of the military officers gave an order, and his men began to hand out weapons to everyone, just in case. "We need to protect ourselves if they find out where we are, so everyone needs to be armed."

While they were handing out weapons, Joe made a point of telling Dominic to make sure he advises them about each state. "The governors need to get their Guard units ready for an assault."

Dominic said, "I informed him of that as you said earlier. He's been connected to the President, but he felt that they had already contacted each state—but some governors thought it was unrealistic, and that their security forces could handle whatever arose."

Joe just shook his head. He knew what was coming. "The governors are at risk, too. I told you what we learned about them detaining each governor so their person could take over. Didn't anyone believe that?"

"That I cannot tell you. We'll just have to wait and see."

Chapter 73

Several hours later

It was just past midnight and nothing had happened. Everyone except the three who had traveled to D.C. were beginning to doubt the whole affair. Joe or Ann could do nothing more to convince people. Everyone in the large room was beginning to get lazy and doubtful.

A military officer came in to talk to Joe and Ann. "Are you sure this is happening tonight? It's past midnight and no one has seen or heard a thing."

Ann responded, "We're sure. We have people inside the organization who informed us. Before you know it, this will happen, and you will be minus several governors."

"That doesn't even sound like anything anyone could possibly accomplish. Each state has its own security and the governors are under the protection of the Dignitary Protection Section. They haven't identified any threats as of midnight, so we think your theory is wrong."

Joe jumped up and looked directly at the man. "This is not a theory. This is going to happen, and you need to be ready. Is the President protected?"

"We'll see."

1:45 a.m.

It took some time, but just prior to 2:00 a.m., activity began to pick up in D.C. No one really noticed because there was always movement, but to those who knew D.C. well, they understood something was up. Word went out, and everyone was on high alert. When the safehouse received the message, commotion picked up there too.

Joe, Ann, and Joette knew what was coming. They grabbed their weapons and told Dominic that they needed to get outside to see what was happening. "Dominic, this is the beginning of the attack. We need to get out there and help. We have people who are at risk."

"We're all stuck in here right now, but if you want, you can come out and watch everything on the screens that we have. There are numerous cameras around D.C., and we have tapped into all of them. You can watch what you want."

They all rose and followed Dominic. And then it started.

Reagan National Airport

The boss was talking to his next in command, not the new boss, but someone he selected to be his right-hand man, "I have given the word. Is it out there?"

"We have connected with all the leaders at every location. The attack is on. It won't take long now."

"The election was always a long shot. We may not need to worry about it if this works. We will head to the White House as soon as we get the word. Then we need to contact the island and let the committee know when I am in power. A few want to fly in and be a part of this. Let me know when all is clear, and I'll give the order for them to land here."

"Right. As soon as we know, we'll let you know. Do you want to watch part of it?"

"Can we?"

"Sure. Just stay in the limo, and I'll get a feed to you."

The boss settled back and watched as the event began to unfold. He was smiling and very happy. He leaned back to watch and said, "Soon, I should be in charge for life. What a relief. I'll have those other bastard politicians put in prison. I will be able to do that. What fun!"

The attack did not unfold as the President and the chief of staff had envisioned. It began with a huge boom. Artillery. Then rapid fire from machine guns mounted on small trucks tore into the Capitol Building. The President had been informed that they should expect an event like 2021, but that was not the case. When about one thousand troops stormed the Capital from all directions, they knew they were in trouble.

The White House was undergoing the same trauma. Mortars landed on the lawn, and tore the façade off the back of the building and destroyed the colonnades.

The boss took a deep breath. "Oh, I hope they don't do any more damage. I've always loved that place. Well, we can repair anything, I guess. Just get it done." Then he spoke to his driver, "Take me to the Heliport!"

Chapter 74

Safehouse

The scenes they were watching were horrific. History was being destroyed by the minute. Then the news from the states started pouring in. Dominic rose from his chair and walked over to Joe, Ann, and Joette. "Word is that several governors have gone missing, and several state capitols are under siege. Some have been taken. Some have imposed new governors. So far, seven capitols have fallen quickly. Someone has really planned this country-wide attack very well."

"We know!" is all Joe said.

They watched as the White House snipers picked off many of the advancing troops, but then a barrage of fire and mortars began to rain down on them, and they had to pull back. The advancing troops were getting very close when four helicopters in attack formation came tearing over the White House, mowing down many troops.

The old boss was watching—and he was getting nervous. This was not supposed to happen. He had people in charge who were supposed to stop any aerial attack against them. His troops were backing up now, and the boss thought, *I might not get into the White House tonight.*

The President and his family were also watching from the bunker below the East Wing of the White House. He was happy to see his plan unfold, but at the same time he was nervous. He ordered as many soldiers as he could to surround the troops making the attack. That was the plan from the beginning, but he and his chief of staff had thought it would only be the Capitol Building.

Dominic was getting more and more information from the states through his partner. It was not looking good in some places. The capitols were seized and the legislatures were told they were no longer needed, and that the new governors would take care of everything. There was no word from the governors who had been taken, and the new governors were preparing to go on television early to tell everyone all would be fine after this evening's events.

The U. S. Capitol Police and National Guard were happy for the aerial assault by the helicopters until they saw two blown apart in midair. One of the officers yelled, "That was antiaircraft fire. What the hell!"

It didn't take long and all four helicopters were out of action. The attack kept getting more furious, and the attack on the White House was also going badly. The military decided to send their back-ups to surround the troops at the White House instead of the original plan to surround the Capitol Building. They just could not let the White House fall.

It took some time to get the soldiers to the White House, but they made it and began an assault. The troops attempting the coup were now surrounded, and they were caught in a cross fire.

Joe was watching everything at once when his phone rang the second time tonight. "Hello, this is Joe."

"Joe, this is Michael. Tony and I are taking cover near the White House. We're hiding in a grove of trees on the West Wing side of the building. We're afraid if this ends that we'll be hunted by both sides. We're surrounded right now and trying to pick off people storming the White House, but we're afraid that soon they'll figure out what we're doing. We need help. We don't want to be taken by either side. We think the good guys will think we're in on this."

"I get it. That's a bad spot to be in. Let me check with people here. I'll explain your situation, and maybe someone can help."

Chapter 75

The heliport

The boss watched as the helicopters were blown out of the sky. *Well, that's better,* he thought.

His men were making progress at taking the White House when the National Guard surrounded the attackers. They began to mow them down immediately. The attacking troops had to turn and fire, and that gave the guards in the White House a chance to regroup and fire back. When the snipers were able to take their places on top of the building, a slaughter ensued.

The old boss had turned to the Capitol Building to watch the onslaught, and he was very happy when he saw his troops enter the building. It was like the soldiers inside had left. His men were all over the place. The Capitol Building had fallen. He turned back to the White House, and he saw the carnage. His men were almost wiped out. He would not be in the White House tonight.

The presidential bunker under the White House

The chairman of the joint chiefs of staff had gotten a message from his people in the South China Sea. They had gotten enough information from the agent they had sent to take down the committee that they felt had initiated the attack.

The chairman asked, "Are you sure?"

"Yes, sir, these are the people who have been financing this campaign."

"For sure."

The chairman turned to the President who had heard everything. Mr. President, "We failed to quietly take down their leadership, those who have been running and financing this coup."

"The group that is meeting on the island?"

"Yes. The agent who tried to take them out has been rescued, and she gave us more information than we need. There are heads of state, billionaires, and some others whom we do not know. What should we do?"

"We've talked about the possibility. You know what I want."

"Yes, sir."

"They are destroying our Capitol. We will not let them destroy our democracy. I don't care who they are. They have attacked our country. That's a declaration of war. We must strike back at their leadership. No more of this taking them down quietly. Are we prepared and in place to send a cruise missile or two in their direction?"

"We are, and we can. We know exactly where they are. We have pinpointed the building."

"Then let them have it as soon as possible. Don't let them escape. Patch us in to the video if you have it, so we can watch."

"You are set up for that. The officers at the bunker know the routine."

"All right. Let them have it. We misjudged this coup. We thought that it could not be as bad as it is, but we underestimated and did not have enough troops or equipment again. We cannot repeat this mistake!"

D.C.

The Capitol Building fell. When the revolutionaries had control, several members of Congress appeared in the building. Apparently, they had been in on the plan, and they began giving directions to the troops. By now it was 5:40 a.m., and the sun would be above the horizon at any time. The leaders at the Capitol said it was time to get ready to inform the public that they were in control.

The President had the same idea. He needed to tell the American people that all was under control, but that there were some revolutionaries they had to subdue until all was safe in D.C. Yet, the President did not know the scale of attacks on the Capitol or on state capitols, and that those in charge of the attacks were also ready to hit the airwaves.

The old boss sat in his limousine. He would not be able to take the helicopter tonight. His security team was all around his SUV. It was quite a parade of military and civilian vehicles. He told the driver to head toward the Capitol, but not to go all the way there. They had to check on whether it was safe or not to traverse the streets. The security team led the driver toward the Capitol Building, and they took the old boss as close as they could. They pulled into a parking garage to wait. It was quite a distance from the Capitol Building, but it wasn't far from the Supreme Court Building that they had easily taken, so they thought he would be safe to wait there.

Safehouse

Dominic's boss got the word that several states had fallen. Dominic relayed the information to Joe and Ann. "It looks like about thirty state capitals have fallen. Several had been ready and repelled the attacks. Michigan is in the best shape. The governor had learned from her past that it was better to be prepared."

Ann said, "We have been working with her for quite some time now, and we warned her about this event. She had enough experience with people like this, and she was not about to let them just waltz in and take over. We know she warned several others, as did the President, but they didn't all take it to heart. Many thought it was just some kind of conspiracy theory. There are so many out there, and if they are believers without the facts, then they would just think it was somebody trying to scare everyone."

The presidential bunker

It was about 7:00 a.m. when the leaders of the coup in the Capitol Building cut into most regular television. They also hijacked some online mediums to get their message out. One of the insurgents, a member of the Senate, said, "I am in charge until the new President arrives. He should be here any time now. We have taken the Capitol Building—and all Senate and House members are no longer needed. They should stay out of the way. Once we have the White House, we will put many of the Cabinet members and Congress on trial for destroying our country."

The President was getting ready to address the nation. He was sitting at his desk in the secure bunker under the White House. He knew that the fighting was not over. One of his closest aids came in. He said, "You need to watch what is on the television right now."

The President turned and watched. He was surprised that the insurgents had somehow gotten control of most of the networks, and they were ahead of him with a message.

The safehouse

Joe had explained what was going on with Michael and Tony. They were hiding and trying to pick off as many troops as they could. He spoke directly to Dominic's boss. "Two people who have infiltrated the group can help your people direct their fire. They know where their light artillery is located, and they could also help direct the soldiers that were trying to defend the White House, but they also need protection soon. They cannot hold out much longer. Is there any way you can help them?"

"Right now, we have control of most of the area around the White House. We still need to finish the fight though, and it will take some time. Where exactly are these guys?"

"Here, let them tell you directly." Joe handed the phone to the officer and Michael was able to tell him where they were.

"Stay put, and we'll get some soldiers there to help."

Joe asked, "Can I help?"

"I think this is a job for some younger guys, but thanks for the offer."

Joe was not happy, but he was relieved to know that Michael and Tony would be rescued soon.

Even though the White House seemed in the hands of the good guys, it was still not safe to move outside of the building. Michael reported that occasionally, along with gun fire, there were hand grenades, mortars, and the possibility of artillery shells being used against the White House troops.

Chapter 76

Parking garage

The old boss was watching the feed from the Capitol. He was happy that there were two down and one to go. He wondered if they could pull back and gather their forces to attack the White House again. He asked one of his assistants, "Can you get me the man in charge of the attack?"

"Yes, just a second. Got him. Go ahead."

The old boss spoke slowly and calmly as he gave directions. "Pull back all the troops and reorganize so we can try another attack on the White House."

"Boss, the problem is that we did not get the three or four hundred troops from the U.P. They must have been delayed or something. We are really hurting for troops right now. Can we get more here soon, or are they on the way?"

"Let me check for you." But the boss knew that the troops were not coming from the U.P. The place had been attacked again, and he feared that they were lost. He knew that any other troops would take hours to get there, but he had one idea that might work, and so he decided to head to the Capitol Building to see if his troops could assist in his plan to seize the White House.

The man in charge of the troops acted quickly, and he had all of them regrouping. He kept enough troops at the Capitol to keep it safe, but the rest he gathered and told them to meet at a spot just south of Constitution Avenue near the Art Museum. He realized if they attacked once the soldiers had surrounded his other troops at the White House that he could shift the balance and gain the upper hand. He had some mortars set up, not far from their position, close enough to reach the U.S. soldiers' positions.

The presidential bunker

The President thought it was important to reach the American people right away. He had every network ready to give him air time, but there were several problems. Apparently, some of the key technicians were with the enemy, so there would be a delay. In the meantime, the leaders at the Capitol kept broadcasting lies and conspiracy theories about the U.S. Government.

As he watched, the President could only shake his head. "They're telling the people lies. Will they believe them?"

The President's people were working furiously to get him a feed so he could address the nation, but the people running the coup had that all tied up, and they had people on the inside working against the President's people.

D.C. was a mess, and people were hunkered down everywhere due to the massive gun fire and artillery. The place was deserted in a sense, but a lot of military personnel and police were everywhere. The problem was that many of the National Guard troops were being held back by people who were in on the scheme to take the Capitol.

No one realized that the attacking troops were regrouping, but they could tell that the small arms fire had diminished. Michael and Tony knew they could not regroup with the troops, so they stayed put until help would arrive. With a bit of luck, they would not be discovered until they were rescued.

The Capitol Building

The old boss had his car take a route that had been suggested by a congressman inside the Capitol. They knew it was a safe route for him. He arrived without any trouble, and he was immediately escorted inside to a safe spot. He was patched into the feed that had been ongoing, and he addressed the people of the U.S., while flanked by members of Congress who had defected to the attackers.

"Good evening, I am the new President of the United States. I have been given the title by these people in the background. Most of the old President's Cabinet have been dismantled or destroyed, and it is necessary for us to take over and quell this disturbance. We have eliminated the need for Congress to meet in the future. I will have full power as Commander-in-Chief of the Armed Forces, and I request that all military officers withdraw their men to stop this abomination of the seat of government here in Washington, D.C."

The old boss smiled warmly to give the assurance to people that all was under control. He said, "I will make sure that anyone who was involved in this travesty of justice will be brought to trial, and any people found to support the old repressive regime will never be a problem again. I will report further this evening when we have quelled all the disturbances, and God bless America and the American people."

It took some time for the enemy troops to reorganize, but they did. They still had a sizeable force, and they were able to include reinforcements that had been transported to D.C. after a few state capitals fell. By the time the troops were ready, the reinforcements were there.

The soldiers under the command of the President had also regrouped. He had the chief of staff give the order to send as many soldiers as were available to take back all the ground and structures that the insurgents were holding.

Chapter 77

The safehouse

As Joe had been watching the television, he realized this was worse than anything he had imagined. *Why wasn't the President addressing the nation?* That's when Joe's phone rang again.

"Joe, this is Michael. These people are regrouping, and we're trying to stay put. They have reinforcements, and they're going to attack again soon. You need to get reinforcements and get them fast, or these guys are going to overrun this place. We're afraid for our lives right now since we didn't regroup with the rest. We're hidden, but when they attack, we'll be exposed."

"Stay put if you can. We have a group searching for you. They are out there now, and you should see them soon. I don't have any more information, but stay put because they are headed your way."

"That's easy to say, but if they storm the building, we are right in the path they tried last time. Hope your people are quick."

"I can't tell you anymore because I don't know. I'm just going on what the officer told me. Good luck."

"Thanks." Michael hung up because gun fire started again behind them.

It was daylight now, and Michael and Tony could clearly see troops headed their way. The gun fire increased to a level that they had to stay on the ground. They realized that they could fit in if the troops got close to them, but *how would they get the hell out of harm's way?* Then mortars started to fall around them.

The presidential bunker

The President had everyone who mattered in on a meeting. How could they get to the American people? They were in touch with everyone who could make a difference, but the key people were not on their side.

"We need to do something. We may have to bring the new system on board. This is what we have been secretly working on for years. Is now the time, or can we get ahold of the Pentagon directly?"

His staff people responded. "We can, but apparently, they're also under attack. The chairman of the joint chiefs of staff was with the President. He had been there from the start, and he was in touch with his people in the Pentagon, and they were sending troops and air cover in the form of more helicopters. The officers in the Pentagon had apprehended several military people who were sympathizers with the attack, and they now had control of their own soldiers' movements.

It wasn't long before the President had all the soldiers he needed to retake the Capitol and secure the White House, but it would be an all-day battle.

The attack on the White House was in full swing, and the troops were gaining ground. They had reached the spot where Michael and Tony were hidden, so the two just fell in as if part of the group. There was so much fire power behind them that they took cover again. Bullets ricocheted off the White House and were destroying it little by little. The soldiers at the White House were overwhelmed, and their resistance was diminishing. They needed help right away.

The troops began pounding the White House with mortars. They destroyed much of the beautiful building, and then they attacked in full force. They were inside in minutes.

Reinforcements ordered by the President began to arrive, and four helicopters were strafing the area in front and behind the White House. Those troops who had not reached the White House would not. They were being wiped out. One of the helicopters was hit and crashed just to the side of Michael and Tony. They kept low, but they were pelted with debris from the crash and the explosion that followed, but they were all right.

Unfortunately, many of the troops were inside now, and they routed the few remaining soldiers who were guarding the President's residence. The insurgents took up positions to secure the building while several searched for the President and his people.

The Capitol
The old boss was again on the news. "I have decided to be in office for the next five years. After that, we will once again allow elections, but I will tell you things will be different. The borders will be completely closed. No one will be able to vote unless they prove they have been a citizen for at least ten years. They will also have to be twenty-five years old. Oh, yes, there will be changes. You will love them. Only real Americans will be able to vote."

The old boss kept up with this fallacious argument for a long time until the President's people were able to cut in, but before they did…

"I also want to express my gratitude to the people of the thirty states that have now been allowed to join our effort to change this country. Thank you to those people. They are in charge and the governors are with me…."

Then the President cut in. His face appeared on the screen along with a number of both left and right members of the House and the Senate. He looked ashen and tired, but he was firm in his presentation. "Good evening. I want to speak to you tonight about what is going on in the nation's Capital. A group of revolutionaries is trying to take over the government. They are doing it violently and have devastated many of our most hallowed buildings. Do not believe a word you have heard tonight. They have been able to take command of the airwaves, but we have gotten control once again. They have also invaded many state capitals, so do not believe what is coming out of those offices unless your elected officials or governor speaks directly to you…"

As he was speaking, his feed was lost and the screen went blank. Everyone just looked at each other. There would not be any more transmissions this evening.

"Find out what just happened!" the President shouted.

His staff began to check with anyone who had anything to do with the tech part of the airwaves, but with little luck. Everything was down, including any Wi-Fi, hot spots, and satellite connections.

The old boss screamed, "What the hell is going on? Is this our doing? I hope so, but it should have happened when I said." He was having the same problems, but he knew what had happened. He was complaining to his people because he wanted to address the nation one more time before they had everything go down.

Outside near the White House

In the meantime, Joe was talking to Michael and Tony, and they were giving information to the soldiers rescuing the White House. They identified where the troops were, where they saw mortars, and where the artillery had been placed. They also notified them that the enemy had helicopters in the area, but no one had seen any yet.

The battle raged. Both sides were in full battle mode. The façade on the White House was pocked with bullet holes, and in several places, mortars had blasted holes in the building, but the information coming from Michael and Tony helped to slow the advance of the troops who were attacking. They had even rescued one of the pilots from the helicopter that had crashed. He was not doing well, but he was breathing. The others who were aboard, two door gunners and a co-pilot, were gone. They were trying to get help for the injured man and to continue to pass along information when suddenly, the connection they had was lost.

Chapter 78

The Island

After the SEALs had liberated Loretta and Gloria from the Island, the committee members were informed about the break in security. They decided to meet briefly as they had been earlier, and there was some panic among some of the members. Several decided that this was the time to leave and head for the U.S. to join the old boss. Many just thought that they would return home. The meeting ended quickly and several members left the island immediately.

Those who left the island and planned to land at Reagan National found out that all flights were now redirected to other places because of the crisis in the Capital and in some other areas of the country. Their flight was now headed to Chicago, and they were forced to land at O'Hare International. They would not be able to meet the old boss right away as they had planned, but they hoped they could meet with him soon. They were not surprised when they landed to find out that all flights were now grounded, but they still hoped to get to D.C. soon.

The island, on the other hand, was another story. Not long after the meeting broke up, there was a tremendous explosion. The building that housed the meeting was partially destroyed, then there was another explosion and the meeting place was destroyed. Two cruise missiles had demolished the building and killed a few members who had not left.

D.C.

Power was lost for some time, so there was no way to contact anyone. Everyone seemed to be in the dark. The auxiliary power in both the presidential bunker and the safe house kicked in. Soon connections were made and communications returned. No one could figure out how they had lost all contacts, but they were glad to be back.

The President's chief of staff said, "We may not need to alert everyone to use the new system. It seems we have a connection."

The President was once again back on the air, and his message was clear. "We have not had this type of destruction to our homeland for over a hundred years. Even 2021 pales in comparison to the loss of life today and the destruction to infrastructure. The Capitol Building has been breached, and the insurgents are holding it for their pretend president. Do not believe them when they tell you that this is what the American people want. You need to understand that they intend to destroy our system of government. We will not let that happen."

The President was about to complete his remarks when once again, the signal was lost and the feed went blank. This time it was devastating. "What is going on?" the President growled as he looked around in the darkness.

No one answered as the darkness enveloped the room. The President could hear people moving around and bumping into furniture. There was a long silence, then the door to the room opened.

"Mr. President, our best guess is that this is a cyber-attack, and we think an attack on the grid too. The tech people said that is why our equipment is down. Even the generators stopped working. Not sure why." A flashlight lit up the man's face, as he handed another to the President. "We need to make sure that our people have this place under control."

In the meantime, the soldiers who had been sent to rescue the White House had overwhelmed the insurgents, and it looked like they could have the area under control in no time. They had taken several prisoners, including Michael and Tony who begged the soldiers to check with Joe who was in D.C., but they just transported them with the rest of the prisoners.

The Capitol was another story. With the precautions taken after 2021, everyone thought this would never happen, but who would have thought that an army of mercenaries would storm the Capitol fully armed with light artillery, training, and preparation that no one could have believed possible, but here it was unfolding.

The President had ordered several thousand soldiers to take the Capitol Building back. It was going to take time, but they would succeed. What would be left of the building would be a mystery since the enemy had fortified themselves inside. Now things would be worse as there was no communication or electricity in the entire capital of D.C.

Several places still had cell service and power. The President had been working with cyber security and cell service for several years, and now was the time to test their system. "Let's get the Genesis system up and running," he blurted out. His closest advisors knew to what he was referring, and they were propelled into action. Only his closest consultants knew about the secret communications system, and now was the time to test it.

It took about thirty minutes, and the President had phone service, power, and he was connected to the Pentagon. He was also able to get back on the air, and he completed his message to the American people.

Capitol Building

The old boss was irate. "How can the President have power? How is he back on the air?"

His closest assistants did not know. "We had attacks on the infrastructure. They should not have any power, nor should they have access to any television stations. We had that covered."

"Yet they are on, and our message is not getting out there. He will turn the people against us."

They watched the program as the President gave assurances that all was under control, and that power would be restored for many communities as soon as the revolution was terminated.

This just incensed the old boss. He launched into a tirade, and those around him were stunned. He was not like this. Then all hell broke loose as the building was stormed by soldiers well trained to take down an insurgence like this. The boss had to vacate the place.

"We need to leave now. This is not going well. We should have had this place secured by now."

His closest assistants all escaped with the boss into the basement, but they were cornered by the advancing soldiers.

Chapter 79

Safehouse

Joe heard the news that both the White House and the Capitol Building were back in the hands of the U.S. Military. He spoke to Ann and Joette, "That's a relief. Now we must find Tony and Michael and get them out of harm's way. We also need to contact Ron to see if he can get a group together to check on what was left of the bunker, and if any troops are still left there that could be a problem. There may also be people who need medical attention."

Ann said, "I should also contact Jerry. He's probably wondering how things have gone here. Aaron too. We should head back as soon as we can and make sure everyone is all right."

Still, Joe was troubled. "The problem remains in the state capitals. What will happen in each state? I hope there's a plan."

Joe readied himself to go out and find Michael and Tony. He was going against the orders of the officer in charge, but he knew he needed to get Michael and Tony to safety. He had fatigues, helmet, flak jacket, and an M4 rifle, a weapon like the M16A2. He told Joette, "Keep your phone on so I can reach you if I need help."

Joette protested and said, "We've come this far together. We need to help each other."

Ann agreed. "We're going!"

Joe wasn't going to be able to stop them, and they were both readied with the same equipment.

Dominic came in and said, "You know we have a group out looking for your guys. They will find them."

"Sorry, we need to do this."

"Then I'm coming along."

Joe had last spoken with Michael and Tony when they were taken by the soldiers. He knew where he had to go. He also had written orders from the commanding officer at the safehouse to allow Joe to take the two men.

White House

The President was back in control, and the military had secured most places in D.C. The shooting had subsided somewhat, and the military also had control of the air space. Planes had been grounded earlier, but now certain planes were allowed to land—and for some—money talks.

At Reagan National one landed and a group of men exited, jumped into a few limousines, and headed for the White House. They would be surprised. They had trouble navigating the military equipment, and then they were stopped at a military checkpoint, but it wasn't their people in charge. They were not allowed to go any farther, so they turned around and headed back to Reagan. They could not contact the old boss, and they realized they had better get out of D.C. before someone put two and two together.

When they arrived at Reagan, they boarded the plane and planned to travel to Canada and land at the London International Airport. The men were safe, but they were distressed about the results in D.C. Their people should have been in charge right now. They had expended huge amounts of cash—and they expected better results. They could not reach the old boss, but they were able to connect to the new boss who was in D.C. coordinating all troop movements. The committee head said, "Hello, where are you, and what is going on?"

"I'm safe and am trying to gather the troops to make another attack. Right now, we are scattered and no one seems to have control of the different groups. I've sent out the call for everyone to gather at a spot that I won't mention over the air, but we have a good number of troops still able to fight even though many are in custody."

"Will we be able to take D.C.?"

The new boss said, "Not sure, but we are going to send many armed drones into the area to see whether we can get control back. We also have a few suicide drones that will crash into the White House and the Capitol. We're not sure where the old boss is, so we need to be careful."

"Why didn't you use these earlier to help take the place? Why wait until now?

The new boss said, "We had a mix up with the people who were in control. They had them hidden all over the city so they would not be found by the government."

The committee head was not satisfied. "That's just not good leadership. They might have made the difference."

"Maybe. We could not coordinate everything like we thought."

"Just get control no matter what. Destroy what you must and take over."

"Got it."

Safehouse

A truck met Joe and the others and took them to the White House. They were shocked at the destruction. The place did not look the same. Craters were around the building, holes were in the walls of the White House, and bodies littered the ground. Joe exclaimed, "What a disaster!"

They were all shocked.

Dominic knew the exact spot where the prisoners were being held, and he directed the driver. It took some looking, but they found Michael and Tony—and they were out of there in no time, heading back to the safe house.

When they returned, they had just entered the building when they heard and saw many explosions taking place near the White House. "What's that?" they heard Dominic exclaim.

"Looks like drones all over the sky. There must be over one hundred!" someone exclaimed.

"Take cover, everyone. I don't know if they will head this way, but they look very menacing.

Joe took one look and decided that they were not coming their way. "They're focused on the White House and farther south to the Capitol, but they are doing some damage."

The U.S. military had antiaircraft and scrambled several F-16s from Joint Base Andrews. Between the antiaircraft battery and the planes, many of the drones were destroyed, but not before they caused serious damage to the buildings.

The new boss tried to have his men rally and attack the White House again, but they were overwhelmed by the soldiers guarding the building, and they were driven back and scattered around the city.

The attack was over, but the drones had caused more damage to the White House and Capitol, and had also caused damage around several of the nearby buildings. The place was a disaster.

The drones and troops eventually were quieted, and a wary peace came back. Except for a few planes and helicopters flying around, the skies looked normal, and there were no further troop movements by the insurgents—and the government once again had control.

Chapter 80

A few days later

Quiet returned to the country, but everything was not over. Several states had rogue governors who had taken over and had control of the capitol buildings. Some of the elected governors had disappeared, and in some places, people were backing the interlopers. It would be a long, weary battle to get the country back to what it was.

Many groups agreed with the attack on the establishment. How anyone could get the country organized under the federal government again was anyone's guess. The President acknowledged that this was not going to be easy, but he had a coalition of Senators and members of the House who would attempt to assist in bringing the country back to what they thought was normal.

The coalition determined that an election at this time was not possible, and until they could get everyone on the same page, an election would not be in the best interest of the country. The rogue state governors had declared the old boss as the president, but the military had him in custody, and he was being held while there were further investigations.

No one knew what would happen in the future, but several countries had begun to take advantage of the conflict in the U.S., and they were making moves that could jeopardize the welfare of the country.

Joe was concerned about the events, but he knew others were working on that, and he and Joette really had to get back to their own lives. The next day, Joe returned to Michigan with Joette. They decided to first check in with their headquarters in Ishpeming, then head back to Colewin to meet with Ron and everyone who had been involved in the effort to end the bunker.

Loretta joined Ann in Lansing where Loretta was now in charge of the FBI post. She and Ann would now be a force for change. Aaron and Jerry were also back, but Jerry decided to retire from duty. He was on full disability and decided to switch careers, which Loretta and Ann had discussed with him many times since his injury.

It was late when Joe and Joette returned to Colewin where they met with Ron and Shanice. So much had happened during these few days that Joe wondered how he had even gotten to Colewin.

The community had gathered to plan an investigation of the area that had experienced the blast a few days ago. Most people avoided the area for fear of further explosions, so it took them several days to get organized. Now they were ready with local ambulances, the DNR, fire departments from several communities, the State Police, and some Colewin residents who had volunteered to take part in finding out what had happened—and to see if anyone might have survived.

The next morning, they drove to the bunker area. They entered from the south off U.S.-2 and drove in a group of vehicles that looked like a mismatched convoy of toys. When they arrived, they were all amazed at the damage. The entire bunker was gone. The barracks that had housed the troops were all destroyed except for the last one farthest from the blast. The armory was gone too. There was such a deep hole where the blast had originated that they could not get vehicles into the parade grounds. They had to proceed on foot, and they found bodies, some partially intact, but many destroyed beyond recognition by the explosion.

Joe and Ron assisted some medical personnel as they searched the area for any signs of life. They wove their way toward the barracks where they found a few men, dazed yet from what had happened, but not in very good shape. They were hungry and distressed. They searched the area beyond the barracks and into the woods and found several troops camped out who were relieved to see help. Other than that, there wasn't much.

Joe looked at Ron, and they both shook their heads in disbelief, but they knew this area would never be a threat to anyone again as it had been. The work to find bodies continued for some time, and Joe and Ron finally decided to leave the area. They knew they had one last stop before they would retire from this business for good.

They met with Michael and Tony who had returned to Colewin from D.C. They all gathered at the town hall with Don, the mayor along with the barber, his son Peter, Tommy and Wendy, Wayne and Cathy, Paul and Sarah, and others for one last meeting before everyone returned to the new life that awaited them in a country that had been torn apart.

The meeting was somber and short, but everyone agreed that they had done the right thing, and they vowed to work together to create a better place to live.

Joe and Ron and their wives left and headed to Marquette General Hospital where Charlie was now under the care of some specialists. He was not doing well.

They arrived after a very quiet two-hour ride and went straight to the hospital. When they were near his room, they were met by Charlie's wife Grace. Several people were there from Colewin, best friends of Grace and Charlie, and Joe knew that several others were on the way from Colewin. Matt was there too with a few of his friends. Matt had not left Charlie and Grace since he had driven them from Charlie's place a few days ago.

"How's he doing?" Joe asked.

"Not good, but he's conscious, and we've been talking. You can go in and see him."

They only allowed a few in the room at once, so Joe and Ron went in with Grace. Charlie looked up, and moaned, but it was a happy moan, if there is such a thing. He said in a very weak voice, "Never thought I'd see you two again."

They both looked at Charlie and knew he did not have much time left. "Hey, Charlie, why wouldn't we visit the guy who has become a good friend?" Joe said.

Ron added, "We had a rough start, but we worked together to do something that was right. We owe you for all you did to help."

"Well, I wasn't a friend in the beginning. Sorry the way I treated you both. Come to find out you two are good partners." Charlie sighed and closed his eyes. His head dropped deeper into the pillow, and Joe and Ron looked at Grace.

She looked back with tears in her eyes.

Charlie turned his head toward his wife and said, "I ain't dead yet. I'm gonna make it outta here!"

They all smiled as did Charlie. Then Grace said, "We should let him rest."

They all agreed, and left. When they walked into the hallway, they saw Tommy and Wayne and their wives headed to the room.

"How's he doing?" Wayne asked.

Joe looked at him and said, "If you want to say anything to him, do it now."

They all shook hands as Joe and Joette and Ron and Shanice walked slowly from the room and out to their vehicles.

"What now, Ron?" Joe asked.

"We're heading back to Virginia with my son and his family. We're going to stay with them for a while and figure this out. My mom gave me the house when she passed, so we're going to stay there. What about you two?"

"Not real sure. Dominic wants us to stay in D.C. for a while as they clean up the mess, but we don't want any more to do with this aside from our best to bring the country together."

"Yeah, so a bunch of rich guys can do what they want and try to destroy this country. I guess money talks."

"I guess. So many people are duped by these guys who just want to take over and run everything. They don't care about us. They just want control. Democracy to them is just a speed bump in the way of their power grab. I hope that we have diluted their power, and we can get back to some common ground in this country where people get along again and can govern from the middle where compromise works, and those in the government aren't always screaming and yelling at each other."

"Big order, Joe, but I agree with you."

"Yes, for those people who always feel someone is about to take their freedoms, this is a good example of what violence can bring. I mean we have people who have loaded up with weapons and supplies, expecting some government agency to turn them into some kind of slaves or something. How do you convince these people to work together and try to be a part of the solution, rather than an antagonist, ready to fight?" Joe asked.

"I know. I hope everyone can find some common ground to make this country a place where everyone feels welcome. It's going to be an uphill battle just getting back to what we had. If we can!"

"What if we cannot do that? These people look at our government and see millionaires running it, so, yeah, they are dubious, because they feel the rich don't understand. Yet, they back some who like controversy."

"True. What's next for you and Joette?"

"I think we might stay in the U.P. for a while with family in Ishpeming. Maybe wrap up the work we started, and then finally try to enjoy retirement with our family."

Chapter 81

Canada

All was not lost, according to the committee. "It looks like the old boss is in custody. We might have to forget about him or take him out if he starts to talk. We still have the new boss who is reorganizing the troops. He has many of them out of harms way and headed to a secure spot outside of D.C. This isn't over yet. Plus, we control ten states."

The committee had lost a few members in the island explosion, but the majority had escaped. Since no one knew about them, or who was part of the group, they felt very safe. They decided to disperse and return to their various countries or homes. No one would be able to trace them to this committee.

Chapter 82

Ishpeming, the next day

Joe received a text from Tommy that Charlie had passed. There would be a memorial at his place in three days, and Tommy said that Grace would like Joe and Joette to attend. She felt Joe had been a better friend to Charlie than a lot of people.

Joe told Joette about Charlie. "We're going to have to go to his memorial. Tommy said Grace would like us there."

"Yes, we need to attend, Joe."

"I guess I better call Ron and Shanice too. Charlie took to Ron after a while. He sure started out badly with him, but they became friends during the last year."

Charlie's place

Everyone was there. It was like a reunion of those who had tried to build a tunnel to the bunker, and who had attacked the bunker two times. Of course, a few were missing, those who had been killed by the troops and their assassins. The most notable was Charlie. He had held the groups together for some time. Many of his old militia members attended. One absence was Sheriff Daryl who had joined the other side.

There was much reminiscing. Joe and Ron stood together in a corner of the kitchen. Grace was sitting in the living room where Charlie's body was. Many of his friends sat around talking quietly. No formal service was planned, just a short memorial. A few people had said some nice things about Charlie, and how important he was to the success of their effort to rid the town of the people who had turned it into a war zone.

Tommy walked into the kitchen where Joe and Ron stood. "I can't help to wonder what the country will be in a year or two. Ten states have still not gotten rid of these fake governors. Can the federal government help?"

Joe looked at Tommy and shrugged. "Not sure what will happen, Tommy. They have people backing them, and senators and representatives from their states saying they are the rightful leaders, so who knows?"

Ron said, "You know what we did was huge, but we can't fight that kind of thinking. I'm not sure the federal government is in a position to either, but we can hope."

Wayne walked in. He looked dejected. "I feel partly responsible for Charlie's end."

"Why is that?" Tommy asked.

"He wanted to drive that truck into the bunker, and I didn't argue with him. I just let him do it."

"He wouldn't have had it any other way," Joe said.

"Absolutely. He wanted to do that." Ron agreed.

Tommy looked puzzled. "But this whole mess. How do we stop this kind of violence against the government?"

"Probably can't," Ron said.

Wayne seemed hopeful. "What we can do is try to work together and end this constant arguing. Our politicians can't work together anymore. They argue and yell, and they bring up false stuff that people believe!"

Joe looked at the three and took a sip of his drink. Then he added. "You know, people are so used to getting their way nowadays they can't see that other people might have a different opinion about things. I wonder if we have gotten soft. We have so much, and we raise people to have as much as they can to do whatever they want. Then they think that they should have that their whole lives. We've become very selfish."

Ron said, "Yeah, think about millions of people with a belief that they have, and they think everyone should have that same belief. People are different. They have different opinions and goals, but we must learn that we need to work together so we can get along peacefully."

Tommy agreed. "I guess you're right. We all need to look at our neighbors and talk, see where we can find how to get along."

Someone in the other room said, "Let's clear a path. We're taking Charlie. His last wish was to be buried on his land near that big maple tree out yonder."

Everyone stepped aside and let the pallbearers carry the casket through the house and out the door. The rest followed. They had already dug the hole. They lowered Charlie's casket. Matt said a few final words, and Grace threw in some flowers she had.

Grace was quiet, but she said, "This should have never happened! Why in the world do people have to be so angry? Why do they have to be so power hungry that they need to overthrow the government? This is the best country in the world. Why do they want to destroy it? What has anyone gained? I'll never know why Charlie had to start a militia in the first place. I kept telling him it was a waste of time. Now I see what he was afraid of. These people have made a mess.

Everyone stood by silently, thinking. It was so quiet that they could hear the breeze blowing through the trees. It was chilly and people were trying to stay warm while they watched as a few of Charlie's friends began to grab some shovels.

"We should all leave," Matt said.

Joe looked around. "This is a beautiful place. Charlie should be able to enjoy it."

"He will," Grace said. They all said their goodbyes and every-one walked back quietly to the house.

As Joe walked away holding hands with Joette, he could not help thinking about how this all started for them. They were living a quiet life until the explosions that got him investigating, and it all led to this point in their lives. His life was changed—and that of so many others too.

Epilogue

Joe and Joette did just as they had planned, and they returned to Ishpeming where they would work to improve the country—and worried less about the bunker in Colewin, or the events in D.C. They kept in touch with Ron and Shanice, who decided to work with Dominic who was involved in the restoration of D.C. as the seat of government.

Others also settled into everyday life, *but they would not forget what happened.* Tommy was back as a bear-hunting guide for tourists. Wayne and Cathy decided to move to Marquette and settle there. Colewin quieted down after the coup. No troops were seen anywhere. Mayor Don returned to a normal life, as did the barber and his son, Peter. Michael and Tony settled down, returning to lives they had left. Grace lived in her home in the woods where Charlie had been buried—and stayed close to her family.

Ann returned to her job, working with Loretta at the Lansing FBI office. She and Loretta dedicated their lives to their jobs, working against seditious activities, and bringing as many insurgents to justice as they could.

Loretta informed her FBI director that "the madam," Gloria, could be an asset in their hunt for the committee members who had financed the conspiracy. On numerous occasions, Gloria had worked for them, and so had valuable information that could lead to some of them.

Gloria agreed to cooperate. Her trade-off was to get all the women on the island to safety. They were rescued by a combined military and private endeavor. Two Chinook helicopters landed, along with a few attack helicopters that provided protection. All of Gloria's women, as well as other women who were there, were rescued. The security force tried to fight back, but the attack helicopters made quick work of them.

The local men who had joined the ranks at the bunker returned to Colewin, many of them disgruntled at how it had all worked out. Several spoke about how they felt dragged into a conflict they did not agree to. However, some were disappointed that they were not successful. Many of them quietly left the ranks of the troops that had attacked D.C., hoping they would not be found guilty of the insurrection as those in 2021 had been.

The young men who were lost to their families were mourned. Some families petitioned Washington to find out what happened to their loved ones—but not everyone received answers.

The new boss lost a lot of men, as droves left for their regular life again, but he thought he had enough troops left to move on. Time would tell. The old boss was in custody, and because the new boss was being sought by the government, he was not out of the woods.

The billionaires and other very-connected committee members were scattered by this time, but their days were numbered as a force. Although no one knew exactly who they were, a search had begun for answers. Some of the U.S. citizens could not return to the country. Some others on the committee returned to their home countries. Although they believed they were safe, their problems were just beginning, since they were not out of the crosshairs of the CIA and other government agencies.

The country was in disarray, and many wondered what would come of the coup. Who was responsible? Had they been defeated? What happens now? Not unexpected questions for a country under siege.

Many great countries have fallen from lofty heights. They usually do so from within. Who knows why? It could be that people believe "freedom" means they have *total freedom*, and they are not willing to understand that freedom is not that, and so they blame others for their problems. It takes efforts by many to remain free from those who would like to subjugate others, and have power and control. Just ask anyone who has had to defend a homeland against coups or outside intruders.

This country has always been run by the rich and powerful, but it is not just the rich who can bring a country down. The country has roots in slavery, and at that time, many ordinary people had believed in the system. Today, common people believe in some lies and conspiracy theories, and they are as lethal as anyone who wants to replace a government. World War II was not just one desperate man trying to obliterate the world order—*it took many to look the other way.*

This is not the first time the people of the United States have had to defend their country, and it will not be the last, unless they decide that this great country—a paragon to the world of how to live together with many diverse people, cultures, religions, beliefs, and individual freedoms—is worth saving. However, it will take work.

Are the people of the United States of America, the greatest country in the world, willing to do that?

Acknowledgments

To my wife, LaVonne, who has been on this ride with me all these years.

I would like to thank my publisher, Ann Aubitz, of Fuzion-Press and Kirk House Publishing. Ann has worked closely with me on three novels and a children's book and has been a huge help in bringing my works to life.

I would also like to thank Connie Anderson, my editor, who has been a wonderful partner. She is careful to allow my voice to come through my works, and also offers suggestions and asks questions that are so beneficial to make the final document the best possible.

I am also grateful for all the teachers in my life, from St. John's School, St. Lawrence Seminary, Northern Michigan University, and the University of Minnesota-TC. They molded me into the writer I am today.

However, there were no greater teachers than my parents, grandparents, uncle and aunts, brothers and sisters, mothers and fathers-in-law, and cousins. Family is so integral to anyone's early and future nurturing.

I would like to thank LaVonne, my children, their spouses, and my grandchildren for making my life so rich and full of fun.

Finally, thank you to all my colleagues everywhere—and to all those teachers who struggle daily to do one of the most important and difficult jobs in the world.